Praise for *A*

"The story of a young woman desperately searching for her mom in a harrowing landscape she barely recognizes. All she knows is that the traveling circus might hold the key. Think *Station Eleven* meets *The Road*, filtered through the prism of Robert Cormier. Ellen Parent has created a world that isn't ours, but could be—that's what gives this post-apocalyptic novel its power."

—David Yoo, author of *The Choke Artist* and *Stop Me If You've Heard This One Before*

"June has a big heart and a truthteller's tongue. Teens will love following her on her quest to seek her mother, to uncover secrets, and to discover a better life in the dangerous and deeply flawed Republic of Vermont."

—Laura Williams McCaffrey, author of *Marked* and *The Water Shaper*

"Ellen Parent truly has the gift of the storyteller's voice. Her modest but robust prose rolls out this lovely story in which dire things transpire, and yet love and persistence prevail."

—Sandra Scofield, author of *The Scene Book* and *Little Ships, a Novel*

"Through lyrical and heart-wrenching prose, debut author Ellen Parent explores the complexities of family, interweaving the unbreakable ties of blood with the bonds of kinship forged through shared experiences and unwavering loyalty. Courage emerges as the defining force that shapes June's path—the courage to pursue her loved ones and the equally formidable courage to let them go."

—Robyn Dabney, author of *The Ascenditure*

"An intricately woven tale by a master storyteller. I was unable and unwilling to escape June's shattered world of hardship and painful longing for better times. If you are enthralled by well-crafted, post-apocalyptic worlds and those who inhabit them, Ellen Parent beautifully written *After the Fall* will not disappoint. It's been a while since I held a true page-turner in my hands."

—Morgan Howell, author of *The Moon Won't Talk*

"We all cling to something: a memory, a fantasy, even a lie. In Ellen Parent's propulsive and emotional new novel *After the Fall*, set in a post-climate-collapse Vermont, teenage orphan June and her adopted brother Thomas, and the dark and troubled disgraced lawman Jacob deal with the visceral aspects of day-to-day survival, but they want—need—more. They need to make the stories they hold so tightly to real. Told with equal parts insightfully emotional and harrowingly vivid prose, the journey June embarks upon through this intricately crafted and detailed world is risky, exciting, and finally deeply human and emotional. In the end a deeper meaning is revealed as each character is forced to come face to face with their inner stories and decide if they can let them go; just like each of us. Poignant, gripping, immaculately drawn, heroically exciting, and deeply relatable, *After the Fall* is a story that will stay with each reader for a long time."

—Jim Naremore, author of *American Still Life* and *The Arts of Legerdemain as Taught by Ghosts*

After the Fall

Ellen Parent

Fitzroy Books

Published by Fitzroy Books
An imprint of
Regal House Publishing, LLC
Raleigh, NC 27605

https://fitzroybooks.com
Printed in the United States of America

ISBN -13 (paperback): 9781646034840
ISBN -13 (epub): 9781646034857
Library of Congress Control Number: 2023949030

Cover images and design by © C. B. Royal

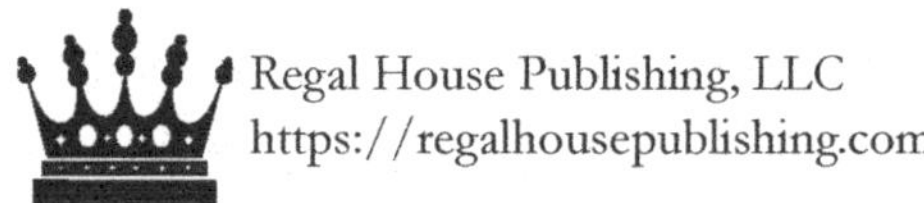

Regal House Publishing, LLC
https://regalhousepublishing.com

Printed in the United States of America

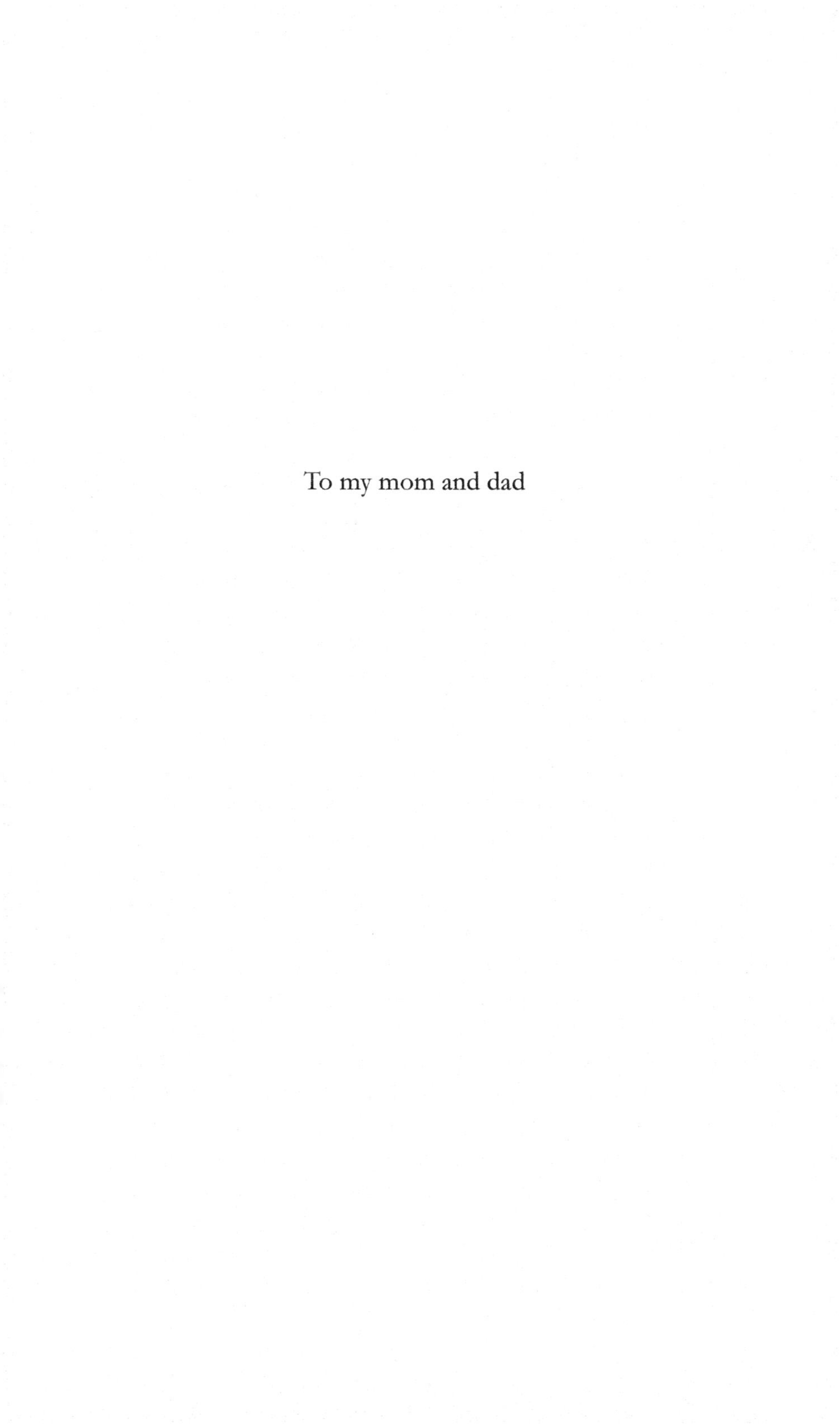

To my mom and dad

1

Two things made me finally leave the Hollow, even though I should've left a hundred times before. One was seeing Jacob again, and the other was the circus.

I'd heard about the circus from Old Bill, of all people, who spent most of his days riding a broken-down old bicycle from place to place, begging work and being a nuisance. I came across him when I was walking back up the hill on the day of the storm. The squeak of his bike sounded through the woods from a ways off, so I had time to think about hiding somewhere till he passed. He wouldn't hurt me, he wasn't that kind of criminal, but he would try to talk to me, and that was almost worse.

"Hey, June!" I heard before I could find a spot to hide. I kept walking, waiting for him to catch up. We were in the poison parsnip field and the tall dry rods of dead parsnip rose up on either side of the path like the bars on a prison. I'd been digging parsnip root out of the muddy dirt for dinner, trying hard not to touch the stinging stems. Past the field, the mountains were gray walls with a little stubble of green at their feet. The sky overhead was gray, too, and the parsnip swayed like there might be some weather on the way. I glanced up and saw low-bellied clouds to the north. Ever since the double winter, it seemed storms were coming more and more often. Like the end of the world wasn't hard enough already.

The squeaking got closer and closer, and I ignored my body itching to run. No reason to run when you're not being chased. Still, I wondered how Old Bill had lived this long, what with his way of showing up when he wasn't wanted. Finally he slowed down beside me, his wispy gray rattail blowing in the breeze. His bike was rusty red and he kept the tires patched with pine pitch and his own sticky spit, probably.

"Didn't you hear me calling?" he gasped, stepping off the bike and then rustling along to catch back up with me.

"Hello, Bill," I said. My teeth were tingling like they wanted to bite. I pulled up my collar, just to make sure all my scars were out of sight. He knew about them—everyone knew—but that didn't mean I liked the staring. I wished I'd worn my mom's old jacket, but I'd left it behind on account of the day's warmth.

Bill was wearing layers of patched sweaters with an oily sheepskin vest on top. It wasn't much different from what I wore, but my clothes didn't stink like his. I wondered if he avoided washing just for effect. Rounded out his scummy image nicely, I thought. He was the kind of tinker who'd clean off your solar panels or patch your roof on a good day, but who'd just as soon steal the tools from your shed if you didn't give him work.

"Your parents up there?" he asked, eyeing me a little hungrily. He'd started looking at me differently lately, in a way that made my hair stand up. Cyrus, whose family lived up above the stream and who thought he was going to be my husband in a few years, would've whacked Old Bill on the head for what his eyes were doing. Cyrus didn't know that I'd take his sister over him any day, and neither did Old Bill.

"Your parents need anything?" Old Bill insisted when I didn't answer.

They aren't my parents and you know it. That's what I wanted to say. But I wasn't in the habit of saying what I thought. I had secrets, things no one knew about. I didn't ever say, *I'm not gonna get married and stuck here forever*, and I didn't ever say, *My mom is coming back for me, and then we're gonna go somewhere you folks in the Hollow probably can't even imagine.* It was simpler not saying, sometimes.

"You can ask them yourself," is what I told Old Bill.

"I never seen you smile," he said next. Just the kind of dumb thing he'd started saying recently.

"Well, I don't drink like you do. What do you want me to smile about?"

He laughed at that. "Just 'cause the world's over don't mean you can't smile!" he said. A rod of poison parsnip got stuck in the spokes of his bike, and he stopped to get it out. I kept walking. When he caught up, we were almost to the house. I could see it through the broken woods—all the trees in this spot were dead, or almost dead, since the drought and the double winter a few years back. But new stuff was growing up in the woods—lots of kudzu, and some hardwood saplings too. So the Hollow wasn't done living yet.

"You'd smile more if you saw the circus," Old Bill said offhandedly, just loud enough for me to hear.

"What circus?"

"Oh, you're probably not that interested, too busy moping around to—"

"What circus?" I said again, louder and harder. I don't think this was the effect he'd intended, but it made him answer.

"A new one. Jeff Quigley said he seen them in Dorset, and they's on a tour all the way up to Middlebury for Town Meeting. Jeff promised they was stopping in the Borough. They got a fire-eater and everything. I could take you, if you like."

It was always big news when something different happened in the Republic. Oftentimes it was something bad: a new strain of flu, a flood, another attack from the Yorkers. But every once in a while, like this time, it was something good. There were a couple of circuses that made the rounds in the Republic. Even hungry folks got starved for a laugh, and they'd pay what they could to see a show.

The thing was, circuses almost always had more than just tricks and juggling to offer. Sometimes they traveled with a tinker—they deal with electricity and machines, and some people think they're in league with the devil. Sometimes it was a peddler, and that'd be good news for me because peddlers always had books to sell. But the really important thing that traveling circuses had was news. Information from far away. They could tell you who they'd met, and where. And that was more important than books.

"Still got your little simpleton?" Old Bill said, looking up at the house.

Thomas was there by the edge of the porch, corncob pipe clenched in his mouth. He'd only just lost his last baby teeth.

That's funny, coming from you, I wanted to say to Old Bill, but I didn't say anything because sometimes keeping quiet made him go away. Thomas watched us from the edge of the house, and even though he didn't move an inch, I could tell he was happy to see me from the tilt of his head and the way his hand was half raised, almost a wave. He must've heard us coming and run around from the greenhouse where Bob had him picking slugs. I grinned up at him and he smiled back.

"I can't see why ol' Bob and Denise keep taking in help that don't do no helping," Bill was saying. He'd taken a white plastic pill bottle out of his fanny pack and was trying to pry the lid off. "The Warrens—now they only bring on orphans that can lift fifty pounds. And they don't have no roof falling in or slug rot. What's the point of an orphan that don't work?"

What's the point of a dirty tramp that steals your hammer when he says he's going to patch the roof? I waved up at Thomas, but Bill was still struggling with the pill bottle. I wondered if his finger joints hurt him.

"You need help?" I asked halfheartedly.

"Think you're stronger 'n me, orphan?" Bill cackled. "Damn thing's stuck."

"Here," I said. I pulled it out of his hand and read the top of the lid. "It says *push down and turn.*" I pushed the lid down and screwed it off. The motion made something uncomfortable flicker inside me, and I handed the bottle back quick. Memories sometimes happened to me like that, like shadows from an unexpected cloud.

"Unnatural, reading," Bill muttered, taking the pill bottle. "Thanks kindly." He shook a blue tab onto his palm. "LoTab dreams tonight… You want in?"

I stepped away quick, wrapping my hands around my bag of parsnip roots. "I gotta go." My voice was wary, but as I turned away I'd already forgotten Old Bill and his LoTabs—I was going to the circus, and maybe they'd have the news I was looking for.

The sky churned with wind and clouds above me as I walked up the yard—I'd been right about the weather coming. The darkening before a storm always made the world look different, like maybe you'd gotten lost and ended up somewhere you didn't belong. Or like you were in a dream you wanted to wake up from. The windows of the house were dark—Denise hadn't lit any lamps yet—and its jumble of plastic siding and tacked-on sheet metal seemed as strange as it had the first night I laid eyes on it. The clearing was still littered with Bob's projects too: a yellow car with the engine pulled out, a big brush pile, a half-built shed for the chickens. Thomas was the only change.

I started up the steps, and Old Bill turned his bike around. "Storm's coming, June. Guess I'll see you at the circus!"

I didn't answer. I climbed over the broken step and onto the porch. I wanted to run, but instead I just made a face at Thomas, who flicked his middle finger at Old Bill's back.

The rain came hard just after dinner—it was our second bad storm in just a couple of weeks, and when the wind picked up, we started to hear the crash of trees falling in the pine stand. Their roots couldn't hold up to it all, not with the dirt already soft from the last rain.

Bob and Denise liked to spend the start of storms in the living room, and it wouldn't do to say no to them. They'd taken me in as a farmhand after I got burned in the fire and lost my mom. I figured I owed a lot to them, and I also figured they'd kick me out to starve or freeze to death in the storms if I got cheeky and stopped doing what they said. But Thomas didn't seem to care about that stuff. Right after dinner he disappeared up the stairs.

Denise clicked her tongue, watching him go. Her legs had gone swollen and red in the past months, and she didn't walk much anymore.

"That boy's gone antisocial, more than usual," Denise said.

Not to me, I thought. She didn't understand him like I did.

"He's just scared of the storm," I said, flipping idly through the pages of *The Spy Craft Manual*; I was waiting for my time to bring up the circus, so I only pretended to read.

"Storm ain't in here yet," Denise said, but nothing more. Storms scared all of us, no matter how often they came.

For a little while we sat quiet, listening hard for trees falling or worse. There'd been a landslide over across the valley last month. I'd seen it from up in the Warrens' high field, a big tear cut down the mountain.

"Old Bill says there's a circus coming this way," I said finally, trying to sound casual.

"Yep, Joe Staples reckons he saw 'em coming down from Dorset Pass. Might be in the Borough by now, if they ain't caught in the rain," Bob said, frowning down at the boot he was resoling with a tire tread from his collection. He was wearing overalls faded soft as lamb's fleece. His hat had *Dorr Oil* printed on it, or at least that's what it had read before the letters started peeling off. I told him what it said once, but he'd looked at me like I was speaking French and said, "It's a *hat*, it can't say nothing."

Now my heart skipped and I closed my lips tight to keep from saying anything. Bob didn't like things happening too fast. I wanted to jump up and out into the rain and run down the Brook Road all the way to the Borough. But I sat and laced my fingers together.

"Cyrus came by when you were out and dropped off a full tin can," Denise said to me. "One of the old ones and no sign of mold. I need you to read it before I open it—it's got no pictures, and I want to know straight away whether it's cat food or peaches."

"I want to go to the circus," I blurted out.

"Did you hear what I said about Cyrus?" Denise said.

At the same time, Bob said, "You're sure as heck not going out in this weather."

"I can go soon as the rain stops, though?" I said.

"Might need to make repairs on the greenhouse after this wind, and I can't do that alone," Bob said slowly, sticking his bone awl through the tire tread.

"Don't you care that your match came by here and left a present, girl?" Denise cut in.

"The circus might be gone if I wait." I swallowed. Had to lay on some sugar too, I realized. "And that's nice Cyrus came by. I'm sorry I missed him." That was about as much sugar as I had in me.

"Why you want to see a circus anyway?" Bob asked.

"I—I want to see if they have books to trade," I said. Better not to complicate the matter with the real reason I wanted to go.

"Joe said he seen an American flag in one of their boxes when he helped 'em cross the river down in Dorset." Bob made like he wanted to spit, but stopped since we were indoors. "You don't want to bother with that kind of folk."

"American?" I asked. My heart fluttered at that. If they were American, I wanted to go even more.

"Oh, don't get him going," Denise said. She sounded snippy but a little worried too. "That circus ain't American. Yorkers wouldn't be able to get a whole circus across the border without the Green Mountain Boys noticing! Now go get that can from the cupboard and read it, girl."

I went to the kitchen. The window over the sink was covered and the cracks were stuffed, but I could still hear a drip of water pushing through. In the other room, Denise clucked at Bob, who was muttering something else about the Yorkers. No one their age talked about America without getting angry. They were bitter and afraid for the Republic, because their grandparents used to get raided by Americans back in the time just after the Fall. But a lot of young folks were more curious than scared of whatever was across the border, since we'd never seen anything to make a fuss about.

I brought the can back into the main room.

"If it's not the Yorkers trying to steal our good soil, it's the New Mainers poaching our live trees for fuel. They're scoundrels, every last American, and I'd know," Bob was growling, punching the awl through his shoe like it was an American too.

"We know, Bob; they're trouble," Denise said, in that voice she used when she knew he wasn't listening to her.

"Stay away from the border, the both of you," Bob said. I didn't answer, and neither did Denise. Bob wasn't talking to us, exactly. He spoke slow and ponderous, but once he got going it was hard stopping him.

"I been on the other side. I been to Old York. Crossed for a grain trade with my dad way back. And I seen horrible things, things I won't ever forget. People strung up like animals, kept in cages. It's their system, see—you break a few rules or you do something to offend one of the governors, that's it. There's no life for you except for work and dying—"

"June, you got that can?" Denise interrupted. She was the only one who could wrangle Bob when he got going with one of his stories.

"I tell you, without the Green Mountain Boys, the Republic would be overrun." Bob didn't want to stop. "They're the bravest of us, keeping our borders safe. Noble, they are. Thomas works hard and gets strong and maybe one day he can become a Green hisself. Bring pride to us."

"June?" Denise said again.

I waited, but Bob waved a hand to say he was done. I was glad. I got an uneasy feeling in my stomach whenever Bob talked about wanting Thomas to be a Green Mountain Boy. My mom hadn't trusted the law, and neither did I. I could remember that much.

"The can says *mixed vegetables*," I announced.

"Well, isn't that nice," Denise said loudly, letting Bob know that the talk about America was over. "After the storm's passed, June, you go up to the Warrens' and give our thanks. Enough about this circus for tonight."

I'm not going up to the Warrens'. I didn't say that.

"There's rain coming in the kitchen," I said instead. I put the vegetables in Denise's hands and left before they could say anything else about Cyrus or tin cans or why going to the circus was a bad idea. I'd heard enough.

2

That night was just like any other storm night, at first. I spent the evening in my room, trying to read by the light of my candle stub to keep myself occupied until I figured out how to get to the circus. Reading was the one thing I'd always had at Bob and Denise's.

They weren't sure I'd live when they took me in six years ago. I was only eight or nine then, and I'd had to lie perfectly still all day long, since every move made my skin scream like it was on fire again. I'd been burned on most of my upper half, the worst of it on my chest and neck. For the first few days I could feel my skin falling off me, and the only thing I remember is the pounding of my heart and the feel of my breath whistling through my lips. A doctor came, and she gave Bob and Denise an ointment to stop infection and told them to keep the burns covered, and that was all she could do.

As soon as my throat opened up I asked for my mom, but Bob and Denise just said that they weren't sure when she'd be coming to get me. The looks on their faces hurt about as much as the burns. They asked what her name was, but I didn't know. They asked where we'd lived, but I couldn't tell them that either.

So I asked for books instead, once I could sit up. Reading was one thing I still remembered. It was one of the gifts my mom gave me. No one else in the Hollow was able to read. Susan Briggs, who kept pigs and lived with her four grown kids, could sound out plenty of words if she tried, but she didn't like it; she said there was a reason books went by the wayside when the world ended—no one had time or need for it anymore.

Bob and Denise had some books they'd been using to start fires in the oven. Bob carried an armload up to my room while I was sick, looking dubiously at them like I'd asked for a pile of old shoes. The books were damp from sitting in the woodshed, and some had earwigs in the pages. Most were ridiculous mysteries with main characters who had pet dogs, or unbelievable stories about Before where characters found their long-lost families or beat the bad guy or got even richer than they already were. Those were the ones I'd give to Bob and Denise for kindling, once I was finished. The books I really loved, which were harder to come by, were manuals, reference guides, and textbooks, full of facts and diagrams, where every little piece fit together and had a name. I had questions I wanted answered, questions that might help me find my mom. And those books had answers, even if they weren't always helpful ones.

Eventually I'd tried to get Bob and Denise to let me go looking for my mom, but they said it wasn't safe, that I couldn't leave the Hollow alone, not with Yorkers and other Americans trying to get past the Green Mountain Boys all along the border of our Republic. But they left me alone while I read, even though Bob told me it was unnatural for someone to spend so much time staring at kindling. And anyway, I knew my mom was still trying to find me, too, even if I hadn't been able to find her. That was one of my secrets, along with the other things I remembered about her—she'd always come back to me, and she'd taught me to be good at waiting.

The storm rattled the sheet metal in my window and a gust hit the house, making water drip in around the cracks, soaking the wadded rags. Once the storm passed, we'd have to scrub the walls and floor dry so the black mold wouldn't come back. That was life in this season—hunker down for a storm, clean up as best you could, then watch the horizon for the next one. It made me want to rattle the windows myself.

But the storm wasn't the only thing keeping me from my book. Another half-memory, flickering around in my mind, wouldn't leave me alone but wouldn't quite come into the light. I was in a car—I could feel the sticky slick of a dusty seat under me. The glass in one window was broken. My mom was there, hunched beside me, wet from the rain. She whispered something—*ghosts, Junie, come to get you*...but before I could remember anything else, the memory sank away, drowned under the sound of rain pounding on the sheet metal.

I tried to catch the memory, but of course I couldn't. Through the years at Bob and Denise's, my memories of the time before the fire never came back. Little bits of them swirled around and visited me in dreams and then faded back into the dark corners of my mind. So I thought about the traveling circus instead. They surely had news from all over, and it would only take one right piece of news, one familiar name for me to go from orphan to daughter again. I couldn't go up to the Warrens' just to say thank you to Cyrus for a can of vegetables; it'd take too much time. What if I got down to the Borough and the circus was gone already? I couldn't follow them across the whole Republic.

Thomas was pacing in his bedroom next door, moving things around and making odd thumping noises. I think he was feeling jumpy too. Storms make people feel all kinds of things they don't like.

Finally I couldn't stand it anymore, so I knocked on the wall—three slow beats. I heard his pacing stop, and then he knocked three times back to me. I knocked twice, and then he knocked once.

Next time I looked up to rub my aching eyes he was there, standing in the dark doorway to my room. He was gangly, all knees and elbows, and I was surprised all over again at how big he'd gotten these last months. He stood so still I might've missed him if I wasn't looking for him. If I hadn't known him, I might have thought he was creepy, but I did and so he wasn't.

No one knew much about Thomas, but I knew that wherever he'd come from had been bad. I'd ended up at Bob and Denise's because I'd been hurt and alone and someone figured the two of them could help me, but Thomas had just showed up under the porch one day about a year ago. It took him a week to come out. Until then, I poked bits of food down through the porch boards for him, and every day Denise would lie on her belly and put an eye down to the cracks and whisper nice things to make him feel safe. When he crawled out, he looked like he was only nine or ten years old, but once he got cleaned up and ate a few meals we decided he might be a bit older than that. And since then he'd done nothing but grow—he was taller than me now. And we'd gotten close too. Bob and Denise weren't family, but Thomas might be.

"You scared of the storm?" I asked.

"No," he said. "I'm scared of this house."

He came and sat on the end of my bed. He didn't have his corncob pipe anymore. It wasn't really a corncob pipe—it was a regular pipe he'd found in the crawl space upstairs. But ever since I'd shown him a picture of Huck Finn with one in *The Adventures of Huckleberry Finn*, he took it everywhere, pretending to smoke.

"I gotta get out of here," he said. He said that every other day or so. "I don't belong cooped up."

"It won't last forever," I said. "It'll be the three of us soon, and we can go wherever you want."

I'd told him about my mom as soon as we became friends. And I'd decided that when I found her, we'd take Thomas with us. I'd always wanted a brother, and he'd always wanted a family. And my mom was the kind of woman who'd welcome anyone into her family—I was sure of it just from the warm feeling I got in my stomach when I thought about her.

"What's she look like?" Thomas asked. He'd asked me that before.

"She's pretty," I said. "Long black hair. Green eyes."

"You said she had brown hair last time," Thomas said.

"No, I didn't. You never remember right," I said, a little too quickly. I tried to picture her in my head. I hadn't said brown hair, had I? It was black.

Thomas didn't say anything for a minute. "We've got to go to that circus Old Bill was talking about," he said finally.

"We will," I said. *Brown hair? Black hair?*

He kept fidgeting, looking at the sheet-metaled window as if he thought he might jump out of it. "Maybe we'll find treasure hidden in a cave and become millionaires," he said after a minute.

That was from *Huckleberry Finn* too. Thomas believed that life outside the Hollow was just like that book. But even I knew that wasn't true, and I hadn't left the Hollow since I was nine. Steamboats sure didn't exist anymore, and people weren't made to be slaves either. At least as far as I knew. I'd read stories that took place after *Huckleberry Finn*, stories where slavery had been outlawed and people weren't so picky about skin color. The trouble was, it was hard to say for sure what the rest of the world was like now, after the Fall. As best as I could tell, people who looked like me and my mom and everyone else in the Hollow were the only ones left, but I hadn't had a chance to see if that was true outside the Hollow. I didn't really know anything about the real world, and the bit that I had seen, I couldn't hardly remember. Everything I read was from Before. Maybe things now, after the Fall, were more like *Huckleberry Finn* than I thought.

"We can share the treasure with your mom, if we find it," Thomas said.

But I didn't want to talk about her anymore, or the color of her hair. "You want to look at Vermont?" I asked. Thomas tore his eyes away from the window and shrugged, and I took that as a yes. "Bring it here."

Thomas went over to the pile of magazines piled against the wall and brought over my copy of *Vermont Life*. He curled up on the end of the bed.

The magazine was one of the only things I had left from before I lost my mom, one of the only things that had survived. The cover was ruined, but I knew what it was called from the inside page: "Vermont Life, Autumn 1991, Volume XLVI, Number 1." And then a stamp: "Middlebury College August 27 1991 Library." I thought a lot about *Middlebury College*. When my mom read this magazine to me, she'd always pretended we were in the library at Middlebury College, not in a tent or a cave or a broken-down car. I wondered if the library was still there.

Thomas and I had tried to calculate how old the magazine was once. The year was 94 After Fall, and the last time people still counted years in the thousands it'd been 2040, or thereabouts. So that made *Vermont Life* a hundred and fifty years old, give or take. No wonder its pages were stiff and the cover was ruined.

"Which pictures you wanna look at?" I asked.

"Colors of Time."

So I turned the pages carefully, the way my mom had shown me. My fingers touched the same spots on the corners of the pages that she had touched before. The story Thomas wanted was about a season called autumn. As best we could tell, there used to be a time when the leaves on the trees would all change color at once, and the whole world would be red and orange and purple for a month. Then the leaves would drop and it'd be winter. That's what the story said, and it had lots of photographs to prove it.

I read while Thomas looked at the pictures, just like I used to do when my mom read to me. I could've said the words with my eyes closed, I'd heard them so many times before.

"Every turning tree carries the ensign of fall, and scatters it across hill and valley. But there are other colors to savor now as well. An ordinary red barn glows with a richer hue in the late October sunlight. On clear autumn days ponds look up at a sky turned impossibly blue, and give the color back again, in seasonal affirmation."

The picture showed a red barn nestled down in a field so green it made my eyes water. The sun coated everything in light, and the trees on the far hillside were green with bursts of red. The only part that looked familiar was the sky, where dark clouds were gathered up on the far horizon. The Republic had barns still, and new ones, too, but none that were red and none with fancy white trim around the windows. Those ones were all piles of rot and kudzu now.

The next page showed a picture of five little kids jumping rope beside a set of big red doors. The American flag hung from the doorframe—back then, the Republic had been a part of America, which was another reason why it was stupid to hate Americans.

"Let's go there," Thomas said. Smiling, I turned the page again. I used to say the same thing to my mom, and she'd always reply that we'd go everywhere together.

"The days shorten, the autumn air turns clear and crisp, and the sun hangs lower in the sky. Gradually, the look of everything changes: the light, the forested hills, the colors that define a suddenly limited world. Schoolchildren bask in the last few days of warm fall weather, enjoying the intense sunlight that makes every leaf and door and clapboard vivid."

"You think the circus is American like Bob said?" Thomas asked. His voice was low and serious now, like it had been when he'd told me he was going to run away down the Mississippi River. I'd had to break it to him that there was no such thing as the Mississippi River, at least not anywhere around here.

"I dunno," I said. "How would they get past the Greens?"

"Yeah," he said. "You ever want to go to America?"

Of course, the right answer was no—at least, that's what we were supposed to say. We were supposed to hate America. But I had a secret that complicated things, a secret I hadn't even told Thomas about, a secret sitting over in the corner of my room, tucked into my backpack.

When I first came to Bob and Denise, I'd been wrapped up in my mom's coat, the only thing she'd left me apart from *Vermont Life*. It was singed from the fire, and part of its collar was burnt bad, but Bob and Denise left it in my room anyway. One night when I was able to move a bit, I crawled out of bed and wrapped myself up in it again, just to be close to her.

It was an old coat, heavy and thick. The fire had burned away part of the lining by the collar, and in bed that night I felt something I hadn't noticed before. I reached my fingers into the coat's inner layer and pulled out a rectangle of paper, thin and fancy. I read it by moonlight: "Treasury of the Reincorporated Federation of America. $50." I found another in the lining, and then another and another. There were dozens of them hidden between the singed fabric.

My mom's coat was lined with American money. That was my secret. I'd thought about it and had decided that it meant one of two things: either she'd spent a lot of time around Americans, or she was an American herself.

"Wonder what it's like to be in a traveling circus," Thomas said. "You could see the whole world!"

"We'll see the world," I said. "My mom and I used to travel all around—we'll do it again."

"When?" he asked, looking at me so intense that I laughed. He didn't crack a smile.

"Soon," I said. "We're doing it already—we'll go see the circus tomorrow."

But just as I said it, Denise appeared in the doorway. "Storm's still coming hard," she said. "And it's coming from the northwest for certain. I don't think you'll get to the circus when this is all over."

I groaned. The circus was out there now, waiting for us. "Can't I go out tomorrow?" I asked.

"No, it's too angry out." Denise limped back to her bedroom before I could get in another word. I had a million things to say to her, but not one of them would come out in time.

I kept turning the pages for Thomas, but I didn't see them. The magazine, the burned coat, and the American money—that was all I had left of her, and it wasn't nearly enough.

"Denise can't tell us what to do," Thomas said.

No one in the Hollow could help me find my mom—it was up to me to find her, and whatever I said to Thomas, I was hoping the circus really was American. If it was, they might know of other Americans in the Republic. Ones that might be hiding, like my mom.

I closed the magazine and crawled under my covers, booting Thomas off the bed.

"We'll figure it out tomorrow," I muttered. "We can't go anywhere in this rain, Thomas." But he was already gone.

The rain hammered on the doors and windows, and on the

roof Old Bill had caulked with pine pitch and ash just a few months ago. I lay in my bed, tossing and turning. And because I couldn't sleep, I heard right away when the pounding on the barricade started.

At first I thought it might be the wind. But Bob came out of his bedroom in his flannel nightgown and hurried down the stairs. Someone was outside the barricaded door, asking to come in.

I slid out of bed and through the dark to the top of the stairs. Bob was standing in front of the barricade, holding the club that he kept propped in the corner.

Sometimes the bad storms blew drifters up to the house, desperate for shelter. We wouldn't open the door for anything during a storm though. And most drifters who were out in a storm were there for a reason—they were mean enough that no one else would let them in either. They couldn't get through the door, but whenever they came knocking Bob would stand there with his club until they left. And I would watch him from the stairs.

The knocking stopped, and Bob shifted closer to the door, listening. I don't know what he heard, because the wind was so loud, but then he did something I'd never seen him do before. He put his club down and unlocked the barricade, right there in the middle of the storm.

Denise must've heard the barricade unlatching, and she limped out of the bedroom. She passed by without seeing me and lowered herself halfway down the stairs.

"What're you doing, Bob?" she hissed.

"It's Jacob," Bob grunted. He swung the barricade out and Denise drew in her breath. The rain was already loud on the roof, but with the door open, it roared. A man stepped through the rain into the kitchen, like a piece of the storm coming apart from itself. The barricade swung shut again, and then all I could see of the stranger was a shadow of wet darkness standing there in the kitchen.

Denise struggled down the rest of the stairs. I followed her partway, but stopped when she flicked on the electric light in the kitchen.

The man standing at the door was covered from head to foot in a black oilskin jacket, dripping with storm rain. Bob and Denise looked like plucked chickens next to him, both of them in their nightgowns and bare feet.

The man looked from Bob to Denise. Then, before I could hide or do anything, he turned his face up to me on the stairs. I shivered. His eyes were shiny under the wool of his hat and scarf, and they got wide when they met mine. I tried to be still, tried to blend into the background like it said in *The Spy Craft Manual.* My hair was covering my shoulders, so my scars were hidden.

"Get that stuff off and leave it by the door," Denise whispered, her voice tight.

The man didn't seem to hear her. He took a step forward, toward me, his eyes still wide and locked onto mine. For that one second, time seemed to stop.

Then Denise stepped in front of him.

"Don't let the rain into the house," she said. The man blinked and looked down at her, and I let out a breath I didn't know I'd been holding. He glanced up at me one last time, then nodded to Denise and stepped back. I stared at him, wondering what had made him look at me that way.

He pulled back his hood and released the fastenings on his jacket. Underneath, he was wearing canvas pants and a clean wool shirt. Something silver gleamed on his chest, a little star. He looked about forty to me, but not an easy forty. There's some people like that, like Denise, who are old even though they're not that old. The man's eyes were gray and his beard was gray and he had lines so deep between his eyebrows that they seemed to have been carved into his face by the storm itself.

But I didn't think about it for long, because as he came into the light, something new shifted in my memory. My heart started racing.

"Don't worry, I'm perfectly dry," he said, and his voice was hoarse as if he hadn't talked in a long time. He unfastened a bag strapped across his chest and put it on the table, rolling his shoulders.

"Come in, come in," Bob said.

"Leave your wet things there," Denise said again.

The man left his stuff on the ground by the door and followed Bob into the living room, Denise following after. I tensed as he came closer. Bob and Denise still didn't see me on the stairs, but the man glanced up again as he passed. He met my eyes for a second, but this time he looked away, as if my face had burnt him. The shadow in my memory shifted again. The man wasn't quite a stranger. I knew him.

"We didn't expect to see you here this time of year," Bob said, sitting down in his favorite chair. He lit up a candle, even though the electric light was still on.

"You were right not to," the man said. Then silence pooled in the room like rain, and I thought they must all be able to hear my beating heart. I knew him. The curve of his shoulders. His sharp eyes.

"So why're you here? Some trouble?" Denise asked finally. She was still standing, even though the stranger had sat down too.

"The Smiths' cattle gone missing," the man said. "Thought I'd be able to help."

"You came up just for a few cattle, Jacob?" Bob asked.

"I was already up," he said, rubbing his hands back and forth across his knees. "The well in Dorset's compromised too. Constable sent me to take a look."

"The well? But how…?" Denise's voice trailed off.

"Surely the Green Mountain Boys ought to be called, eh?" Bob asked.

"Isn't a border matter. Constable's got it well in hand," Jacob said.

"'Course she does. You all do good work down in town," Denise said, shooting a glance at Bob.

"The Greens might want to know. It might have something to do with the Yorkers!" Bob insisted. Denise huffed.

Jacob turned his head while they bickered, his eyes finding mine again. The candlelight flickered on his face, and finally, the memory that I kept tucked away in the darkest, deepest place came spilling out.

I smelled the dark barn, all smoke and flame. I heard screaming, close and shrill. And I saw his face, flickering in firelight.

Bob said something that made Jacob turn away from me again, but I didn't hear any of it.

I forgot about *The Spy Craft Manual* and being sneaky.

I ran back up the stairs and into the dark of my bedroom.

The blankets were cool against my scars. Bob and Denise had called the man Jacob. That name didn't mean a thing to me, but I couldn't get it out of my head. The barn was burning again in my memory, and I was sure he'd been there. And now he was in the room below me. I fumbled with the candle and lifted *Motorsports Monthly* from the floor and tried to read, but the words swam under my fingers. I tried harder but couldn't concentrate. The candle flame flickered in the wind through the cracks and the words on the page turned into Jacob's face, and then my mom's face, and then the memory came loose and broke over me, clearer than ever before…

The candle flickered in a hush of dry wind that blew through the cracks in the barn's walls. Bales of hay rose up around me, their shadows moving like monsters when the flame guttered. My mom was coming back, she'd have to come back soon. I'll only be gone a few hours, *she'd promised when she left. She'd left me the candle to keep the dark away.*

I thought I was dreaming the fire, because it was so cold and I wanted so badly to be warm. It crackled, quiet and gentle, and I rolled over, pulling my mom's coat closer around me and trying to sleep, to stay in the warm dream.

I'd cried when she left. I can come with you, *I'd said. I always said that when she left. But she'd said,* Hush, stay quiet, *and she'd tucked the ends of her coat closer around me and then I was alone.*

The smoke caught sharp in my throat. I coughed and opened my eyes and saw the walls burning, and the bales burning, and everything either dark and smoky or too hot and too bright to look at.

I was screaming, and I didn't know when I'd started. I screamed for her until I didn't have enough breath to scream anymore, because the smoke was in my lungs and the fire was licking at my legs. I didn't know why she hadn't come, how she couldn't hear me. Then something exploded below me and the whole barn shook, and Jacob's horrible face was there, surrounded by fire and twisted up with anger or fear or both.

3

By morning the storm was gone. I hadn't slept much; I'd had too many dark memories spinning in my head. I woke up from the kind of night that feels like a battle and hurried down the stairs, but Jacob was gone like the storm.

I went into the kitchen, feeling queasy and clammy and not sure if I would've had the guts to talk to him, anyway. Not sure what I would've asked him, even. Nothing in the house was different, but I felt different. The walls seemed closer and darker. Denise and Bob talked too loudly.

Denise had turned the electric light on in the kitchen again. The narrow bulb flickered and steadied, an evil yellow glow. The last few days had been fair up till the storm clouds rolled in, and Old Bill had cleaned the solar panel a few days before, so we had some charge. I pulled the sheet metal off the kitchen window to let in some real light. No one was out in the yard or on the road.

"June, careful," Denise said. "Storm might not be full passed—might start raining again."

"I'm going to the circus." I kept my eyes averted from the hanging bulb—it was bad luck to look right at electric light.

"You'll do no such thing. Not today. Too dangerous to go out. And you can't go to the Borough anyway." Denise was filling a bucket from the well pump in the kitchen shed, which connected to the kitchen through a heavy wooden door.

"Who was that man last night?" I asked.

She carried the bucket past me and kneeled down in front of the door. I thought she might be praying, but then I saw the can of potash beside her. She wet a rag and started scrubbing the floor where Jacob had stood. Rainwater was bad luck in Denise's book, not electricity.

"That was Jacob," she said. "He's a deputy in town—the very one that brought you to us, matter of fact."

So I'd been right. He had saved me from the barn fire, and then he'd brought me here. And now he was gone again. I tried to picture his face, to think if I'd seen it before the fire, but I couldn't remember him any better than I remembered anything else from before.

"Why didn't you tell me about him?" I asked. The bulb was still shining bad luck in my eyes.

Denise glanced up. "Nothing to tell. He's got nothing to do with you. He was just doing what all deputies do, taking care of a problem."

"Wasn't a deputy back then, though," said Bob, coming out from the back room with an armload of wood. "Night he brought you was the first time we'd seen him. Came from up north, he said. Constable in the Borough made him a deputy 'bout a year later." He stumped across the kitchen and dumped the wood in the box next to the stove.

"Well, if Jacob can go out, why can't I?" I asked.

"He goes where he wants, and it's none of our business. But you—you stay. You work for us, and I say no." Denise's voice was tight again, and I knew what that meant. She squeezed her rag into the bucket.

"You know the well water comes from the rain, too, right?" Then I darted past her and flicked the switch to turn the light off, holding my sleeve over my hand so I didn't have to touch it, like my mom had taught me. I ran back upstairs before Denise could say anything.

Up in my room, I pulled the metal off my window and looked out. The morning was misty and hushed, like it was holding a secret. It was cold, too, but the sky wasn't roiling with clouds anymore. Downstairs, I heard Denise fitting the cover back on the window I'd opened.

I couldn't stop thinking about the one thing I didn't want to think about. Last time I'd seen Jacob had also been the last time I'd seen my mom. Six years, almost. Six years I'd been waiting for her, looking for her in books and strangers' faces. I had all kinds of stories about why she'd been gone so long: she'd been captured by outlaws; she'd been given a secret mission she couldn't refuse; she'd gone blind and was searching for me by sound, listening for my voice in every town. But seeing Jacob—someone who'd been there, at the very place I'd last seen my mom—was bringing up a sick feeling… Six years was too long. We should have found each other by now.

I grabbed a book from the floor and opened it. *Cattle Husbandry, Volume II.* Cyrus had brought me the book when he started coming to see me. The words on the page were the same old words I'd read before. I threw it against the wall. I didn't have anything to read. I didn't have anything here at all. And the circus might be leaving the Borough today, now that the storm had passed. The house felt too hot all of a sudden, and the air too heavy to breathe. I put my head out the window, where the air was cooler and a breeze rustled the dead leaves on the trees.

I wasn't a prisoner. I might live with Bob and Denise now, but I wasn't their kid. Anyway, the Borough wasn't so far. If Jacob could come and go in the rain, why not me?

I grabbed my backpack from the corner and tossed in whatever I thought I'd be able to trade, plus all the food I kept stored in case I needed to leave in a hurry. I packed my mom's American money, too, hidden in a knitted sock. I wouldn't leave it behind for Bob and Denise to find. Then I pulled on my mom's old coat, which hung down to my thighs, stained and burnt and bulky. It covered my scars entirely, plus most of the rest of me too.

I held *Vermont Life* for a second, then dropped it back on the bed. It was too precious—I was afraid I'd ruin it on the road. If I found my mom, we could come back for it together.

When my bag was packed, I knocked hard three times on the wall. I paused, knocked two more times, and then crawled out the window onto the tin roof. The tin was already dry, and that made me even more mad at Denise for keeping me in.

When I looked back, Thomas was standing in the doorway of my bedroom.

"You coming?" I whispered. He grinned.

We ran until we got through the aspen stand and past the Hastings farm. Then we slowed to a walk, right where the road opened onto the field. The yellow-gray sky loomed above us like the palm of a hand cupped over an ant. Below, the Hastings' fields gave way to scraggy woods. Somewhere in those woods, the Borough and the old quarry road lay hidden. And below that, just visible from up here, the Otter Creek river valley stretched north and south through a corridor of mountains. I could just see the ribbon of Route 7, the old road that Bob said had been overrun by *the good for nothing Alt-Zs and their thieving ways.*

We stopped to rest a moment, and I breathed deep, trying to let my lungs fill up. The fire had damaged my lungs, too, so they didn't work as well as before, but the air was crisp and every gasp felt wonderful. In the early light of the morning, I could see green stalks coming up through the dead grass in the field. I let my mom's coat hang open, taking in the morning air. Behind us, the woods were dark compared to the open field. I wondered if Denise had figured out we were gone yet, and what she'd do when she found out. Would she send Bob out into the wet to come after us, or would she wait until everything was dry to open the door?

I shifted my own pack and turned back to the valley. The bag was heavy with the books I'd brought to trade. But I felt light. We were finally doing what we'd talked about doing, even if we were only leaving for a day. We'd find the circus, and if I was lucky I'd find Jacob, too, and ask him if he'd known my mom. I might be hours away from a real clue about her, and then I'd know what to do next.

"We're lighting out for the Territory!" Thomas whooped, and he danced ahead of me on the road. He had a full pack with him, too, as if he'd been ready to go before I even thought to knock on the wall. He hadn't looked back once. I laughed at him, the way he bounced around like a little kid. But I felt the same way. We could do anything—we could go anywhere. I followed Thomas, almost skipping myself.

We walked quickly until we passed down into the trees at the bottom of the Hastings' field. A blue jay screeched somewhere in the branches. We slowed up, sweating a little, and soon we swung around a bend in the old road and stepped into a ghost town.

A dozen or so cellar holes gaped at us from under the half-dead mess of brush, all that was left of the houses that used to stand there. One house at the end of the row hadn't fallen in yet, but its windows were like empty eyes and half its roof had caved in. A sickly-looking tree grew right up through its middle, and puckerbush grew thick in its doorway. Rusted relics of cars were pushed up on the side of the road every fifty feet or so. Some of them still had color on their sides, but the wheels had been long since scavenged for rubber.

I'd seen all this before, because Cyrus had started taking me to market days a few months earlier. Before the Fall, the Hollow had been the outskirts of a bigger town that had some other name. But when the population dropped, the towns shrank like puddles drying out in the sun. Now the Hollow was separate from the Borough, and I'd only ever been to the Borough twice, with Cyrus, since coming to live with Bob and Denise. And this part of the journey always made me remember how much we'd lost, and how much we'd forgotten.

Up ahead, the trees on either side of the road were all torn up from a tornado or something like it. A few of them were freshly fallen, big ones that must've come down in last night's storm. On the other side of the valley, I spotted a broken church spire, next to a few crumbling buildings. That was the old town, and all that was left of it was the Borough.

"I don't get what happened," Thomas said. He was looking at the old church spire too.

"What d'you mean?" I asked.

"The Fall. I never got it."

I didn't know what to tell him. I didn't get it either. "Bad things happened," I said. "Our ancestors messed up. They got it wrong."

"Got what wrong?"

"Everything," I said, shrugging. They'd broken the planet, somehow, and ruined the soil and killed each other in wars. For the first generation after the Fall, it had looked like no one would survive at all. Some people, I knew, thought it was a religious thing, the Rapture or the End of Days. Made people feel better, I guessed, thinking that it was all part of some greater plan. It was easier than believing it had all been pointless. Personally, I didn't think about it much.

The sun had gone behind the clouds again, and Thomas and I were at a crossroads. The legal way to get to the Borough was to follow the road down along the stream all the way to where it joined up with Otter Creek, and from there to head up the old marble quarry road so everyone could see you coming and the road guards could check your pass. But we didn't have passes, and it was a lot quicker to cut through the woods and down through the solar field and into town that way.

"I've taken the shortcut before, with Cyrus," I said, looking down through the woods.

"Oooo, Cyrus," Thomas said. I blushed.

"Shut up. You know I'm not going to marry him."

"What about Gemma?" he asked, and the thought of Cyrus's sister made me blush even worse. I felt a little tug of guilt—I hadn't told her I was going to the circus, that I might not see her for a little while.

"Come on," I said, to stop Thomas from laughing at me and to shake off the thought of Gemma. I led the way around a rusted skeleton of a car lying on the edge of the road and into the woods.

"Won't we get arrested in town, 'cause we don't have passes?" Thomas asked after a few minutes, his corncob pipe clenched firmly between his teeth.

"Cyrus says that once you're in the Borough, the only people who'd check passes are the Green Mountain Boys, and they don't come into the towns unless they've got a reason."

"They're awesome," Thomas said. He'd found a stick that he thought looked like a gun, and he was shooting imaginary enemies through the trees. I rolled my eyes.

We walked downhill for ten minutes or so through scrubby woods, till the trees got taller and older and I figured we must be getting close. I was trying not to laugh at Thomas, who'd just done an army roll under a fallen log, when I heard a voice.

I stopped, listening through the rush of wind passing overhead. Thomas stopped, too, mid-roll. The voice sounded again—deep, yelling something long and loud, but too far away for us to make out the words. It was coming from farther downhill.

"What's that?" Thomas whispered.

I looked behind us, but nothing moved except the branches of the half-dead trees all around us, swaying in a high breeze. I slipped a little on the slick leaves and stood still for another minute.

"Guess it's nothing," I said finally. So we kept going, and Thomas didn't run around pretending to be a soldier anymore.

A few minutes later we passed a maple tree, so big around that it had to be from Before. I was pretty sure I remembered it from when I'd come this way with Cyrus, and it made me calmer until I heard voices again, more voices than before. Some of them were low and mournful and some were high and shrieking. They weren't human voices, I realized suddenly, a chill prickling down my spine. Something wasn't right.

"What is that?" Thomas whispered, and I turned to tell him to shut up.

And then I saw what was sitting against the base of the old maple tree, the one we'd just walked past. And my words died in my throat.

I backed up quickly, pulling Thomas with me and almost

tripping as I went. The thing lying against the tree was a person—a girl, curled up with her arms wrapped around her stomach. We'd made plenty of noise walking past her, but she hadn't moved. I blinked, not understanding what I was seeing at first.

The girl's hair was spread over her face and tangled up with leaves, and she was soaking wet; she'd been out all through the last storm. Her pants were too short for her legs. Her bare ankles were hooked carefully around each other as if she'd arranged them that way. She wasn't even wearing a jacket.

Then I saw the line of ants crawling over her foot. My eyes followed the line across her hand, up her shirt and onto her neck and her face. They were in her nose and mouth, I realized. And that was about enough for me. I tried to cover Thomas's eyes, but he pulled away from me.

"Is she dead?" Thomas asked.

"Quiet," I said, trying to think straight.

The voices we'd heard earlier were back, louder than before, all talking at once. A bell rang nearby. The sounds didn't make sense to me. The girl was dead—she'd been dead for a while, and she was out here where no one would find her. My heart beat hard, and I could feel ants, hundreds of them, crawling over my body, into my ears... I couldn't stay still anymore. I pulled Thomas away from the dead girl and we ran down toward the voices and the bell.

We didn't stop until we got to the edge of the solar field that covered the hillside above the Borough. There I crouched down, breathing hard, and still brushing my hands to be sure I was free of ants. I wondered what the dead girl's eyes looked like under her hair, and then I had to stop thinking about it. Thomas stood over me, looking back into the woods.

"What happened to her?" he said. He sounded calmer than I felt—curious, almost.

I didn't answer. I'd seen a dead person before—Ezekial Hastings, who'd been sixty or even older than that when he dropped dead in the field while we were all picking beans. And I was pretty sure that before then, before the Hollow, I'd seen a few dead bodies. Death didn't feel new to me. But unexplained dead bodies weren't normal, not here anyway.

"Look," Thomas said, pointing.

A herd of sheep was trotting away through a long, sloping field of solar panels. Their voices, the way they carried on the wind, sounded like people yelling, like people saying, *Help, heeeelp* over and over. One of the sheep wore a bell. So that's what we'd heard in the woods. Beyond the solar panels, the rooftops of the Borough rose up over the trees.

But Thomas crouched down then, and I saw he was looking at something else over in the field: a man kneeling on the ground, his back to us, bent over like he'd lost something in the grass.

I caught my breath, but the man was too far away to notice us. Even so, I didn't want to move while he was so close. We'd already broken the rules coming into town from this direction, and we'd be in trouble if we got caught. Especially if whoever caught us also found the girl and thought we had something to do with it. My mom always said that when a crime happens, it's best to split so no one gets the wrong idea.

Thomas and I crouched in the puckerbush at the edge of the field, and the man didn't give any sign he'd seen us as he stood up and stretched his back. He had the stalk of some leafy plant in one hand and a hunting knife in the other. He wore an oilskin coat, but the hood had been thrown back and his face was uncovered. When he turned, I couldn't stop a quick hiss escaping my lips. The man was Jacob.

4

Jacob put his hand to the small of his back and rubbed it, looking down the field at the sheep. They'd stopped running now, but they were all watching him. Thomas and I watched him, too, trying to be invisible. Jacob tucked the plant into his pocket and wiped his knife on his thigh. Then he walked down the field, headed for the Borough.

"What was he doing up here?" I wondered.

"Who is he?" Thomas asked, standing up and glancing back into the woods again.

"A deputy. He…I guess he brought me to Bob and Denise, when I was hurt."

Thomas looked at me then. "He knew you before you got hurt?" he asked.

I shrugged. "I dunno." I didn't say it, but I was sure Jacob knew something about me, something about my mom. The way he'd looked at me during the storm told me so. "Maybe he did."

"D'you think we should've told him about the girl?" he asked, gesturing toward the woods.

"I dunno," I said again, and then I wished we had, trouble or no. We had to tell someone—why not him? And if we told him, I'd be able to ask him about the barn too.

"Let's go," I said.

We headed down the hill. The image of the dead girl at the maple tree followed me the whole way, her face clear as day in my memory, the ants tracing a black path across her cheek.

If I had to guess, I'd say at least a hundred people lived in the Borough, and that's not counting all the hill folks that came down for market days a few times a year. On those days, the place swarmed. I had a hard time getting used to so many people talking and laughing and arguing all around me. When Cyrus had brought me with him, I'd wear my eyes out looking at all the faces, trying to recognize my mom among them. Trying to recognize anyone I might have known from before the fire.

To get to the proper town, Thomas and I had to pass through a crowd of rough shanties in the thin woods of the lower hillside, where people who didn't farm but couldn't hold on to real houses lived. The neighborhood was quiet, almost deserted. Twice we walked past people slumped on the ground, their eyes open and empty, smiles twitching across their faces. They were high, on salts or maybe LoTabs, like the ones Old Bill had yesterday. Drugs went around the towns like flu outbreaks, Denise said. Supplies flowed in from the border towns and then dried up, and people got high when they could. Thomas and I were quiet now, tired out by the excitement of running away and the fear we'd felt in the woods.

As we came down into the town, I pulled my mom's coat tight around my neck. When I was here for market, my scars always got attention. But today wasn't a market day, and the Borough was quiet when we finally came out onto the quarry road that formed the backbone of the town. The houses here were neat and square like ones from Before, almost like the houses in *Vermont Life*. Most of them had solar panels on the roofs, and a few even had wind turbines shooting up between their greenhouses. Electric light shone out of some of them. The sky had started to darken since we'd come out from the woods.

Thomas and I stopped on the edge of the quarry road. It was white with marble crush and led right up to the mouth of the old quarry from before the Fall. No one was around, and there was no sign of a circus anywhere.

"I think the jail's up there," I said, pointing up the road to where the houses got closer together. "Jacob probably went there. We can ask him—I mean, tell him about the girl."

I didn't like the idea of going to a jail, but it had to be done if we were going to talk to Jacob.

"Maybe they can tell us if the circus is here too," Thomas said. "It's so damn quiet—where is everyone?"

Soon as he said it, a group of people came out of a building farther up the road. They wore green uniforms and flat-brimmed hats, and a few of them carried guns. They must be a Green Mountain Boy squad, and they were headed our way.

My stomach clenched up with worry. Cyrus had said we didn't need passes, so long as there weren't any Greens patrolling. He'd said they hardly ever came through town.

Thomas wasn't thinking about passes and towns. He spotted the Greens and said, "Look, June!" Bob and Denise wanted him to be a Green Mountain Boy, and that was the one thing they all agreed on. Thomas liked any idea that involved adventure.

"No, don't—" I said, but before I could stop him Thomas waved his arm at the Greens, and the man at the front of the group saw us. I thought about running, but that'd make us look guilty for sure.

"Don't tell them anything," I whispered to Thomas as they got closer. The man in the front had a big black mustache and matching eyebrows and his green uniform was working hard to hold him in.

"You need something, kid?" he asked. His eyes were hard, like shiny pebbles. Something about his face made my stomach turn. My fingers balled themselves up into fists inside my pockets.

"Are you Greens?" Thomas said, a little breathless.

The man turned and looked back at the others. "Who's asking?" he said, and then he laughed like he'd just said the funniest joke in the world. The others laughed too.

"Thomas," Thomas said, straightening his back and stepping past me. "You catch any Americans?"

The man laughed again. He didn't seem to mind stopping to talk, though the others kept shuffling along the road like they had somewhere to get to.

"Tons, kid. Strung 'em all up by their toes on the border."

"Yeah, I'd do that if I caught an American too," Thomas said. "I patrol the border too sometimes, just in case." He was lying, of course, trying to impress them, but I didn't like it anyway. I put a hand on his arm and squeezed.

The Greens laughed. "You been to the border, huh?" the man with the hard eyes said, nudging the man next to him. "Sure you're not an American in disguise?"

Thomas shook his head. But the lead Green looked past Thomas, still grinning, and his eyes landed on me.

"You like Greens, honey?" he asked. His eyes flicked to my neck, and I knew he was seeing the scars that threaded around my neck, under my chin, visible over the collar of my mom's coat. I didn't move. Something about his face scared me bad, though I couldn't quite put my finger on what it was.

"You from around here?" he asked when he saw I wasn't going to answer the first question.

"C'mon, Lee. We gotta get camp set up," said a man with a big red beard.

"I'm establishing connections with locals, Greg. It's our job," Lee said, still looking at me. "You local? Got a boyfriend?" He looked at my scars again, and grinned like he'd said another joke.

"None of your business," I said finally, wanting to get away from him as quick as I could. I didn't like him seeing my scars, and I didn't like his questions.

Lee's posture changed. "It is our business," he said, his hand moving to the strap of the rifle slung over his back. "That's the Greens' job—keep the Republic safe from trespassers. Best not to be smart with us."

You're one to talk.

"I'm not being smart," I said.

He frowned. "Let's see your passes."

We didn't have passes, of course. Beside me, Thomas was drifting backward, not so sure about the Green Mountain Boys anymore.

"We're locals," I said, trying to sound polite this time.

Lee stepped forward, and the red beard followed him. "Passes, missy."

He reached out like he was going to take my arm, but then out of nowhere Thomas jumped forward and knocked his hand aside.

"Leave her alone," he said.

Before I could move or even make a sound, the red-bearded man grabbed Thomas by the shoulders and knocked him to the ground. One of the other Greens leapt forward, and the two of them wrestled Thomas until he was flat on his belly, his arms behind his back.

"What are you—?" I started forward, but Lee grabbed me by the arm, twisting it hard behind my back.

"Passes, or we'll have to assume you're trespassing," he whispered in my ear. He smelled bad up close, as if he'd been on the road a long while without washing.

"Lee—" one of the other Greens said, touching his other arm. "We don't have time—" It was a woman, I realized, with long brown braids under her flat-brimmed hat. I hadn't known women could be Green Mountain Boys.

"It's our responsibility to hold folks accountable, ain't it?" Lee shook her arm off. "Well, kid, what's it going to be?"

"Let him go!" I shouted, looking down at Thomas, his face in the dirt. His eyes were wet, and I knew he hated to cry in front of people.

"He accosted a Green," Lee said. "He ought to know not to struggle."

"He's a kid!" I said. "You're a coward if you got scared by him. And you're a coward for having those two knock him down!"

Lee's lips went white and he pulled me close again. "Don't insult me, bitch," he hissed. "I can make you regret it." Then he backed up and said loudly, "And what's in your pack? You dealing LoTabs?"

"What—no, I—" If he looked in my pack, he'd find my

mom's American money. And that was worse than drugs, I was pretty sure. I had to stop him from looking.

"Might have to search under that jacket too," the red beard said, leering.

"Please—we just came to see the circus, and we don't have passes," I choked out.

Lee grinned down at me. "So you are unauthorized trespassers."

I nodded. "We're sorry," I said, the words sour in my mouth.

"Lee, they're just kids," said the woman who had spoken before.

"I seen kids younger 'n this slit a man's throat for a piece of bread," Lee answered. Then he smiled at me, his mustache flexing on his thick lip like a black caterpillar. He must've seen that I was shaking, and he thought it funny.

"All right, honey, you're under arrest for trespass and under suspicion of malicious intent."

Lee pushed me forward, gripping me hard by the arm. Beside me the two Greens holding Thomas lifted him up and pushed him along too. His chin was bleeding and he looked scared and mad and he wouldn't meet my eyes. I was breathing hard. My mom's coat had fallen below my scars, but I couldn't fix it with Lee tugging me forward.

I heard a sigh behind me from the woman who had tried to stop Lee arresting us. "We're gonna be late," she muttered to one of the others. "No point in this."

The Greens led Thomas and me up through the middle of town. Up closer to the quarry opening, the buildings got bigger and bigger. These ones weren't for living in—they were stores and a meeting house and a church. They blocked out the trees and the sky and all the shacks and shanties out beyond the quarry road too. The buildings made me feel small and stupid—We'd lasted about five seconds out on our own before getting caught. And now the town was going to eat us up, toss us into the dark of one of these big buildings, and leave us there to rot, if the Greens had anything to do with it. The circus would leave town, or maybe they'd already left, and we'd have nothing to do but wait for Bob or Denise to come take us back to the Hollow.

We headed toward a log building with one window and a door in front. Lee dragged me up the steps, but before he pulled me inside, I twisted around to look back. The sky was already rusty red with evening light. The wind was a quiet whisper, and everything was still in the Borough. Way back along the road, among the shanties, a lone voice rang out, calling someone in for supper. Thomas whimpered as Lee opened the heavy wooden door, and we all stumbled over the threshold.

5

First thing I saw when we walked into the log building was an electric light bulb—the biggest I'd ever seen—hanging down over a cast-iron wood stove in the middle of the room. The whole room was bright with its light, and I couldn't look at it straight without my eyes hurting. I tried to keep my gaze down, but I was too nervous and kept glancing up again.

The room was big and cluttered. Old desks from Before lined the walls, covered in dusty computers and piles of rope and a mishmash of junk. A jumble of wires snaked up the wall and out through a crack in the corner, and I wondered how much electricity they were managing to pump in. It made me uneasy, being in a room with so many wires. An echo of my mom's voice flashed in the back of my mind, so quick I almost missed it: *Electricity was what ended the world, Junie. We oughta turn it off forever.*

"Didn't expect a visit from such es-teemed guests," said a voice from the wood stove. A man sat with his back to us, creaking slowly in a rocking chair. I thought for a second it might be Jacob, but then he turned his head to squint at Lee, and I saw it wasn't him at all.

"Wilson," Lee said. He sounded like his teeth were stuck together. "Where's the constable?"

"Out," the man named Wilson said. He wasn't wearing a uniform, just a patched shirt and overalls. He was drinking something out of a battered plastic cup, and that made me remember how I hadn't had anything to eat since morning. I was still holding my pack, and I could almost smell the food I'd gathered from my bedroom before I left.

"I got a couple trespassers," Lee said loudly. "They both tried to get into town past the watch, suspicious-like. You want 'em, or should I take care of it?" Then he knocked my backpack out of my hands. I'd been reaching inside, trying to feel for any of my food. The bag hit the ground hard on account of all the books, and *Parable of the Sower* fell out, but I didn't dare pick it up—it was too close to Lee's boot. My chest was feeling tight again, like I couldn't get a proper breath in. The edge of a woolly sock was just showing under the book, and if Lee looked inside it, he'd find the American money.

Wilson twisted around to see Thomas and me, then heaved himself out of the chair. He wore glasses that made him look like a confused old owl, his hair a feathery fringe around the bald dome of his head. He blinked at us like he'd never seen kids before.

"Trespassers, are you?" he asked me. It was the first time I'd been asked a polite question since we'd started out that morning.

I looked at the glass discs of his glasses. It was easier than staring straight in someone's eyes.

"No, sir."

"Protocol is they gotta be questioned by the constable." Lee crossed his arms and shifted back and forth as if he'd gotten bored with us already. "You local cops gotta do something to pass the time, after all."

"I know how it works, Lee," Wilson snapped. "I'll see the constable talks to 'em when she gets back. You can get on with whatever it is you're doing here, so long as you leave folks alone that don't deserve your trouble. Or better yet, get a head start on your trip to Town Meeting."

Lee snorted and shook his head. I thought he was going to put up a fight, but instead he turned on his heel.

"Carry on, *deputy*," he said, drawing out the word. "And you best get rid of that electricity before I come through here again. It's bad luck." He stomped out.

My lungs relaxed a little when Lee left, but only a little. The room was still stuffy, and even though I knew the heat was from the stove, it felt like it was coming out of the light bulb instead, like it was about to burst into flames. The last place I wanted to be was stuck in a cell under the nose of the law. This was exactly what my mom had warned me about. Things had gotten out of control, and I couldn't do anything but stand there and keep a hand on Thomas's elbow.

Wilson took his glasses off and wiped them with a cloth from his pocket. His eyes looked like tiny pinpricks without the glass to magnify them. I stood straight, even though my hands were shaking from being tired or scared or I don't know what. Thomas kept looking at the light bulb and then rubbing his eyes, and then looking at it again. His chin was still bleeding, but he was just letting it drip.

"Your book fell out," Wilson said to me finally. I bent down automatically and shoved *Parable of the Sower* back into my pack, then stood up again to face him. As I did, I saw him see my scars. I yanked my mom's coat up.

"Can we go?" I asked. Wilson shook his head.

"But don't worry, constable oughta be back soon," he said, smiling a little. He looked us over as if we were the most mysterious things he'd ever seen, and his eyes disappeared behind the gleam of the electric light when he put his glasses back on. He sighed. "But you two look like you're about to fall over. Come on."

He walked through a dark hole in the wall I hadn't noticed before, and another lamp—a regular oil lamp—lit up in the next room. Thomas looked at me. I shrugged and we followed Wilson.

The other room was full of jail cells. All of them were empty except for low cots and empty chamber pots, which they must have gotten from a proper jail, because the metalwork was too fancy to have been made after the Fall. Each cell had a bed, and Wilson gestured toward the closest ones.

"Don't worry," he said again, and I think he said it especially to me, seeing the look on my face. "I won't even close the door."

He walked back out and I heard the chair creak as he sat back down by the stove in the other room. Thomas and I looked at each other, and for some reason it was easy to walk into the two closest cells and sit down on the cots. I took a bit of bread out of my pack and we ate it without talking. Out in the main room, Wilson's chair squeaked as he rocked, and no one else came into the jail. I thought about going to ask where Jacob was, but instead I lay down and stretched out on a cot, just to catch my breath for a minute, and Thomas did the same. I didn't think I'd be able to sleep, and I was right. So I lay there and tried to match my breathing to Thomas's, listening as he slowly drifted off.

I wonder sometimes if things could've turned out differently if I hadn't made so many mistakes that first day in the Borough. It's easy now for me to think I should've been braver and smarter right from the get-go, but then I have to remember how little I knew then, and how alone I was. Anyway, I didn't feel very brave or very smart when I woke up and I was in a cage and Thomas wasn't beside me anymore. I just felt panic.

I sat up quickly. I hadn't realized I'd fallen asleep, and my brain was turning itself upside down trying to figure out where I was and what was happening. I was in a shadowy room full of cages, with electric light filtering through the door. There were no windows, and I thought I smelled smoke. I heard voices in the next room. The darkness was all around me, and I just wanted to hide. I pushed myself to the end of the bed, right up against the wall, and listened.

"I really don't see this as necessary," someone said in a smooth voice, carefully sounding out every part of every word in a way that seemed strange and foreign.

"I'll decide what's necessary," a woman replied, her accent clearly from the Borough. "If you've done nothing wrong, you'll be on your way again soon as we find someone who has."

"But really, is this the way justice is supposed—"

"Wilson, sign these folks in and get 'em in the back."

"You got it, ma'am," said Wilson, and when I heard his voice I remembered where I was and that I wasn't really a prisoner, that the door of my cell was open. I whispered Thomas's name but he didn't answer.

Then a whole crowd of people walked through from the other room. I slipped to the edge of the bed and sat down on the ground next to my bag. The hard dirt floor smelled like dust and sweat. I curled up small, but then I remembered the girl I'd seen in the woods. She'd been sitting just like this, in the same position. I straightened my legs out again, and as I did I heard a hiss from under the bed in the next cell.

There was Thomas. I should have known—he was stretched out under the bed, grinning at me and pointing at a little hole he'd scraped out of the dirt floor.

"I'm digging us out," he whispered. I put my finger to my lips, because there was no time to tell him that we'd die of old age before he dug a hole to freedom.

Wilson followed the crowd, raising his oil lamp high. The light spread across the crowd and sent shadows crawling up the walls.

"Two to a cell," he called back to all the others.

The group of people stopped, filling the hallway, but none of them so much as looked at the cells. I was starting to wish the door of my little cage had been closed and locked after all.

"Sir, I strongly object to your methods," said the man at the front of the group, the one who had spoken in the strange accent earlier. He was tall and thin, and had a get-up on the likes of which I'd never seen before. His pants were pinstriped in blue and white, and his jacket and tall top hat were red and covered in white stars. I could see patches on his elbows and frayed thread at the cuffs, and the fabric looked thin and too fancy to do much good against any kind of wear. His face was pale, his cheekbones sharp. He looked smart, and he also looked like he knew it.

"Just get in there," Wilson said, like he was just about done being nice. "If you're innocent, you'll be out again soon."

Nobody moved. A couple of men in the crowd were really big, and I thought Wilson was pretty brave to stand up to them.

"You heard the man," came another voice from the doorway—the constable. It was easy to tell who she was. For one thing, she had a brass star pinned to her chest. For another, she was holding a rifle at her side. Right away I knew she was the most confident lady I'd ever seen. The stranger closest to her was a giant, with big muscles and a face all screwed up like he was about to spit, but the way she glared at him you'd have thought he was a little kid who didn't want to go to bed.

The giant was the first to move. He looked the constable up and down, then twisted his mouth back into shape and backed into the cell across from ours. He sat down on the bed so hard I was surprised it didn't collapse under him. Then the rest started shuffling into cells, and the constable just watched them all, her mouth a thin line. I could almost feel the heat coming off her glare.

Wilson walked back down the room, locking the cells with a big key as he went. When he got to Thomas's and my cells he looked a little surprised to see us.

"Oh, constable," he said, "got these two trespassers or something—Greens found 'em in town without passes. Lee says you gotta talk to 'em."

The constable came and looked in at us—well, at me. I tried to meet her eyes, to keep my shoulders back like she did. She was the law, and my mom and I didn't trust the law. She crouched down and peered under the bed at Thomas.

"What time they get here?" she asked.

"Couple hours ago."

The constable looked at me again, and I blushed. She had dark blond hair cut short to her chin, and a line between her eyebrows from frowning. She didn't look mean, but I could tell she didn't trust anyone who was a stranger, including me.

"We didn't do anything," I said. "We just came for the circus; we didn't mean to be in town without passes."

"But you were," she said, gently enough.

"Can't you let us go?"

She sighed, turned to take another look at the crowded jail cells.

"We'll hold on to them all for now," she said to Wilson, calm and certain. "Gotta clear this matter up. These kids don't look like killers, but you never can tell these days."

She straightened back up and motioned to Wilson to follow her out. He went right along with her, no questions asked. And even though she was the law, I would've followed her too. I didn't even know her and I wanted to make her proud.

"Where's Jacob? We need him," I heard her say as they left. My ears pricked up at that—Jacob was going to be here soon, and he could vouch for us. He'd seen me only last night at Bob and Denise's, and he knew I wasn't a criminal. I might be able to talk to him, then ask him what he'd seen the night he saved me from the fire.

But then I remembered the other reason I had to talk to him—the dead girl was still out there, tucked into the maple roots. And now we'd been arrested, it didn't seem so easy to tell a deputy that we'd been in the woods with a dead person just a few hours ago, especially when the constable was talking about killers. I crouched to look under the bed at Thomas, and he stared back at me from his hiding place, and I didn't know what to do.

"Who are all of them?" Thomas whispered. I looked around.

I had a pretty good idea who the folks in the cells were. The man in the pinstriped suit shared a cell with a woman wearing a red dress that tied up tight around her waist. She was so beautiful I found it hard to look away. In the next cell a teenager skinny as a sapling was stretching one leg, wearing pants that were too short for her and a loose blue shirt. Her skin was the color of soil after rain, darker than anything I'd seen outside of books, and her hair was pulled into a thousand intricate braids. So not everyone left in the world looked like me after all.

She was with another woman dressed all in black. Then there was the giant, who had a tiny mustache and big muscles, and another man with shifty eyes and a real leather vest. Finally, in the last cell, a man and a woman wearing matching green shirts.

I glanced back at the man in the pinstriped suit. We'd found the circus after all. Problem was, we were all locked up.

"Runaways, hm?" said the beautiful woman in the red dress, breaking the silence and smiling over at me. She had a nice voice, and talked like she was always just about to laugh. I didn't hear voices like that too often, and I wanted to hear more of it. She had curly black hair and lips that were painted a bright red. I felt plain and bedraggled in my mom's burnt coat and Bob's old flannel.

Thomas crawled out and sat on his bed, staring at the woman just like me.

"Well, we might have found you just in time," she continued, like it was perfectly natural that I wouldn't answer. "We're a runaway's dream. Don't all runaways want to join the circus?"

"You're in the circus?" I asked, even though I knew that already. I blushed.

"This is the grand ensemble," the man in the pinstripes said, still pronouncing each word with syllables I'd never heard before. "The musicians, the strong man, the contortionist, the knife-thrower," he pointed to each person, making fancy spins with his hands so it all seemed very grand, "and finally, your ringmasters, Sebastian Aguera and Alexandra Delamonde," he finished, taking the beautiful lady's hand and whipping his top hat off. The two of them bowed.

"We were looking for you," Thomas said, and Alexandra beamed at him.

"What a treat! Why were you looking for us, sweetie?"

"I thought you might have some books to trade and stuff," I said, before Thomas could answer. Best to start off slow—I'd learned that from Bob.

"Books?" She smiled as if I'd said something funny. "The kind with pictures, you mean?"

I blushed again. *I can read. I could read to you,* I wanted to say. But Alexandra was still looking at me so closely that I got shy.

"Why're you here? In jail?" I blurted instead. The constable had said something about killers, but I didn't think they'd found the dead girl, not when she was out in the middle of nowhere in the woods. So who else was dead?

It was as if I'd lifted up a flat rock without realizing a hundred centipedes were sleeping underneath it. The room positively rustled—the musicians turned to look at Sebastian, the knife-thrower stood up and started pacing, and Sebastian danced his hands at them all, making some kind of signal I didn't understand.

"We don't know," Alexandra said, and her voice was cool and level like a breeze over water. Everyone else quieted down. "The constable came by our camp and asked us when our last performance had been. We told her, and she said we all had to come with her. She said some kind of crime had been committed, and that any visitors to the town were suspects." She made everything seem reasonable and simple.

"This is just a charming example of local law," Sebastian said, careful and precise. "We are a defensive folk, but the constable doesn't mean any harm. I'm sure we'll be sent on our way very soon. We've done nothing wrong, and we're simple citizens like anyone else."

"You're…from here?" Thomas asked, sounding disappointed. But Alexandra smiled at him with her red lips and crouched down with her hands on the bars so she was level with him on the bed.

"But of course," she said. "Where else would we be from?"

Thomas opened his mouth and glanced at me. I thought of the American money in my pack and my stomach sank. If they were from the Republic, the most I could hope for was whispers and rumors, and maybe some books I could trade for. But if they'd been Americans, it would've been a sure thing that they could help me find my mom.

"Go ahead, sport, tell us what you mean," Sebastian said, like all this talking through prison bars was a lot of fun. All the circus folk turned to look at Thomas too. He shrank away from all the eyes on him, but then he scuffed a foot and spoke again.

"You're wearing an American flag," he said to Sebastian.

"Now why would you say that, bud?" Sebastian asked, sounding impressed.

Thomas reached inside his jacket and pulled out a rolled-up magazine.

"Thomas!" I hissed angrily as he unrolled my copy of *Vermont Life*.

"Sorry," he said. The magazine was damp and the back cover was half torn along the fold. He smoothed it out and opened it up to the article "The Blue and the Gray in Vermont." The page had a black-and-white picture of an American flag flying over a tombstone. He held it up to show Sebastian and Alexandra.

Sebastian smiled, his eyebrows arching right up to the brim of his top hat. "I suppose my suit is like the American flag! You're a sharp kid. And you know, that used to be the Republic's flag too."

"Put it away, Thomas," I whispered.

"Nothing wrong with talking about the American flag." Alexandra winked, and a lock of dark hair fell across her face. She tucked it back behind her ear with the backs of her fingers. "It's not a crime, is it?"

Her offhand comment made me want to smile—I'd been thinking the very same thing. Who said America had to be bad, anyway? My mom wasn't bad—it shouldn't be a crime to be from across the border, or to have money from somewhere else.

Still, I pulled *Vermont Life* out of Thomas's hands and slid it as carefully as possible into my bag.

"You shouldn't take my stuff. You can't keep things clean," I said to Thomas before I could stop myself.

"You shouldn't have talked back to the Green Mountain Boys and got us arrested," Thomas retorted, turning his back on me with a huff as he sat down.

"That's okay, kid—we're all in this mess together now," Sebastian said, smiling.

"Don't be a baby," I whispered at the same time. Thomas just rolled his eyes.

I was about to say more, but in the lamplight I could see the bruise coming in on Thomas's forehead from where the Greens had held him on the ground. And that made the fight go out of me a bit. He'd gotten big, but he was still a kid. And it must've been scary for him, sneaking into town with me.

"They're gone, at least," I said to Thomas, keeping my voice low. "And now we know to stay away from Green Mountain Boys."

"If you hadn't talked back..." Thomas insisted, digging a toe into the dirt floor.

"Come on," I said. "They were wrong to arrest us and you know it." Thomas loved soldiers and warriors, but I couldn't believe he'd defend bullies who'd made him bleed. Greens were supposed to protect the borders, but from what I'd just seen they were more interested in hurting people than in doing right by the Republic.

"Imagine what they'd have done to us if they'd found us up in the woods," I said, nudging Thomas through the bars so he had to look at me. "Think they'd have waited to hear our side of the story? They just want to catch people, no matter if they've done something wrong or not."

"You don't know that," Thomas said, shifting away from me.

"What's up in the woods?" the man in the cell across from us asked suddenly, the only one Sebastian hadn't introduced. He was wearing a leather jacket and the knuckles of his hands were stained dark as he clenched his fists around the bars of his cell.

"This is our tinker, McLean," Alexandra said. "He's good at fixing things."

I didn't much care who he was—I didn't want to tell him what we'd seen. But Thomas made the choice for me.

"Someone died up there," he said. "A girl. We saw her."

The others all went quiet at that. I glared at Thomas but couldn't think how to get him to shut up without making the circus think we were hiding something. And I wanted to stay on their good side, so they'd help me.

"How horrible," Sebastian muttered, then sighed as if the whole world disappointed him. "It's not unheard of, but what a terrible thing for children to see. Was it someone you knew?"

Thomas shook his head. "A stranger."

"You poor things," Alexandra whispered, looking at Sebastian and then back at us. "You must've been very frightened. Did you tell the constable about it?"

When I didn't answer and Thomas didn't answer, Alexandra smiled like she understood us perfectly. "I know how you're feeling. It's hard to trust someone who's just thrown you in jail—I get it."

"We just haven't had a chance to tell her yet," I said quietly.

"I don't blame you, given what can happen to people who are just in the wrong place at the wrong time," Sebastian said, nodding again. The other circus folks were listening, and a few nodded along with him.

"What do you mean?" I asked.

"You must know what I'm talking about," Sebastian said quietly. "We've seen it all over. Down in Williamstown, a kid not much older than you said he'd seen a pickpocket in town—and what does the law do? They arrest *him*. Cut off two of his fingers, just 'cause he'd tried to point them to a criminal." Sebastian's face twisted with disgust, and another of the circus folk—the knife thrower—made a *tsk tsk* noise.

"Why would they do that?" I asked.

"Easier that way," Sebastian said, with a sigh. "They're pressured to arrest criminals, and if they can't find the actual culprits, it's simple enough to find some innocent bystander who happened to be there, and lock them up instead. Who knows—maybe this constable is different. But I don't blame you for hesitating."

I didn't know what to say to that. I wanted to tell the constable about the dead girl all alone up there. What if her murder had something to do with whatever the constable had locked the circus up for? But I hadn't forgotten how the Greens had treated us—my mom had taught me that someone looking for lies would find them. So maybe the circus was right and we were all just innocent bystanders after all, and the killers were still at large.

"It is a pity that girl died, but she won't be any worse off for you waiting till you're sure," Alexandra said softly. She made it all seem so simple, her words turning knots into perfectly straight lines.

"Or maybe the authorities will find her on their own," Sebastian said hopefully. "Where'd you say her body was?"

"Up past the solar field," I said.

"Well, that doesn't mean you're responsible for her," Alexandra said soothingly. "You focus on figuring your own situation out, and then help her when things have calmed down a bit here."

"I suppose," I said, scuttling back into the darkness of my cell, trying to get all their eyes off me. I didn't care for so much attention all at once, and my mind was busy enough as it was without having to work its way through a conversation with a bunch of strangers. I expected Thomas to lie back on his bed, too, but he stayed where he was, watching the circus while they said quiet things that I couldn't quite hear.

6

Don't touch it, *my mom said. I wanted to touch it, though. It itched so bad that all I could think about was itching, itching. When she looked away, I scratched my arm where a long red cut throbbed. My skin burned where my fingernails touched. I couldn't stop, though. The itching was too bad. I scratched until the cut bled, and then kept itching. Then my mom was there again, pinning my arm down.* Don't touch it, don't touch it, *she whispered.*

Shuffling footsteps in the other room woke me from a groggy sleep.

The oil lamp had gone out again, so the only light in the cells came through the half-open door. Thomas was curled into a tight ball on his bed, his back to me. I couldn't be sure if the circus was asleep or just quiet, but I knew they were there and it made me uneasy. The room was too dark, too crowded, and I didn't know if it was daytime or nighttime outside.

I heard a heavy thud from the other room, and a hissing of voices like rain on a glass window.

For a second I was scared that someone might have locked the cell while I slept, but the cell door was open. Hidden by the darkness, I crept over and peered into the other room.

Three people stood close around a table, a dead sheep lying on its surface under the flood of electric light. Like my day wasn't strange enough. The sheep's head was twisted back at a queasy angle, its eyes a dull black that glittered in the light from the bulb hanging overhead.

"Strangled, you think?" Wilson was saying. "Never seen eyes like that."

"What do you say, Jacob?" the constable asked, after a minute of silence. So the third person, the one with his back to me, was Jacob. I recognized his oilskin coat, the curve of his shoulders. I took a half step forward, but couldn't bring myself to tell them I was there just yet.

Jacob pried the sheep's mouth open, peering down to have a closer look. He sighed. "Can't say for sure," he said. "Looks like its insides are swollen."

"So what does that mean?" Wilson asked.

"Might be poison," said Jacob.

"Poison?" Wilson sounded confused. "Who'd have poison?"

I was breathing low and careful, trying to stay quiet. This must be the crime we'd all been locked up for. It was just like Sebastian had said—we'd just been nearby, and now we were in jail for something we didn't do. Killing livestock was a serious offense, not something I wanted to be accused of. I stepped back again, trying to fade into the darkness, but the floor under my feet creaked.

The constable, Jacob, and Wilson all looked around. Jacob's face was already grim, but it darkened even more at the sight of me standing in the doorway.

"What's she doing here?" he asked, sharp and quick.

"Come on out, girl," Wilson said gently. "The Greens brought her in," he told Jacob. "They been making folks show passes while they're here. Guess she didn't have one."

"Greens will have to arrest half the town if they're looking for passes," the constable muttered. "They don't even have jurisdiction. I'm sick of them stepping on our toes."

"Surprised they bothered stopping anyone. Said they were in a hurry to get to Town Meeting up in Middlebury," Wilson said. "Anyway, does she look like a sheep poisoner to you, Jacob?" He laughed a few wheezy hacks.

"No, we should let her go—she's no one," Jacob said, and I felt a little stab of hurt I couldn't quite understand.

"Never can tell from a person's looks," the constable said mildly, but she didn't seem too interested in me. "Why poison, Jacob?"

But Jacob didn't answer, his eyes still fixed on me. The constable said his name again, and finally he turned back to the table, blinking, like he found it hard to focus. The small window by the door was dark, and I wondered if he'd been pulled out of bed to come here. I couldn't tell how old or young the night was.

"I found some plants up in the solar field that I don't recognize," Jacob said slowly.

The constable whistled. "I guess the end times really are here. A plant you don't recognize?"

Jacob smiled, quick as a flash, and the sight reminded me of a memory stuck in my mind—his bared teeth in the fire. The constable smiled, too, her eyes warm.

Wilson prodded the ewe uncertainly. "So that's it, Jacob? Weird plant, maybe poison, case closed?"

"Not quite," Jacob said. "I've almost got it, though. Look."

He lifted a book off a nearby table. Was it his book? I couldn't quite read the title from where I stood by the door.

"Look at this—this is it. Same leaves, same flowers. Look." Jacob put the open book on the table, alongside the leaves I'd seen him gather in the solar field. He pointed, and I saw that his hand was mottled with burn scars, just like my neck, back, and shoulders.

"Shit," Wilson said. "What good's that?"

"If we could just find out what it says, it might tell us what happened."

The constable sighed. "Seems a thin hope. You want us to get one of the Millerites down here to read a little thing like that? We'd have to turn the electricity off, and go through their prayers, and we don't have time for that with a jail full of strangers."

I leaned forward on my toes, trying to see the pages of the book.

"It's here, though, Sarah," Jacob said. "This time it's right here. We can figure this one out."

The constable crossed her arms, and the men waited to hear her thoughts. I could tell from the way she held herself that she knew folks would listen when she talked.

"What about her?" Wilson said suddenly, pointing at me.

"What *about* her?" Jacob repeated warily.

"She's got books in her pack—I saw them," Wilson said. "Can you read, honey?"

I nodded.

"Can you read this?" the constable asked.

I nodded again.

"Come over here and have a look," Wilson said coaxingly, like I was a stray dog he was trying to charm.

"She's not—" Jacob started, but then he stopped himself.

"Jeez, give 'er a chance. What's the problem?" Wilson said, gesturing me forward.

I walked across the room, which seemed like a long distance, and stood at the edge of the electricity's glow.

"Go on," Wilson said. Jacob pushed the book a little closer to me and I picked it up, feeling the heat rise to my cheeks as they looked at me. Reading wasn't exactly private, but I didn't read with just anyone.

The book's title was *Wildflowers of the Northeast.* It was open to a page with a picture of the plant Jacob had found in the solar field, labeled *cowbane: Oxypolis rigidor.*

I read the words in my mind, and then they were mine. The constable and Jacob and Wilson stared at the page with me, but the words didn't come to them. For that short moment I was stronger than them, richer than them. I knew what the plant was, and I knew what it had done to the sheep, and they didn't.

"Will you let us go if I read it to you?" I said. I looked up at the constable just in time to see the flicker of something changing in her face—her expression hardened and her gray eyes focused in on me, because now I was bartering instead of helping.

"We're going to let you go either way," she said coldly. "Now will you help or not?"

That hit me like a slap. I'd just embarrassed myself bad. I looked back down at the page, and it took a second for the words to come into focus again. I wasn't used to the electric light, could feel it burning on my skin where it touched me. I read the words quick, the pleasure of it gone.

"*A herbaceous wildflower indigenous to a wide temperate range within the contiguous United States, cowbane has compound odd-pinnate leaves widely spread on glabrous, veined stems—*"

"The heck are you talking about?" Wilson cut in.

"It's what it says," I said, even though I didn't know what the heck I was talking about either.

"Is there anything about what happens if you eat it?" the constable asked.

I searched the box of words, feeling pin pricks in my armpits. What if I didn't find it? What if I missed it?

"Here—um…*must be avoided as a source of food.* And before that…*the foliage and roots are highly toxic and have been known to kill livestock as well as domestic pets. Symptoms include vomiting, hypersalivation, loss of muscular control, and dilated pupils.*"

I looked up. "That's what you wanted, right?"

"That's what we feared," Jacob said quietly. He'd been right. I wasn't sure how he'd guessed that one strange plant had poisoned the sheep—I wouldn't have been able to do that.

"And you found that stuff up in the solar field?" The constable shook her head. "We'd best send someone up there and clear it out before any more of the flock gets into it."

"So it was all an accident?" Wilson said slowly, squinting down at the book like he was reading. But he was looking at it upside down. "That traveling circus sure ain't gonna be happy we dragged them up here on suspicion of sheep murder."

"That's the way things are," the constable said stiffly. "We get strangers in town and five sheep die; we can't just ignore it. And they've only been in there a few hours."

She glanced out the window, and I looked too, trying to see if the day was coming yet. It was hard to tell with the weather being so temperamental and the window so small.

"Is there anything else?" she asked suddenly, and I glanced over to find her staring at me.

"What?" I choked out. Of course there was—that girl up

in the woods. She'd faded away while I read, but now she was back. This was the time that I should tell the constable what I knew.

"Anything else in the book, about the cowbane?" she said. I looked down, and then back up again. I saw the girl's hands, curled up in her lap and wet with rain, the ants marching a trail across her pale cheek. And then I heard Sebastian's warning again: *It's easy enough to find some innocent bystander, and lock them up instead.*

I closed the book. "No, that was it."

They were sending someone up to the solar field anyway. That was pretty close to the woods where we'd seen her. Odds were that they'd find her without my help. Those were some of the lies I told myself while I stood there with my hand on the book.

7

"Okay," the constable said to me. She looked tired, but her back was straight and her hands were planted on her hips. "No reason to keep you around anymore. The Greens don't like it, they can file a complaint."

She looked down at the sheep for a long minute, then sighed.

"What's happening in this town? Sheep, cows, wells...makes me wary to leave just now."

"All the more reason you best go to Town Meeting, Sarah," Wilson said. "Find out what's going on, and if it's in the other towns too."

The constable shook her head. "I worry 'bout leaving. But I suppose you're right. You two can hold things in place the few days I'm gone." Wilson nodded, but Jacob was still staring at the sheep.

"You okay, Jacob?" the constable asked.

Jacob flinched like someone had pinched him, and blinked a few times. "Fine," he muttered. The constable studied him, looking a little worried, before turning and walking back to the jail cells. I tried to summon up the courage to ask Jacob what he knew about my mom, but he'd turned to listen to what was happening in the back room. So I turned to listen too.

We heard the jingle of keys and the shuffle of feet.

"You're free to go," the constable called.

"Just a dreadful accident, hmm?" I heard Sebastian say.

The circus filed out, straightening shirts and squinting in the brighter light of the outer room. The constable returned, followed by the man Alexandra had called a tinker.

I turned to Jacob again, but he was watching the tinker with narrowed eyes. The man paused while the others headed for the door.

"You going to apologize?" he asked the constable.

"What're you talking about?" she asked.

"Not very nice, locking us up for no good reason," he said. He stood close to her, closer than she probably wanted.

"We were doing our job," she said, her voice light and even. She made to walk past him but he stepped in front of her.

"C'mon, sweetheart. One little apology won't hurt anyone."

"Get out of my way," the constable said.

Then something happened fast. The tinker did something—touched her in a way that strangers aren't supposed to touch—and before a second had passed, she'd taken a step back and kneed him hard in the crotch.

The tinker swore and sank to the ground. In a second Jacob and Wilson were there, heaving him up by either arm.

"You want him back in the cell, Sarah?" Jacob asked.

"Nah. Toss him." The constable wasn't even breathing hard. She looked just as composed as she had a second before.

"Better out than in," Wilson said, and they dragged the man to the door and tossed him out. Through the door I saw the other members of the circus look back as their tinker fell in the dirt. Jacob and Wilson were both chuckling as they came back into the room.

The constable saw me staring at her. "What?" she asked.

"How did you—?" I wasn't sure what to ask. I'd never be brave enough to do what she'd done. But she'd made it look easy.

"Don't seem so surprised," she said. "World like this, you gotta show folks what the rules are. Better yet, make 'em feel it."

"But what if they fight back?" I asked.

She shook her head. "It's safer in the long run to draw a clear line. No local would've tried what he just did. They know me too well."

I nodded slowly. Then I heard the sound of a book thumping shut behind me and I whipped around. Jacob was heading for the door, the plant guide under his arm.

"Wait!" I said, hurrying after him.

Jacob barely paused. "I got places to be," he said, trying to step past me.

"Well, I got a question for you," I said, putting a hand on his arm. He looked down at my hand and then up at my face.

"I can't tell you what you want to know," he said. But even though he looked again at the door, he didn't move. The pale electric light made him look old—his beard mostly gray, the lines around his eyes deep. He didn't look like a man who would run into a burning barn to save a little girl.

"But do you…? Did you…?" Now that I had him, I found it hard to say anything at all. He didn't help me figure it out, he just looked over my head at the door.

"Do you know where my mom is?" I finally asked. And then, for no good reason, my eyes misted up and my throat got swollen and I had to blink and glance away so he wouldn't notice. When I turned back to him again, he looked as bad as I felt.

"I don't know your mother," he said.

"But you were at the barn when it burned, right?" I said.

He paused. "Yes. I was there, but—"

"You got me out."

Jacob took a step back. "I got places to be," he said again, clearing his throat and shuffling a little, like he didn't quite know how to leave without being awkward. He rubbed his hands together, and I looked more closely at the burns, thinking about where he'd got them.

"Didn't mean to scare you, up at Bob and Denise's the other night," he said finally.

"You didn't scare me," I lied. "I seen plenty worse than you."

Jacob's mouth went thin at that. "They're good folks though, Bob and Denise? Treat you good?"

"They're fine," I said, starting to get annoyed. "But I'd rather have my mom back, which is why I want to know if you—"

"I don't, though, Leah," Jacob said, firmly this time. Then he stepped around me and headed out the door.

Who was Leah? I looked around at the constable and Wilson. They'd heard it too. They looked at each other, understanding something I didn't.

"Why'd he call me that?" I asked.

"Heck, I barely know your name either," Wilson said, chuckling. "Now don't you have somewhere to be?"

"But—"

"That was the polite way of saying *get out*," the constable said, raising her eyebrows at me.

"Okay, I—I'll just get Thomas." I hurried past her into the back room, not wanting to annoy her. The room was still dark, so I had to feel my way over to Thomas's cell.

"Thomas, time to go."

He didn't answer. "Thomas?" As my eyes adjusted to the dark, I could see his cell was empty. He'd gone.

"Did you see Thomas?" I asked the constable and Wilson when I came out into the main room, pulling on my backpack. I tried to keep my voice calm, to be as composed as the constable.

"He went with the circus," Wilson said, back at his post beside the wood stove. "Walked out with 'em."

But I barely heard the last of what he said, because I was already out the door.

I didn't see Thomas anywhere when I burst out onto the street. Morning had arrived, the air damp and soft compared with the electric buzzing in the jail. The town was coming alive again—workers heading out to the fields, kids on the street knocking around something that might have been a soccer ball once upon a time. A pair of women in brown robes walked past, dragging an old computer through the mud by its wires and chanting the sing-songy prayer of the Millerites.

In the distance I spotted a few people I thought might be from the circus, heading up the road toward the quarry. I was about to go after them when I heard a laugh from the other direction, drifting on the breeze like robin song. I recognized

Alexandra's laugh and swiveled to see another group of folks turning down a side path through a thin scrum of shanties and into a tree linc.

I took off running after them, but by the time I got to the side path, Alexandra and the others were in the field on the other side of the trees. Beyond them a red tent rose up tall as a house, surrounded by a flock of carts and wagons like chicks clustered around a hen. A little pack of horses grazed beyond the camp. I had to fight my way through the milkweed and tangleroses choking the path, and my lungs were so tired out I could barely yell "hey!" at their backs.

Thomas was there, right beside Alexandra. When I finally caught up with them, I was panting and sweating and mad enough to hit someone, but Alexandra just spun in her red dress and beamed at me.

"This is the Big Apple!" Alexandra announced, smiling up at the red tent.

"Thomas, don't you ever run away like that again!" I gasped. We were supposed to be a team, and now he was following Alexandra like a silly puppy.

"Oh, sorry." Alexandra laughed. "He didn't run away—he just came ahead with us. No harm in that, is there?"

Thomas glanced my way, a little guilty but not remorseful enough for my liking. I wanted to shake him.

"He's my brother. My little brother. We stick together," I said to Alexandra. I'd never called Thomas my brother before today, and now I'd done it twice. And I felt it too. We were in this together. We had to keep each other close, like my mom had tried to keep me close.

"Do you want to see the circus tonight, Tommy boy?" Sebastian asked, sidling over to us in his swishing coat. The rest of the group had faded away, gone into the tent or covered wagons, I supposed. Now that we were up close, I could see that the Big Apple was travel stained, but it still loomed taller than any tent I'd ever seen.

"Don't you have a mom and a dad who'll be worrying about you?" Alexandra said gently.

"No," Thomas said. "I do want to see the circus." He had his corncob pipe out again, so he was trying to impress them.

"Well, we can take care of that!" Sebastian laughed, pulling off his top hat and twirling it around a finger. Thomas watched it spin, his expression serious.

"As long as his big sister approves?" Alexandra smiled at me in a way that made my stomach get all knotted. I pulled my coat up around my neck, just to make sure my scars were hidden from sight. Alexandra spoke like we were friends, but I still felt like a stick in the mud, like I would ruin everything if I said no. But of course we were going to stay. I had to talk to them, to ask if they had any news of an American, of a woman searching for her daughter. If Jacob wouldn't talk to me about my mother, the circus folk were the only chance I had left. I'd jumped out the window thinking I'd be gone for a day or so, but now I realized that I didn't want to go back to the Hollow. Not tomorrow or ever. I wanted to find her.

I nodded to Alexandra, and watched her smile grow.

"Oh, bravo!" Sebastian said, as if I'd done something impressive.

"Let's give them a place to wait, just until the show. They've come so far, and they're so sweet." Alexandra petted Thomas's shoulder. Her fingernails were red, like her lips.

"Of course! What's the circus for if not charity?" Sebastian's voice had laughter in it. The top hat spun suddenly up into the air off his finger, and he leaned forward a bit so it fell right on his head. His expression became serious again the second the hat landed. "And then we need to talk. Gather up the others once you're done with our runaways."

Alexandra led us to one of the bigger covered carts, dancing a little in her bright red dress. I caught myself wondering what it'd feel like to wear something as beautiful as that. I pictured myself in a red dress, my skin smooth and scarless. But it was just wistful thinking; Alexandra moved her body in a way I never could.

She opened a little wooden door at the back of the cart and led us in. A wall of warm air hit me like a pillow pressed to my face. The room smelled of flowers, but stronger than any real flowers could be. Afternoon light filtered red through the fabric hung over a little window. I felt dizzy from all of it.

"You're special guests," Alexandra said, her voice a little muffled by the fabric and the heat. "You can stay here in my cart until the show. There's some candy in the drawer if you get hungry." She smiled down at Thomas, and she was so beautiful with the red light all around her that I forgot to breathe for a second. I followed her pointing finger and saw a little table beside an enormous bed covered in shimmery fabric just like what she was wearing. Every surface glittered. I felt rough and lumpy, and I was glad I had my mom's coat on so she couldn't really see me.

"Where are you going?" Thomas asked Alexandra, and a little flicker of annoyance went through me again. He didn't like talking to anyone except me. Or at least he didn't used to.

Alexandra stood in the open door of the cart, all lit up from behind.

"I've got a meeting with the fairy council, sweetie. I have a marvelous story to tell them about my new runaway friends." She met my eyes and held them for a moment longer than I expected. Then she winked, a secret one just for me, and swept back down the narrow stairs.

The door closed behind her. I didn't have time to ask her anything, not about my mom or anything else.

"Thomas, what's got into you?" I snapped instead, dumping my bag down on the ground and turning on him. Everything had happened so fast, I felt like I'd been trampled and was only now able to get to my feet again. I was starting to sweat in the warm cart.

"I like her," Thomas said. He was looking at the shimmery fabric on the bed. "She's nice."

"I'm nice, Bob and Denise are nice, and you don't go running off wherever we tell you to go."

He shrugged, his lips pressed together. "The Hollow is stupid, and everything in it is stupid."

"Jeez, what about me?" I said, trying to keep my voice light. He didn't answer.

"I'm serious, we gotta stick together while we're here." I was getting angry again, and hurt by what he'd just said. "How are you gonna be safe without me?"

"It's not supposed to be safe—that's the adventure!" he snapped.

I tore off my flannel and shoved it in my pack, but kept my mom's coat on. We'd jumped out the window expecting an adventure. But this wasn't what I'd planned on. All we'd gotten was arrested. And now we were in a stranger's cart and I hadn't gotten up the nerve to ask the circus a damn thing.

Thomas reached over for the chest of drawers. "Don't touch anything," I hissed.

"She said there's candy," he said, and pulled open the top drawer.

Even in the dim light, I saw right away that the drawer was full of books. Thomas started to close the drawer, but I pulled his hand back and opened it the rest of the way.

"They're not yours, they're hers," Thomas said, trying to push me aside. I opened the next drawer down and found the candy. I scooped a few brownish packets out and tossed them to Thomas. He stopped trying to push me and inspected the candy.

I pulled four books out of the top drawer and spread them out on the bed. Three of the books were familiar: *The Holy Bible, The Grapes of Wrath,* and *American Gods*. They looked like all the other books I knew: worn, yellowed, battered.

But the last book was different. Blue, white, and red stripes wriggled across its hard cover, and the colors were intense in a way I'd never seen before. I picked it up and opened it. The spine was stiff, every page creamy white and shiny. I put it up to my face and smelled something sharp and bright.

And then I understood, and my breath caught in my throat.

The book was brand new. The world was over, but right in front of me was something that might have been printed yesterday.

I flipped to the cover again. It was called *Manifesto of Unity*. On the first page someone had stamped a picture of an eagle holding arrows and a branch of green leaves. The words around the eagle said, PRINTED IN THE YEAR 73 AFTER FALL BY THE NATIONAL PRESS OF THE REINCORPORATED FEDERATION OF AMERICAN STATES.

I sank to the bed, Thomas beside me, chewing noisily on the candy. I turned the pages until I found the start of the first chapter.

8

The book started like this:

It is our belief that the Fall of American society since the Last World War and subsequent Five Years' Famine was a necessary culling of excess and decadence. Our government and culture had indeed bloated into a machine of monstrous intent and appetite, and though we do not celebrate the suffering and loss of life endured by our parents and grandparents, nevertheless we submit that The Fall was a necessary and just expulsion of diseased ideology. Just as flesh grows over a healing wound, we will rebuild stronger than before. And where we find continued infection, we will strive ceaselessly to excise the sickness. Thus will our new order rise, whole and untainted, from The Fall.

I turned the page and saw that my fingers were shaking just a little. This was it, the exact thing I'd been looking for. The only kind of person who'd have a book like this in their bedside drawer was an American. So the circus had lied at the jail, and all the rumors Bob had heard had been right. They must be American.

I looked up. The cart was full of nooks and crannies, drawers and shelves that might hold all kinds of clues.

Thomas was lying on Alexandra's bed now, eating candy and staring at the ceiling like he was a hundred miles away. He didn't know about my mom's American money. He thought all Americans were criminals, just like Bob and Denise. And he was so young; if he found out about the circus, he might want to turn them in just for the adventure of it. So I couldn't tell him.

"I'm bored," Thomas said suddenly, making me jump. I shut the book.

"Thought you liked the circus," I said.

"This ain't the circus. We're just sitting here."

"Isn't. And why don't you go find something to do?" My fingers toyed with *Manifesto of Unity*.

"You coming?"

"I'm tired. I'm going to stay here for a bit. Go see what the circus is up to."

"They said they're in a meeting."

"It'll be fine. Just don't go anywhere but the big tent, okay?" It was nearby, and I'd easily be able to check on him.

"Fine." He sprang off the bed, tucked a few more candies into his pocket, and took his corncob pipe out again. "Bye!"

As soon as he'd clattered out the door, I put the book down on the bed and stood up. I'd read the section in *The Spy Craft Manual* on finding hidden codes and secret compartments. I knew how to search without making a mess. And as long as Alexandra didn't know what I'd done, it wouldn't hurt her.

I started with the rest of the drawers in the bedside table. I rifled through decks of cards, crystals, and a surprisingly sharp switchblade that nicked my finger. Nothing useful. Next I went to the little sunken shelf in one wall of the cart. *The Spy Craft Manual* said to always wear gloves when searching, because otherwise they'd find your fingerprints. But my fingers didn't leave any marks I could see. Before, folks had machines that could find things like that. I guess that was one advantage of the end of the world for me.

I found another book on the shelf, but it was just full of directions for how to wire up electric things. I put it down quickly. A chest at the end of the bed held nothing but brightly colored clothes made of fabrics I'd never seen before. They smelled like Alexandra.

How long had I been searching? I went to the door and looked out, but no one was coming. Then, even though I was getting nervous about getting caught, I checked under the bed and found rope and a box of tools I couldn't make heads or tails of. So I sat for a little bit, looking around and feeling stumped. Finally I remembered one more thing from the *Spy Craft Manual* and checked under the mattress.

Nothing there either.

I felt a low, sick ache rising up in me, the kind of disappointment that you only get after a rush of stupid hope. I could still ask Alexandra what she knew. I could trade her for information. But if she'd lied before, I wasn't sure how I'd get her to tell the truth this time.

I picked up *The Manifesto of Unity* again. I wanted to take it with me. I wanted to keep reading it. But I'd found it when I shouldn't have. I'd been snooping, and I didn't want to make the circus distrust me before I'd even had a chance to find out what they knew.

I slid it back into the drawer with the other books, thinking I'd go out to find Thomas and try to talk to Alexandra. But just as I was about to close the drawer, I remembered that I hadn't looked properly at the other books yet. I took out *The Grapes of Wrath* and flipped through the pages. Someone had written notes in the margins, little comments I could barely read. I'd hardly ever seen a real person's handwriting before, since almost no one wrote anything these days. *American Gods* was the same, the printed words surrounded by handwriting, like the printed words were a herd corralled by cowboys.

I picked up *The Holy Bible* last and opened it. Some bibles were fun to read, with lots of stories and magic. Some were depressing. This looked like one of the depressing versions. I flipped through the pages. No writing in the margins.

I was about to put the book back in the drawer when a piece of paper fell out from between the pages. It was folded up small, and looked so innocent that I almost didn't even bother to open it. Almost.

The single page contained a list of some kind. I read it slowly and carefully, trying to understand:

Ty Madison, Plumber—Ludlow—Water systems—Est. 85 AF
Ruth Nguyen, Shepherd—Dorset—Food systems—Est. 88 AF
Neil Delamonde, Tinker—New Bennington—Electric grid—Est. 87 AF
Effie Freeman, Runner—New Rutland—Vice—Est. 79 AF

The list went on, but I stopped reading there. My heart about stopped too. I heard her voice, echoing out from the dark place of my memory: *Pleased to meet you. I'm Effie Freeman, and this is my kid, June.*

Effie Freeman was my mom's name.

I forgot I was in a stranger's cart. I forgot I was snooping, that I should get out of there before anyone saw what I'd found. *Effie Freeman. Effie Freeman.* I read the line over and over, trying to figure out what it meant. Runner? The other names were linked with jobs, so maybe that had been her job. But what was a runner? I remembered us running, but not getting paid for it. And *Vice* didn't make sense either. The year, 79 AF, was a year before I was born. The only thing that made perfect sense was the location: New Rutland. Every name on the list had a place next to it; so maybe that was where they lived. And if that was true, then this was the clearest clue I'd ever gotten.

My mom was in New Rutland.

I was breathing hard, trying to take it in. New Rutland was just a few days' walk north. I'd never gone there, not that I remembered. But there was a lot I didn't remember, and she and I had always been on the move, camping out and keeping a low profile. Maybe we'd lived near New Rutland, and maybe that was where she was still.

I looked over the rest of the names, but no one else seemed familiar. I went back to my mom's name over and over, like it might disappear if I looked away for too long.

I'd been right. The circus was American, and my mom was American too. That must be why she hadn't been able to find me! She'd been in hiding. But the circus knew her name. Maybe they knew where she was and could take me to her.

I stood up and ran my fingers over my mom's name one more time, making sure to memorize the words, then slid the paper back into *The Holy Bible.* Then I grabbed my pack and left the cart to find Alexandra.

The air was heavy outside and the mountain behind me

looked hazy and distant. Another storm was on its way. We'd seen more this season than ever before.

The colorful flags on the wagons swayed in the breeze and the walls of the Big Apple rippled, but otherwise everything was still. I didn't see Thomas, or Alexandra, or anyone. But a whisper of voices floated out from the big red tent, so I hurried across the grass and through the open door.

I'd never been in a tent so big before. The air felt eerily quiet compared to the wind outside. The light, filtering through the red walls, was the color of fire. On the far side of the tent, the folks from the circus stood around a wooden stage, their low voices echoing across the open space.

I followed the curve of the tent wall, recognizing Alexandra's bright dress among the crowd. Sebastian was nowhere to be seen, and neither was Thomas. I hoped he was hidden behind the stage, hoped he hadn't run off again.

It seemed like the circus folks were planning an act.

"William, you'll be on the pulley," Alexandra called, "and the band, you'll be down in the back." Everyone went where she asked without question. The strongman waited beside a length of rope hanging down the back wall. The tinker and the knife thrower stood against the walls near the entrance. I took a step forward, hoping to get Alexandra's attention, but she was too focused on whatever it was they were practicing.

"Let's see," Alexandra said. "The flying entrance is ready, and the liberty act. We'll do just those tonight, to get some practice in. But everyone needs to know their positions for the grand finale, so we'll be ready when the time comes. The VIPs will be in the chairs there, right in front of the stage. We'll tell them to stay seated, though the charge should work even if they're standing close by. All ready? Now call out your blocking."

"Torch sequence," the contortionist called.

"Throw and light," Alexandra said, miming throwing something into the air.

"Close and secure!" the tinker called from the tent entrance.

There was a little pause. "Tommy?" Alexandra called.

I didn't know who she was talking about at first. But then his voice piped up from behind the stage.

"Oh—flip switch!" Thomas said.

"Thomas?" I whispered. I circled around behind the stage and saw an opening in the tent wall that led to another room in back of the Big Apple. Thomas was there, standing at attention in the empty space with his pipe in his mouth and a black top hat on his head. The hat looked just like Sebastian's, only more battered.

"What're you doing?" I hissed. Alexandra had seen me now, but she was still saying something to the others.

"I'm helping," Thomas said. He didn't look happy to see me and kept glancing over my shoulder at the others.

"What do you mean?" I said. "You're going to help them with the show?"

"I dunno," he said.

"Just for tonight?" I felt a meanness in me, and realized I didn't like how easily he'd made friends with the circus. They'd let him join in, no questions asked, and meanwhile I was just some stranger, sitting alone in Alexandra's cart. But I was the one who was connected to them, even if they didn't know it yet.

"Yeah, just for tonight," Thomas said, looking at me with his big, innocent eyes. He smiled.

"That was great, sweetie," Alexandra said, coming up behind me and laying a hand on my back, right below my shoulders. "Wasn't he great, June?"

Her touch sent a jolt through my whole body, a complicated sort of shiver.

"What're you practicing for?" I asked, trying to cover up the way I'd jumped by turning toward her.

"A new show. We're just rehearsing, of course." Alexandra laughed. "Tonight we'll do our normal act, not this more complex one. The world premiere we're saving for Town Meeting up in Middlebury."

"Oh," I said.

"I think we'll have time for one more run-through before the show. Ready to try again, Tommy?"

"Wait, um—can I talk to you?" I asked. My mouth felt unwieldy, every word rounded and dull compared to her crisp pronunciation.

"You are talking to me," Alexandra answered, smiling at me like she had before, like she already knew we had a secret together.

"I mean, about—I have some questions."

"I love questions," Alexandra said. "Let's meet after tonight's show. You can come to my room, have some wine with me."

"After?" I said, and then I blushed at how slow and stupid I sounded.

"I assume you and Tommy are going to stay the night?" Alexandra said, looking between me and Thomas. "It'll be much too late for you to go home after the show."

"Oh," I said, and then I smiled too. They wanted us to stay. I felt my shoulders relax. I'd talk to Alexandra tonight, and then she'd help us find my mom. Maybe we'd find her together.

"Excellent! Back to first positions!" Alexandra called, her voice ringing to the farthest corners of the tent.

They'd just finished another full run-through when Sebastian's voice came floating through the tent door. I looked out the tent entrance and saw him trotting down the path from the Borough on a black-striped horse. I thought for a second that it was a real zebra, like in books, but then I saw that the stripes had been painted on, and that the paint was running down its belly. Sebastian was shouting into a megaphone. "Come one, come all, to see the Greatest Show on Earth! Forget your woes, come see the circus! The world's over, but the show must go on! The spectacular, the strange, the lost secrets of the Before Times! Watch our performers fly and delight! We take all trades in exchange for a glimpse of our magnificent circus! Come one, come all!"

Even for me it was hard not to feel a little stir of something giddy when Sebastian flipped his hat into the air and caught it again. He was so bright and loud and full of happy energy, energy we didn't usually see around here. And people were actually following him back from town. Sebastian kicked his striped horse into a trot, circling the Big Apple and shouting into his red megaphone, and before long a whole stream of people started flowing into the tent. At first it was kids, younger than me and some even younger than Thomas, who came running in little packs and pairs. They all looked more or less the same: mops of long hair, patched clothes, runny noses. Every kid had a runny nose in the Republic.

The musicians started playing, and the tunes swam through the air and filled the evening up with noise. Some of the kids shrieked and ran around after Sebastian and his horse, and some hung back, shy. They kept looking over their shoulders for the grown-ups, who came trailing behind them.

The grown-ups looked a bit more like I felt: tired and a little wary. Some of them wore masks, and some had crosses around their necks. One little boy, one of the shy ones, ran back and grabbed onto the legs of a girl not much older than me. I guess she was the little boy's mother, since she scooped him up and held him tight. I wondered how old she was—how old mothers usually were when their kids were that little. I wasn't even sure how old my mom had been, when we'd been together. I looked for her face in the crowd, as usual, but for the first time her absence didn't hurt, because now I knew where she was. She was in New Rutland, not here.

And then the tent was full, and Thomas swaggered back over to me from the back room, still wearing the black top hat. I tried to feel amused instead of annoyed, and finally settled somewhere in the middle. It was hard to stay focused on any one thing anyway. The strongman and the tinker jostled around, taking trades for the show. A lot of people had brought dried apples to pay their way in, since, I guess, last year was a good apple year. But some people traded other stuff too. One man pulled a cracked computer tablet out of a sack, touching both shoulders with two fingers to ward off bad luck before handing it over to the tinker. Thomas and I kept inching out of people's way until we were backed up against one of the outer tent walls. The light outside was fading, but someone had lit a few oil lamps around the perimeter of the tent.

I looked over at the door just in time to see Old Bill come in, holding a bottle and cackling with a few other drifters I recognized from the Hollow. I was glad we were pressed against the wall then, because I didn't want him to see me and try to talk to me again.

I was watching him weave through the crowd, stepping on toes and shaking everyone's hand, when I spotted Jacob leaning against a tent pole, his silver deputy badge pinned to his coat.

The happy glow in my stomach faded a little. I couldn't tell if Jacob had seen us or not. He was looking at the far end of the tent, toward the curtained back room. He hadn't told me the whole truth earlier, I was sure of it. But then I hadn't told him the truth either. The dead girl was still up there in the woods, alone—I'd almost forgotten about her in the excitement of the circus. I looked away, hoping he wouldn't notice me.

Finally, when the tent was full to bursting, a row of electric lights flared on and lit up the stage. The musicians started beating on drums, louder and louder until all the voices from the crowd died. The patch of sky through the wide tent entrance had gone dusky with evening, so it felt like we made up the whole world, with nothing but empty space beyond us.

Then the drumming stopped and Sebastian stood in the middle of the stage, his hat in his hand. His striped pants and starred jacket shone in the electric light, and the crowd broke into whispers. I saw people looking at each other and an old man shaking his head. So they remembered what American flags looked like too.

Sebastian's face was as serious as death. He looked out over all our heads like we weren't even there.

"The end, friends," he whispered, and a few people shrieked because somehow his voice was coming from all around the tent, from a hundred places at once. I spun around—his voice was right behind me, hissing out of a black box attached to a tent pole. An electrical cord snaked up out of the grass, around the tent pole and into the box. He was using electricity to talk.

The wind gusted under the tent wall but I barely noticed it. I grabbed Thomas's sleeve and pulled him sideways, as far away from the black box as I could get. The whole crowd in front of me was looking up at Sebastian again, and all I could see was the backs of all of their heads.

"The end is hard, friends," Sebastian said again, and his voice came out of the speakers louder this time. His eyes swept across the crowd. "We don't have much hope left. We prob'ly don't have much time left, either." His voice was different than it had been before, his sharp accent replaced by the drawl of the Borough—he sounded like us. I bet he fooled the other people in the crowd, but not me.

"What we do have, folks, is today. Right now. And in this tent, the end of the world ain't so close anymore. We've got the start of something. And you've got it too. So lean back and prepare to be amazed. I bring you wonders from beyond the Republic!" Sebastian's voice was so loud at the end that lots of people looked around at the speakers again, some covering their ears. I pulled my mom's coat higher around my neck, though I knew fabric couldn't hold back electricity.

When I looked back up at the stage, Alexandra was floating down from the dark roof of the tent. At first it looked like she was flying, but when I blinked hard I saw she was holding on to a rope. I followed it up into the canopy and then back down to a corner of the tent, where the strongman was slowly reeling her down. But no one else seemed to see him—they were watching Alexandra. She had changed out of her red dress into a green one, one that draped around her body like a curtain and hung down past her feet. A crown shone on her head and a lit torch burned in her free hand.

She reached the stage and Sebastian said, "Here is the Lady of Liberty!" and then he backed up, leaving Alexandra alone on the stage. She lifted the torch above her head and swung her hips around in a kind of dance.

"Will the torch go out?" she cried. "Or will it shine on through the night?"

"It'll go out!" Old Bill shouted from the floor. The crowd laughed, but Alexandra smiled.

"You think so, do you?" She laughed, and her teeth were shiny white against her red lips. "But my light is special. It's strong enough to stand on its own!"

She lowered her hand, but the torch stayed above her head, floating in midair. The crowd gasped. Alexandra laughed again. She reached into the folds of her dress and pulled out a book. It looked just like *Manifesto of Unity*, and I almost missed what she said next because I was suddenly worried that she knew I'd looked through her books.

"The world is not as it seems—there is more beyond the horizon than you can imagine. Look!" She opened the book and a white bird, bursting out of its pages, flew up and hit the canvas of the tent roof, then fell down behind the crowd. I tried to see where it had fallen and saw Jacob instead, still leaning against the tent pole. His sharp gray eyes met mine, as if he'd already been watching me.

The crowd was shouting and clapping. Alexandra laughed again, then reached up and plucked the torch from the air.

"Let's try something else, if you still don't believe me," she said. I tore my eyes away from Jacob and watched as the tinker carried a bucket onto the stage and put it on the ground in front of Alexandra. She dipped a finger in the bucket and brought it to her mouth.

"Water from your own streams—surely the flame cannot survive this, you say!" she cried.

"How do we know it's water?" Old Bill yelled.

"Come, by all means, taste it!" Alexandra said, swinging her hips and beckoning with a finger. Everyone laughed, but no one went up to try the water.

"Watch—will the water douse the torch?" Alexandra held the torch high, then dunked it in the bucket; when she pulled it out again, the flames flickered even higher than before.

The crowd was getting rowdier. I heard Old Bill's signature cussing, louder than anyone else. The people up front pressed against the ones behind them. A lot of folks made the sign of the cross—though surely that was for warding off electricity, not magic. I grabbed Thomas's sleeve again, just so we wouldn't get separated.

"Yes, the flame is strong!" Alexandra cried, holding the torch above her head and the book to her chest. "And the flame grows!"

Then the contortionist, the brown-skinned girl around my age, ran onto the stage. She was wearing a bright orange suit as tight as a layer of skin, so bright it almost made my eyes water. She flipped in midair, then stretched one leg up above her head and held it there. She reached over, took the torch from Alexandra, and put it on her lifted toes. The torch balanced there, high above her head on the pillar of her leg.

And then the flames of the torch started to grow. I couldn't see how it happened, but one minute the flames were low and flickering and the next they were licking the air four feet above the torch. The light shone on the roof of the tent, and sparks flew off the torch in all directions. I started to sweat. What if the tent caught fire? I could almost see the oil lamps hanging around the perimeter exploding, sending boiling oil onto people's hair, shards of hot glass into their skin. We'd burn before we could get out, or we'd be trampled by the panicked crowd.

The contortionist reached up and lifted the torch down from her foot. She held the flames right up to her face and an explosion of fire burst up into the air from her mouth. People in the audience screamed as the flaming ball grew up around the contortionist's head, shining on the red tent so it looked like the whole place was on fire, and then I couldn't help it, I couldn't stop the barn from building up around me—

A rush of cold wind brushed against my back, and without

thinking, I turned to it and rolled under the bottom of the tent wall. I looked back as I rolled, just long enough to see that Thomas hadn't moved, and that he hadn't checked to see where I'd gone. I stumbled away into the damp night.

9

I didn't stop running till I was far away from the Big Apple, out in the open field with the wind all around me. I was panting, even though I hadn't run long, and my head was spinning so I leaned over and tried to think about something else.

I hadn't expected the show to scare me like that. I worked around fire all the time—coals in a cook stove, at least. And the memory of the burning barn didn't bother me so often anymore. Sometimes I went days without smelling smoke and feeling my body tense up. But fire like the stuff Alexandra and the contortionist had been playing with, fire that wasn't trapped in a metal box or a glass lamp—that was different.

I knew I had to pull myself together. I had to talk to Alexandra, to find out for sure what she knew about my mom, and why an American circus was in the Republic in the first place. But I couldn't go back into the Big Apple, not until I was sure all the flames were gone.

The evening was chilly and windy, with big gusts coming from unexpected directions. The sky was huge out here, black and empty. I'd read about how Before, the sky was full of airplanes, even at night. On clear evenings I sometimes saw moving stars that I thought might be satellites. They must still be up there, even though whatever they'd been doing was pointless now.

Music started playing in the tent, and laughter drifted to me on the wind, so I figured the act had changed. Shivering, I watched as someone came out of the tent, opening the flap in a flash of light that disappeared when the canvas fell down again. I wondered why they'd left the show, and if they were coming my way. Maybe they'd just come out to take a leak.

"June? You up there?" It was Old Bill.

I kept quiet, but he caught sight of me anyway in the dim light from the Big Apple. He stumbled toward me, his bottle sloshing against his leg.

"You came after all," he said. "Couldn't resist a little fun, huh?"

"Yeah," I answered. "You're missing the show, though."

"We could make our own show up here," he said. He lifted the bottle over his head and danced closer. It would've been funny if he hadn't been drunk and we hadn't been alone in the dark.

"No thanks," I said. I tried to step around him to head back down toward the Big Apple, but he grabbed me by the waist and swung me around, trying to make me dance. His stale sweaty clothes reeked, and I smelled the moonshine on his breath too.

"I still got those LoTabs, Junie," he slurred into my ear. "We could forget together. You got plenty you want to forget, right?"

I pushed him away and he stumbled back, dropping the bottle and cussing. Then he reached out to grab me again, and I had a moment of dark sinking fear. I knew what happened to girls who found themselves alone in the dark with men. But then I remembered what the constable had said earlier that day: *Show folks what the rules are. Better yet, make 'em feel it.*

I wasn't sure where all Bill's parts were in the dark, but I kicked my knee out anyway. It hit him in the stomach, and he reeled away. I stepped back, too, which was good because a second later he retched and heaved a spray of sick on the ground.

"Dammit, bitch," he said, feeling around on the ground for his bottle. He staggered to his feet, bottle in hand, and stumbled down the hill.

I barely had time to take a breath before I was on my guard again, because someone else was hurrying up the hill now, passing Old Bill and coming straight for me. I clenched my fists and planted my feet.

But it was only Jacob.

"What'd he do?" he said, coming right up to me. "You okay?"

"I—I'm fine. How…"

"Saw you leave. Saw him follow you," he said, turning to watch Old Bill meandering out past the Big Apple and into the dark. I couldn't see Jacob's face, but he held his shoulders up tight, as if his back hurt him.

"I'm fine," I said again, not sure what else to say. Was this normal work for a deputy, following drunks just in case they got into trouble?

"Well, all right," he said. He stuffed his hands in his pockets, then didn't say anything for a minute. I was feeling ruffled from Old Bill's game, and I didn't know what to make of Jacob's hovering. I wondered if he'd remembered something about the fire, or if he was ready to talk to me now.

"What—" I started to say, but he was already turning back toward the circus.

"Best be getting back, then, if… Well, you're okay," he said gruffly.

"Wait—before…about…" I tried. He paused, and I took that as a good sign.

"Now you're out here," I said, talking fast before he could leave. "You should tell me what you know about the barn fire. I don't remember what happened. I want to know."

"There's nothing to tell," he said, looking up toward the dark mountain and the darker sky, his frown deepening the lines in his face. But he didn't leave. Something in him wanted to talk.

"Would you tell me something if I told you something?" I asked, bartering again, like I'd tried in the jail. But this time I wasn't going to mess it up.

He looked down at me. "What d'you mean?" Behind him, the audience in the Big Apple cheered. Behind me, the wind howled and I couldn't help seeing the dead girl's hair blowing in the coming storm.

"I know something you might want to know," I said. "Something bad I saw."

"What?" he said, more interested than I'd expected. Almost urgent.

"I won't tell you unless you tell me about the barn," I said.

But my voice was faltering already. He was a deputy. It was his job to solve crimes and bring crooks to justice. So if I didn't tell him about the girl, wouldn't I be as bad as a criminal?

"June, whatever it is you know, it might help us." Jacob was deadly serious now, serious as the deputy badge on his chest. "There's something going on that we haven't figured out, something not right." His gray hair was blowing a little in the breeze, but his eyes were steady on mine. We weren't talking about Old Bill or the barn fire anymore, and I knew I'd lost the barter again. *I need information first.* That's what I should've said. But I didn't.

"There's a dead girl up in the woods." It didn't even feel bad, giving it up. Soon as I said it, I breathed more easily.

Whatever he'd expected, it wasn't that. "Where?"

"Up above the solar field," I said. "Saw her when I came down from the Hollow."

"Who did you tell?" Jacob demanded.

"I didn't tell anyone," I said. "I've been in jail all day, remember."

"Why didn't you tell the constable?" he asked, almost angry now.

"I—I just didn't. I'm telling you."

Jacob looked off toward town, then up through the trees in the direction of the solar field.

"Can you bring me to her?" he asked finally.

I didn't want to go back to the looming old maple tree, especially not in the dark. But that girl was up in the woods alone. I'd never had much patience for wondering about what happens after we die, but I knew plenty about what it was like to be alone and scared, to wait for help when no one's coming. No one deserved to get left behind like that. Plus, if I went with Jacob I could keep wearing him down, get him to tell me something about the barn fire.

"What about Thomas?" I asked.

"Tell him to wait here. Or bring him. I can take you back up to the Hollow after, if the storm doesn't come in."

I didn't say anything to that. I wasn't planning on going back to the Hollow, not with Jacob or anyone. "Hang on a minute," I said instead, and hurried down the hill and back under the edge of the tent.

Thomas was still there, right where I'd left him. Up on stage, the musicians were playing a song and the knife thrower was juggling blades high in the air.

"Thomas, I'm going to show the deputy something," I whispered. Thomas's eyes were wide, fixed on the knives. His corncob pipe was hanging loose from the side of his mouth, like he'd forgotten it was there.

"Thomas!" I said louder. He blinked and nodded, still fixated on the juggling.

"You stay right here until I get back, okay?" I said. "Even if the show's over, wait for me right here. I'll be back soon. And tell Alexandra I'm coming, if she asks."

Thomas nodded again. I looked around—lots of kids were sitting together all around the tent, and none of them had grown-ups with them. Thomas looked like he was rooted in the ground, his eyes still on the show. He wasn't going anywhere soon.

"I'll be back in a bit," I said again. "Don't worry."

Finally he looked at me, and he even smiled a little. "Yeah, okay."

That's all he said. And I didn't say anything else, even though I should've. I just squeezed his shoulder and turned away.

Jacob was standing in the dark, waiting for me. After the bright noise of the tent, the night was as dark as a grave.

"Come on," he said, and led me away across the field. I followed him, stumbling on tufts of grass until my eyes warmed up to the darkness.

"Don't we have to go back to town?" I asked, when I realized we were walking toward the woods instead of taking the path back to the quarry access road.

"There's a path, goes right to the solar field," he said over his shoulder.

When we got to the trees, Jacob fumbled in his pack and lit up a little lantern to show the way. A thin trail snaked up the wooded hill toward the solar field.

I looked back at the Big Apple glowing red in the field, the only light in the world apart from Jacob's lantern.

"Come on," Jacob said.

Pretty soon the music from the circus faded and the woods noises took over: creaking trees and rushing leaves and a hissing that I thought at first was the wind. But then I felt a few drops on my face, and I realized I was hearing rain.

10

"Where is she?" Jacob asked over the pattering rain. We'd climbed up the path and out into the solar field, scaring the sheep so they shuffled off through the dark. The solar panels loomed over us, dark squares as big as roofs that sheltered us from the rain as we passed underneath. Even so, my jacket was soaked through by the time we arrived in the woods.

I pointed up in the direction of the old maple. It was hard to remember exactly where Thomas and I had come from, because it was dark and I'd been so scared when we ran away from the body. But I knew it was uphill, and I knew I'd recognize the tree when I saw it. The girl would be wet again from the storm, just like me.

"Where?" Jacob said again, after we'd climbed for a little while. He'd shuttered the lantern, and it was hard to see in the dark at first.

I looked around. Had I jumped over that log? Broken that branch on the ground? I walked a little farther and then saw it: the maple tree loomed high and dark a little ways up the hill. I knew it was the right one.

"There," I said, pointing. Jacob passed by me and headed up toward the tree, but I didn't move. I was shaking from the cold rain by now, and from the wind. The storm had picked up in the last few minutes, howling above us while the rain came down so hard that it sounded like a roar on the canopy high above our heads.

Jacob stopped in front of the tree. He'd be able to see her by now, crumpled at the base of the trunk. I wondered if he'd seen a lot of dead bodies before, if maybe that kind of thing was normal in his line of work. He started walking around the tree, and I guessed he was looking for clues. Was this what it was like to be a deputy? Solving mysteries like the detectives did in books? It seemed impossible that anything as old-fashioned as a mystery could happen in the Republic.

"There's nothing here," Jacob yelled down at me over the wind. I thought I must've heard him wrong, so I made myself go a little closer.

"She's right there," I yelled back, pointing at the base of the tree. But all I could see was the shadow of the trunk. I went closer, sure at any second that I'd see her slumped head, her feet tucked up to her body.

But Jacob was right. She was gone.

I walked around the tree, like Jacob had. It had to be the right tree—there wasn't another one like it in these woods.

"Did you see anyone else up here?" Jacob asked.

I shook my head. "Just you," I said. I looked at him, and he looked back at me.

Then a gust of wind whipped at me and flung my hair in my face, and when I raised my hand up to pull it back, a falling branch hit me on the arm.

I staggered sideways and another branch of the maple tree dropped to the ground where I'd just been standing. The wind was picking up.

"She was here!" I shouted over the wind at Jacob. "I swear she was here!"

Jacob glanced up at the top of the tree and opened the lantern again. He crouched down at the roots and swung the light across the ground. It just looked like dirt and dead leaves to me, but Jacob touched a few spots gently with his fingers, as if he saw something special there. The maple was creaking and groaning now, and far off I heard the crash of another tree falling.

"Jacob, the trees!"

Jacob stood and turned away from the spot where the dead girl had sat, faster than I'd ever seen him move. He grabbed my arm and started pulling me back down the hill toward the solar field.

By the time we got to the edge of the field, big chunks of ice were falling among the raindrops. One hit my cheek and left a burning spot behind. I kept my mouth shut tight and my eyes narrowed, to keep out the rain. I hadn't been out in a storm in six years, and I'd forgotten how strong they could be. It was like the storm was a monster, something that could get angry and show it.

The solar panels in the field were screeching and groaning. Jacob held me back for a second, squinting through the driving rain and dark. But I shook him off and started through the field. What would the strong winds do to the circus tent, and what would Thomas do if I wasn't back soon?

The first solar panel I passed screeched so loud that I had to cover my ears. I looked up and saw that it was shifting back and forth in the wind, teetering on its spindly stand. It didn't seem right. I looked back and saw Jacob, still standing where I'd left him, staring up over my head. He yelled words that I couldn't hear over the wind, and then something big smashed to the ground behind me. I turned and one of the other solar panels was flying through the air toward me, tumbling over and over and crashing into other panels as it went. Before I could move, I felt a tug on my pack and stumbled backward, out of the path of the panel. It flashed past me and into the tree line, crushing a stand of saplings and disappearing into the darkness.

I hit the ground and heard a grunt as Jacob fell beside me. He'd dragged me out of the way just in time. He pulled me up and we ran back into the trees. Behind us, more panels were coming loose and whipping away into the darkness.

"We have to get back to the circus!" I yelled, but the storm snatched my voice from my mouth. Jacob said something I couldn't hear. A flying tree branch smacked him in the arm and he pushed it aside, looking all around. Then he grabbed one of the straps of my pack again and pulled me farther into the woods.

We followed the curve of the hillside, through the trees in a direction I'd never gone before. I thought we might be heading toward the Borough, but I wasn't sure we'd be able to make it that far through the storm. Then Jacob stopped, looked around, and doubled back, a little higher up the hill this time. He was searching for something.

I heard another crash from the solar field, but otherwise the world was a dark, wet howl. And then Jacob shouted something that sounded far away, even though he was right next to me, and pointed ahead to a dark emptiness in the hillside. A cave, or something like it.

The wind dropped away as soon as we passed into the dark earth. I looked back and saw rushing leaves and branches, and then smelled a damp, stale breeze that was different from the storm, that came from deeper in the cave. Jacob let go of me and disappeared through the dark.

"Where—?" I said, but just then the lantern bloomed up out of the dark again, blinding me. I blinked and saw smooth greenish walls, a square tunnel cut into marble. We were in a quarry shaft—I knew it right away, even though I'd never seen one before. I'd read about them, and I'd seen pictures in a magazine called *The Danby Gazette*, before it crumbled to dust.

The tunnel went about ten feet, then ended in a pile of stone and roots and rubble. I was happy enough to be out of the worst of the rain, even though the wind still gusted down the tunnel and water pooled underfoot. Jacob strode to the edge of the wall alongside the rubble and disappeared.

"Back here," his voice drifted out of the darkness. I went to where he'd disappeared, to a crack in the rubble just wide enough to pass through. A damp wind flared up from the darkness, and I hesitated, but then Jacob called again. Taking off my pack, I squeezed through the hole into a tunnel that burrowed down into the mountain. "Jacob?" I called into the dark, hands feeling my way along the wall.

Then, suddenly, a bright light overhead flooded the space. Jacob had flipped a switch on the wall. Blinking in the bright light, I now noticed the cable snaking in from outside and the stack of electric boxes and batteries piled in the corner. The electricity buzzed and a second light bulb flickered to life on the low ceiling.

"Wait," I said as Jacob went to blow out the lantern. He glanced up at me, then at the bulbs overhead.

"It's okay—" he said, but I was already backing out of the room.

"It won't hurt you," he said. I didn't answer. My mom wouldn't have let me come within ten feet of all that electric stuff.

"Look," he said, gesturing me over. "I want to show you how it works. We're only scared of what we don't understand."

I was scared of a lot of things I understood pretty well. But no one had ever offered to explain electricity to me before.

"I can see from here," I said, trying to sound annoyed instead of nervous.

He showed me the cables, how they came in from a little solar panel outside and fed into a battery. Then another cable that snaked its way up to the light bulb.

"This cable has one wire that takes the electricity up, and another that brings it back down. But it's wrapped up in this rubber insulation. You can hold it all day and the electricity won't get to you. It's just the bare wires you need to look out for, and there aren't any bare wires here."

"Just being close to it is bad for you. Bad luck," I said.

"I can't argue against superstition," Jacob said, pulling off his oilskin coat. "But you strike me as a person interested in facts, yes?"

I looked around, trying to keep my eyes away from the battery that held all the electricity. A neat row of canned food was stacked against the wall, next to a folded pile of blankets that might make a nice enough bed. The ground was covered by an old rug.

"Is this all your stuff?" I asked. I was shivering now, wet through from the storm. Jacob tossed me a blanket.

"Yep," he said. "Keep it here just in case."

To some people, that might've seemed an odd thing to say,

but not to me. My clearest memories of my mom all involved us hiding or waiting in spots we'd found *just in case.* Just in case something like this happened. I wondered whether Sebastian and Alexandra had a plan for bad storms, and where they'd shelter.

"What'll the circus do?" I asked, leaning against the wall. I hoped Thomas was with them. They'd invited us to stay the night, so they must have a place for him.

"They'll be fine," Jacob said. "We'll go back when the storm lets up. I need to interview them again anyway."

"Why?"

"Dead girl shows up same time they do? Can't be coincidence."

"They're not like that," I said, looking back at him. "They wouldn't kill anyone."

"I hope not." He didn't sound convinced, which annoyed me.

"I gotta get back to Thomas," I said. And I needed to get back to the circus, though I didn't tell Jacob that. I didn't want him to know about their connection to my mom, especially if he thought they might be murderers.

"You can't go back till the storm lets up."

"I told him I wouldn't leave him there," I said. "I can't wait too long."

"You'd rather die on your way to check on Thomas than wait till the storm passes?" Jacob asked sharply. "It's not worth leaving him all alone forever just 'cause you're feeling impatient right now."

He sounded more upset than he should be about anything I said or did. I didn't know what to say, and a long silence passed before he spoke again.

"June, I got to ask," he said, gentler now. "You won't be in trouble. What else do you know about that dead girl?"

I shrugged. "Nothing."

"Something's not right here," Jacob muttered. "Everything going wrong at once. Those solar panels have been through storms worse than this without a problem. I worry someone loosened the brackets on purpose."

"Who'd do that?"

"There's some folks in the Republic that don't like electricity, even more than you. The Millerites—they think it's the devil. But I can't see the Millerites killing livestock or poisoning Dorset's well. I need answers, but I just keep getting more questions." There was a tightness in his voice that I hadn't heard before, and it made me remember that I didn't know him any better than he knew me. And now we were stuck in a quarry hole together. But even though I should've been nervous about being alone with a stranger, I wasn't. He'd saved my life from the solar panel, and he'd tried to stop Old Bill from bothering me.

"I told you about the girl, so why won't you tell me about the barn fire?" I asked. "You were there. You said so."

I glanced up and saw him rubbing his hands together. He sat down against the marble wall and took his time getting comfortable.

"All right," he said finally, not looking at me. "The barn was out near Wallingford. Just south of New Rutland. I wasn't a deputy then. I was just passing by, and I heard you screaming."

"And no one else was there?" I asked, trying to keep my voice from sounding breathless.

"No one," he said. "You were alone." His hand rummaged in his pocket, but he didn't take anything out.

"What else?" I asked, watching him closely.

"Nothing else. You were all alone, so I brought you here, to the Hollow. Heard Bob and Denise were good people who'd take orphans. That's all there is to it."

The storm was loud on the far side of the cave-in. Water dripped somewhere close by. This was the first time anyone had talked to me about that night. Jacob hadn't told me anything I couldn't have guessed, but each word was still precious. And each one hurt.

"My mom told me to wait for her there," I said. "She was going to come back."

Jacob didn't say anything. He was staring at his hands.

"It's my fault," I blurted out. "I lit the candle because I was scared. If I hadn't, she'd have come back and I'd still have been there, waiting." My voice caught in my throat. I remembered the candle clearly now; it had been red. I'd used its flame to read stories from *Vermont Life* that night. Then my eyes had gone heavy and I'd watched the flame until I fell asleep. And when I woke up, the wax was a red puddle on the floor and the barn was on fire.

Jacob shifted and shook his head a little. "You ever think that maybe your mother shouldn't have left a little girl alone in a dusty barn with a candle?"

"I knew better," I whispered.

"She should have too." Jacob's voice was hard now, his fingers locked together, his knuckles and wrists ridged in twisted knots of scarred flesh.

"You don't even know my mom," I said quietly.

"I know enough," Jacob said. "I know I wouldn't risk my daughter like that."

"She had to hide me," I protested. "People were after us."

Jacob frowned, glanced at me. "People?"

"I don't remember. I can't remember." I hadn't talked about this before. About how the fire had muddled things in my memory. I wasn't sure exactly what our life had been like before the fire. But I knew my mom had been doing something important when she left me, and that she wouldn't have left me unless she absolutely had to.

Jacob looked like he wanted to say something else, but he didn't. The silence grew between us and filled the quarry. Still, his words echoed around in my head, and I didn't like them. Mom hadn't done anything wrong. It was me who'd started the fire.

The storm was still howling just as hard as before, and I thought of Thomas. I hoped he was somewhere warm. Probably he was holed up with the circus, eating candies and listening to Sebastian tell funny stories. I tried to tamp down the tickle of resentment at the thought, to feel glad instead. I'd be back with them soon, and I'd ask Alexandra the questions Jacob couldn't answer. Then I'd find my mom and tell her that I was sorry for all the trouble I'd caused us.

11

I opened my eyes to a slash of brightness. At first I didn't know where I was, but then I remembered. Daylight was streaming in through the narrow gap in the rubble, but the storm wasn't quite over. I sat up amidst my pile of blankets and realized that Jacob was gone.

Shivering and stiff, I grabbed my pack and slipped through the gap in the cave-in. Jacob was there, on the other side of the rubble, sleeping under his coat. His pack sat beside him, its flap partially open.

I needed to get back to Thomas and the circus, but the open pack stopped me; maybe it could tell me something Jacob hadn't been willing to share.

I inched over and tapped his pack with my foot, so that if he woke up it could seem like I'd knocked it accidentally. I tapped a little harder, and the flap fell the rest of the way open. *The Spy Craft Manual* called this *recon.*

I glanced at Jacob one more time. Then I peered into his pack. The first thing I saw was a pill bottle like the one Old Bill had. That surprised me. I'd always thought of LoTabs as the mark of a criminal, but Jacob was a deputy. The bottle was right at the top of the pack, like he'd taken one just last night.

The rest of the pack was filled with clothes and rope, from what I could see. Nothing useful. I was about to give up when I saw the corner of something small and made of leather, poking up from under the pill bottle. Jacob was still dead asleep, so I pinched the leather corner and pulled before I could think better of it. It was an old-fashioned wallet, just like people from Before had used to hold money and money cards.

Inside was a smudged and faded charcoal drawing of two faces: a woman and a young girl. That surprised me again. I didn't think Jacob had a family. There was another piece of paper behind the picture, something handwritten. I was about to pull it out, but just then Jacob rolled over—I snapped the wallet shut and dropped it back into the pack. Something about the smudged faces in the wallet made me feel bad for snooping. Before I could tell if he was really waking up or not, I hurried out of the quarry shaft.

The woods were a mess, with green leaves and branches strewn all over the place, but everything was quiet apart from the trees whispering in the gentle rain. Last night might have seemed like just a nightmare, if it weren't for part of a smashed solar panel caught in the branches of a tree. I edged around it, thinking. I'd get Thomas, and then the two of us would talk to the circus folks and figure out how to get to New Rutland to find my mom. If we were lucky, the circus would let us go with them.

It didn't take me long to find my way back to the solar field. The panels were ruined. Only one still stood on its post, tilted sideways. The rest littered the ground, tangled up in wires and twisted metal and broken glass. The sheep huddled together at the bottom of the field, still as statues and staring at me.

I tried not to think what the Big Apple might look like. Hopefully Thomas was dry and comfortable, waiting for me with the circus. I hurried around the edge of the solar field to the trail we had followed last night. The trees here were thick with fog that made everything look unfamiliar and eerie. I felt my body tensing up, even though there was no reason to be afraid.

I ran the last stretch of the trail and burst out into the field, but it was so filled with fog that I couldn't even see the Big Apple. I walked slowly, squinting through the fog and trying to ignore the fear rising up in my stomach. Soon the trees behind me disappeared in the swirling fog. Where was the circus?

Noises came to me from strange directions: a banging sound that echoed all around, a rustle of leaves that seemed too close to be the woods.

I walked faster. If I could find the edge of the field, I'd get my bearings again. I felt a cool breeze, and soon I could see glimpses of field through the fog. I finally hit a line of dead trees, and then turned around and started to run back across the field. The fog was lifting, and I still didn't see the circus.

"Thomas!" I yelled, my voice echoing across the empty field.

I stopped and looked down. The ground beneath my feet had been beaten down by a crowd, and wagon wheels had rutted up the wet grass.

The circus must've left after the show, right in the middle of the storm.

And I had no idea where Thomas could be now.

I ran all the way back to the Borough, my lungs screaming for air, the path muddy from the circus crowds. I kept thinking about Alexandra dancing through the field with Thomas, pulling him along. She'd been too friendly with him; she should've realized he'd get ideas.

But there wasn't any reason to think anything bad had happened to him. He was probably up in town, happy as anything, having a great adventure in last night's storm. The circus had probably dropped him off in town on their way out. I was gasping for breath, but I didn't slow down.

The Borough was bustling. A few folks were out in their gardens, trying to get a sense of the damage, wearing oilskins against the rain. One man stood on his roof, fastening a jagged leaf of plastic across a spot that must be leaking. I looked all around but I couldn't see Thomas anywhere. Sweating in the cold air, I had a terrible thought—what if the circus had taken him? It was ridiculous, but I couldn't get the idea out of my head. Thomas wouldn't have gone back to the Hollow alone. He wouldn't have gone anywhere without me. But he'd liked the circus folks. He'd liked them too much.

The jail came into view at the top of the quarry road. Thomas would be waiting for me there, I told myself. And if he wasn't, the constable or Wilson would know where the circus had gone, and if they'd taken Thomas with them.

I was almost to the jail when I looked farther up the quarry road and saw the same pack of Green Mountain Boys as yesterday walking toward me from the open mouth of the main quarry. They were leading saddled horses packed for a journey.

I sped up, wanting to get out of sight before they saw me. But that wasn't smart, because as soon as I started to run again they spotted me. Lee, the one who'd arrested Thomas and me, shouted something, but I ignored him. If I could get to the jail before they got me, the constable would tell them to leave me alone. She liked them even less than she liked me.

I raced up the stairs to the jail and ran through the door and slammed it shut behind me. The voices of the Greens faded. I breathed in relief and looked around, hoping I'd see Thomas sitting by the fire with Wilson, smiling over at me.

But the main room of the jail was cold and dark and quiet. The fire had gone out, and the hanging electric bulb was dark, too, so only a dim light came through the one window.

No one was there. My relief evaporated just as quickly as it had come. I was cornered, and the Greens would be coming through the door any minute. I glanced around for somewhere to hide.

Then I saw the constable sitting hunched over in a chair with her head on the table. She must've fallen asleep right where she was working. She'd looked so tired yesterday, I wasn't surprised. But I was surprised she hadn't woken up when I'd barged in.

"Constable?" I said, but it came out too quiet. "Constable?" I tried again. She didn't answer.

I stepped forward through the dim light, full of some new fear I couldn't quite place. Everything was so quiet, too quiet. The doorway to the jail cells was a black hole, and the boxes piled against the wall looked big enough to hide people. For the first time I wished the electric light was on.

I took a few more steps, and my foot hit something soft and heavy that I hadn't seen in the dim light. I tried to jump away but stumbled and went down hard onto the ground.

And then the Greens opened up the door and came barging in.

"No use hiding, kid," Lee said. Someone switched on the light bulb.

The first thing I saw was Wilson's face about a foot from mine, twisted and pale like ash in a dead woodstove. White foam dripped from his mouth. His glasses were broken, and his pupils were so big that his eyes looked black. I jerked away from him and slid back against the wall. Then I saw the constable at her desk, and the puddle of foam pooled under her head. And then I stopped breathing and stopped thinking and stopped everything for a little while.

"Jeezum," someone said. Then again, "Christ and Jeezum."

Lee took three quick steps over to the constable's body. He grabbed one of her shoulders and pulled so her head rolled over to show her face. She was pale like Wilson, and her eyes reminded me of the sheep from yesterday. Its head had rested right there on that table, just like hers did now.

I leaned over because my own head was spinning. Then, before I could stop it, my chest heaved and I barfed on the floor. Tears dribbled down my nose, but I was too dizzy to wipe them away.

"Shit, kid," a voice right near me said. "You didn't drink out of one of those cups, did you?"

I looked up. It was one of the Greens, the one with long brown braids. She was pale under her green hat, and she wasn't looking at the bodies. She pointed at a mug on the floor, the same one Wilson had been drinking from when I first saw him.

"You didn't drink any of that, did you? 'Cause if you did, you'd better keep chucking."

I shook my head, barely understanding what she was saying.

"What was she doing in here?" one of the others demanded. They were talking so matter of fact, like they weren't standing over two dead bodies that used to be alive just yesterday. I straightened up, trying to steady my breathing. Then I realized that the sweet, sickly smell in the room was coming from the constable and Wilson, and I lost it again.

Lee stopped inspecting the constable and looked at me. He even smiled, like he thought it was funny that I was shaking and wiping vomit from my mouth.

"Kid keeps getting in the way, don't she?" he said. "Someone toss her out of here before she blows again."

"Wait," said the woman with braids. "Don't you think we ought to get her story?" She put a hand on my shoulder. "You see anything when you came in? Anything suspicious?"

"We ain't got time for this," Lee cut in. "We're late enough for Town Meeting as it is. She got in here about a second before we did, she didn't see nothing."

"But—" the woman started.

"Get her out of here!" Lee said again, louder this time.

The woman clicked her tongue but gave me a little nudge toward the door. The man with the red beard tugged me the rest of the way by the forearm.

"But—I'm looking for Thomas," I blurted, remembering right when he tried to push me through the door. I looked back at Lee, and at all of them standing there in the electric light with Wilson at their feet. Lee squinted at me.

"That boy you was with? Lost him, huh?" He laughed once, like a slap. "We don't run a charity, little girl. Our work's more important than chasing runaways." He squatted down next to Wilson, reaching out for the mug carefully, as if it might bite him.

Then the red-haired man pushed me out the door and closed it.

I don't know how long I stood outside the jail in the rain. I had nowhere to go. I couldn't think straight. I heard muffled voices through the window, but they were in another world, on the other side of the door. Then I pictured Thomas, his mouth foamy and his eyes big and black and still. I hadn't checked in the jail cells. What if he was back there, lying in the dark, hurt or dying or dead? And then I thought that my mouth was too wet, and maybe it was foamy, and I spit on the ground until I couldn't spit anymore. After that, I sat down on some covered porch steps at the building beside the jail as the rain slowed and finally stopped.

The last place Thomas had been was with the circus. That was the only thing I knew for sure. Maybe he'd been confused, agreed to go with them because he thought I was going too. Or maybe they'd taken him. Could they be kidnappers? I didn't think so, not if they were working with my mom. And they'd been so kind. I wondered for a second if he'd gone with them for the adventure, but he wouldn't do that without me, would he? None of it made sense, but one way or another he had to be with them.

This was how my mom must've felt when she came back to the barn and saw nothing but burned rubble. I'd just been gone, like Thomas, and she wouldn't have known why. I thought about the feeling in my chest, the helplessness and the emptiness, and I realized right there on the steps of the jail how hard it must've been for her all these years that she'd been looking for me. She wouldn't have been able to stand it, just like I couldn't stand it that Thomas was gone, taken away by the circus.

12

I sat on the covered steps until my head stopped spinning, and then I sat some more. People walked by every once in a while. Some of them looked at me, but no one said anything. A few old men drifted onto the road and started raking out the gravel, filling in the parts that got swept out by the storm. None of them knew yet that their constable was dead.

Then the door to the jail opened and the Greens came filing out. Their horses were still tied under some pine trees just to the left of my porch steps, but I was hidden from their view.

"Go'dammed inconvenient, this whole mess. Lost half our day's ride already," Lee was saying over his shoulder.

"Yurp," muttered the man behind him, pushing his hat tighter onto his head.

"If we ride fast, we can make New Rutland tomorrow morning, I'd say," the red-haired one said. "So long as there wasn't any feckin' washouts from the storm."

Startled, I looked up, leaning closer. They were going to New Rutland—my mom was there!

"Alt-Zs'll give us trouble if we take Route 7," the woman with brown braids said.

"Dammit, the other patrols'll be tucked up in Middlebury by tonight, and we'll be camping in the mud. Screw this town, and screw the Alt-Zs. We're taking Route 7, and if the Alt-Zs try to stop us, well, that's their mistake." Lee untied his horse's lead, and it shook its head against the bit.

"You sure it was that Jacob who done this, Lee?" the woman asked, gesturing back at the jail.

"We didn't even talk to him," the woman continued.

"It was him." Lee swung onto his horse. "Easiest case I ever worked. He had that cowbane crap in his hand yesterday—I seen him with it. Case of unrequited love, you ask me. Snuffed the constable 'cause she was sleeping around and Wilson 'cause he was a sunnuvabitch."

"Yeah, I heard lots of stories about that Jacob, truth told," the red-haired man growled.

"He was in with the Alt-Zs for years—can't see why the constable'd make him a deputy. She was asking for it," Lee said.

"But how'll they bring him in? Constable's dead and Jacob's the only deputy left," the woman insisted, tightening her horse's saddle.

"Don't worry about that," Lee said. "We'll spread the word on the way out. I'm sure the good folks of this town know what to do with a freakin' murderer. They'll take care of him."

A few of the others laughed, and they rode down the quarry road. They hadn't ever noticed me.

I stared after them, my mind coming to life again. They were going to tell everyone that Jacob had poisoned the constable and Wilson. And he hadn't, had he? I remembered him up in the solar field, tucking the plant into his pocket. But he'd only done that to show the constable what he'd found. And anyway, he'd been with me last night. He couldn't have gone out into the storm to kill the constable, then come back and gone to sleep. One thing I knew for sure—you couldn't trust a Green.

I stood up. My legs were stiff with the cold, but my heart was pounding warmth back into them already. Even so, I didn't move right away. I guess there was a chance, right then, for me to go back. There was a place for me in the Hollow. Bob and Denise could take care of me, and whatever had killed the constable and Wilson might drift away like a storm. Maybe Thomas would come back in a few days, say he didn't like the circus after all, and then we'd all be together again. Maybe Gemma and I could meet up in the woods like we'd done a few times before, and maybe Cyrus would get the hint and marry someone else. Maybe my mom would fade away into a memory that didn't hurt so much. I could go back to the Hollow and wait for the world to end a little more, and a little more, one person at a time. It'd be easy.

But I wasn't going to do that. I'd come this far. I was going to get Thomas back, and then the two of us were going to find my mom. And I thought I knew who could help me do it.

The circus field was clear of fog now, the spot where the carts had torn up the grass gaping like an open wound. As I came up to it, I swear I caught a whiff of Alexandra's sweet-smelling cart. Then it was gone, brushed away by the wet, empty air of the dying world. Up on the hill I could see more dead trees than living ones, and big swaths where the wind and washouts had knocked them down. The sky was ashy gray, low and heavy even though the rain had passed.

I found the trail and headed up through the solar field again, trying to rehearse in my head what I was going to say to Jacob. It took me a while to find the old quarry tunnel—I had to go by the tree where the girl's body had been. Even though she wasn't there anymore, I felt bile rise up in my throat at the thought of all the death I'd seen lately. Then I kept wandering uphill until I smelled a cook fire and spotted the dark hole in the side of the hill.

"Jacob?" I called. No one was in sight, just a little fire dying down in the mouth of the tunnel. I thought maybe he'd left, but I'd barely caught my breath when he came squeezing out from the hiding spot, holding a bowl in one hand. He blinked like he didn't recognize who I was for a minute. Then he frowned.

"Thought you'd gone home," he said.

"I need your help," I said. "And you need my help," I added. It sounded odd coming out of my mouth, but I tried not to let him see that.

"Bartering again, huh?" Jacob said, with a strange smile.

"I'm serious," I said.

"All right," he replied distractedly, looking around like he'd misplaced something. His eyes were unfocused, just like the day before in the jail. I thought of the pill bottle I'd seen in his pack, but I didn't say anything about it.

"Some people are coming for you," I said instead.

"Oh? Who's that?" He lowered himself down by the fire, still smiling like he didn't have a care in the world.

"People from town. They think you committed a crime and they'll be coming for you."

That got his attention. He looked at me sharper than before. "What crime?"

Even the word *crime* made my skin shiver after what I'd seen. But I wasn't here to mess around or feel sorry for myself. I forced the constable's pale face out of my head. "I'll tell you that in a minute. But first I need something from you."

"June, if there's something going on—"

"I said, I need something from you."

Jacob frowned, looking past me down the hill. "What is it you need?" he asked. He motioned for me to sit next to him.

I ignored his gesture. I couldn't sit.

"I need you to go with me to save Thomas," I said. My voice almost broke on the last word, but I managed to keep it in line.

"What's he need saving for?" Jacob asked.

"He…he went with the circus," I said. "I left him too long last night and they took him, or he went with them, and I…I gotta get him back." My voice did break that time.

Jacob looked closely at me. "Why are you coming to me with this?" he asked. He looked down the hill again, and with every passing second I saw him coming back to himself from wherever that pill bottle had taken him. "Why didn't you get help from Sarah and Wilson?"

My breath caught in my throat when he said their names. My face must've shown what I was feeling, because Jacob's expression changed too.

"What's happened?" he asked, rising to his feet.

"I'll tell you when you promise to help me save Thomas," I said. I hated the sound of my voice quivering. "Will you promise?"

"Tell me what happened," he said again, his voice low this time. And I couldn't hold it back anymore, because I was a terrible barterer and because I felt too bad about what had happened to the constable and Wilson, and about what it was going to mean to Jacob.

"I went to the jail this morning," I said, fast as I could. "I found the constable and Wilson. They're dead."

Jacob blinked. "Who's dead?" He stared at me hard, like he could change my answer just by wishing it.

"I'm sorry," I said, trying to get the words out. "I think they were poisoned like the sheep."

Jacob was quiet then, and I barely breathed. I didn't know what to do, so I looked at the few coals left smoldering in the ashes. Finally Jacob exhaled heavily, like he'd been holding his breath too. He took a few steps, holding on to the tunnel wall, and looked out into the morning woods. His breathing was coming faster and faster.

Then he stepped forward and kicked the fire past me so hard that charred sticks flew out into the woods. He kicked at it again and again, until there was just an ashy smudge left and the coals were scattered around the mouth of the tunnel. I closed my eyes for a moment, and when I opened them Jacob was crouched on the ground, holding his head in his hands, making sounds that could have been sobs. He needed comforting, maybe, but I didn't know how to do that.

I watched him for a little while, trying to figure out what to do. He was saying something into his knees. I stepped closer and heard it: "No, no, no, no, no, no, no, no…"

It was too sad for me to do nothing. I could see that whoever Sarah and Wilson had been to Jacob, they had been more than just coworkers. I remembered The Greens had said something about love, even. My hand floated out and I laid it carefully on his shoulder.

Jacob flinched at the feel of my hand and leapt up, and for a second I thought he was going to attack me. Something in his eyes was different—they were empty and wide. I stepped back, but he just let out a huge breath and blinked and turned away, stepping over the crumbled embers of the fire.

"Where is she now?" he asked, his voice hoarse.

"The constable? She's still in the jail, I think, but—"

"You shouldn't be here," he said. "Go home."

"But—" I started.

"Did you see Lee and the Greens?" he asked.

"I—They stayed in town last night. They followed me into the jail and they—"

"They're still in town?" Jacob said, quick and sharp.

"That's what I came to tell you!" I shouted, trying to make him hear. "They're gone, but they're trying to put the blame on you, Jacob. They're telling the town that you did it. I heard them planning it."

Something flickered in Jacob's face then—he looked out toward town again, and I saw what he was thinking.

"You think the Greens killed them?" I asked. It didn't surprise me at all, not after all I'd seen the Green Mountain Boys do. Maybe they'd been pretending to be surprised in the jail, just because I was there.

Jacob stopped pacing and looked at me.

"Dammit," he said. It was just one quick word, but it was the saddest word I'd heard in a long while.

My head was spinning now. "What if they did something to Thomas too?" I said. "They hated him." Maybe he hadn't gone with the circus after all.

Jacob shook his head. "They didn't hate Thomas. This has nothing to do with him."

"How do you know?"

He put his hand up to his head again and grimaced. "I know Lee. The head of that crew. He's in with bad company. Takes bribes, thinks he's above local law. Sarah wouldn't play that game. That must be why—"

"Then Thomas has to be with the circus," I said, barely listening. "Will you help me get him?"

"You say the circus left this morning? You see them by the jail?" Jacob asked.

"No, they're gone. They're heading north to Town Meeting, and they took Thomas," I said again. He wasn't getting it, and he still wasn't listening. He stared around at the woods, then finally looked at me again.

"Right. You gotta go home. Now."

"No, I—"

"You don't understand what's going on here, June. This is serious. You need to go home."

I stepped back. I'd come up here thinking he'd help. But now he was doing the opposite.

"I told you about what the Greens said," I said. "Now you owe me."

Jacob snorted. "This is exactly why you need to go home."

He kept saying that word. The Hollow had held me for the last six years, but not for one minute had it been home.

"I'm getting Thomas, and then we're going to find my mom. I'm not going back to the Hollow ever."

That got Jacob's attention. His hand started twitching against his leg again, like it wanted to do something but he wouldn't let it.

"You can't do that," he said.

"I can do what I want," I said, backing away another step.

"No. You can't go chasing the circus on your own. It's not safe. The road… You don't know what's out there. And you don't know the circus, either. They might be dangerous." Jacob stepped after me, like he was afraid I'd run before he'd finished.

"I know more than you think," I said.

"Wait," Jacob said. "Just wait a minute." He stared at me, his eyes flicking from me to the woods behind us. Then he rubbed a shaking hand over his eyes.

"I've…I should get to New Rutland, catch up with Lee and the circus," he said finally. "Gotta question them both about Wilson and…and Sarah." He was struggling to put his words together, and I could tell whatever was happening in his head was important, so I waited quietly.

"So I'm going, anyway," he mumbled. "Better than you going alone, getting yourself killed."

"You'll take me with you?" I breathed.

"As far as New Rutland, and no farther. Everyone'll stop there on the way to Town Meeting in Middlebury. We'll get your brother, and then I'm sending you straight back to the Hollow," he said, clearly refusing to believe I wasn't going back.

"What about my mom?" I asked.

"No," he said, too hard. Then he took a quick breath through his nose. "She could be anywhere. She could be dead, June."

He kept doing this, kept trying to get me to forget about her—in the jail, at the circus, here in the quarry tunnel. She wasn't dead. I'd feel it if she were dead. And she wasn't just anywhere. I'd seen her name in Alexandra's book, next to the name *New Rutland*.

"You just don't want me to find her," I said.

"Please listen," he said, grimacing like the words hurt him. "I know what you're feeling." He stopped and turned away, and even though I hated what he'd said, I knew he was telling the truth. I'd seen how he felt, just a few minutes ago.

"The past won't always come back. And trying to change that—well, you can't." His voice was level and empty now, and his hand was twitching again.

But he didn't know what I knew—I had a clue, and I was sure she was in New Rutland.

"Fine," I said, clenching my fists. "We'll go home once I find Thomas." I was lying, but it wasn't hard to make it feel like the truth. I'd say whatever I had to.

13

There were two ways to travel north in the Republic, Jacob said. You could take the mountain road, potholes and washouts and downed trees and all—that's what most folks heading to Town Meeting were doing. They'd left weeks ahead of time, to give themselves time to persuade their mules and carts through the muck. That was the safe route. But the fast route was Route 7, and that's the way we were going.

Jacob said the Greens had traveled that way, since they were armed and Alt-Zs usually wouldn't give them trouble. And he said the circus would have gone that way, too, or their big carts would get stuck or break an axle on the mountain road. And we had to get to New Rutland fast if we were going to catch them, so we had to go the way they'd gone. That sounded fine to me.

We walked most of the way down the quarry road without running into anyone. Right near the bottom, however, where the old town used to be, the Borough had a roadblock to keep bandits like the Alt-Zs from coming up the quarry road. The base of the barrier had been built from big river rocks, and on top of that an even bigger pile of the nastiest trash anyone could find—mangled cars, old bicycle frames, railroad ties, broken glass bottles, and a bunch of other unfriendly items I didn't have names for. The roadblock stretched between two crumbling buildings from Before. And two men were standing on the close side, watching the road up to town.

Jacob propelled me behind a burnt-out car when he spotted the guards. I peered out from the other side—the men hadn't seen us, but they were looking up the road, as if they were waiting for someone trying to escape from the Borough. As if they were waiting for Jacob. The Greens, it seemed, had told them about the murders and who they thought had done the killing.

"Can we go around?" I whispered. That'd mean inching our

way through the rusty skeletons of cars and hidden cellar-holes from Before, which stretched through the woods here, left over from when the forest was a town.

"Might not have to," Jacob said, easing his pack off his back. "Get this wet." He passed me a square of greasy flannel.

I pressed the rag into a murky puddle so I wouldn't have to waste any of my drinking water. When I looked back up, Jacob had a fist full of tinder. "Here," he said, and took the rag back from me. He wrapped it loosely around the tinder, which didn't make sense. No reason I could see to make a fire that'd get stifled right away. Even so, I watched what he was doing. Jacob knew things I didn't.

He took his lamp and poured a few drops of oil into the bundle. Then he made a spark with a chunk of flint and coaxed the tinder to light up. Once it was going, he tossed the whole ball as far as he could into one of the collapsing buildings on the roadside. It made a little thump when it landed, but the men guarding the roadblock didn't seem to notice.

They did notice, though, when a plume of smoke rose up out of the building a minute later. They looked at each other, then ran over toward the smoke.

Jacob and I inched around the car to stay out of sight, and I was glad we didn't have to get any closer to the fire. As soon as the men reached the house, we ran for it.

My heart flew as we slipped by the edge of the roadblock and kept running. Jacob was even better at sneaking than I was. Soon we'd left the old town behind, and the only thing ahead of us was the valley with Route 7 running through its belly. I wondered where he'd learned that kind of trick. It wasn't in *The Spy Craft Manual*, that was for sure.

The light was already fading when we stepped onto the old highway. I breathed in the road and felt a memory swirling up at the taste of dust on my tongue. The road stretched away left and right, and the memory tingled and grew—I'd been here before. I let it open up inside me: *We walked quickly along broken pavement, a dry wind brushing our skin. My mom was talking to me in a quiet voice, telling me one of the stories in* Vermont Life *from memory. But I was crying, even though she kept trying to shush me.*

Now I was in her arms, and she was running, and telling me I had to be quiet. We were being chased. And now we were hiding in a ditch beside the road, and I breathed in the smell of her hair and she rubbed my cheek with her finger. And then the memory faded, and I was standing on Route 7, breathing hard.

I'd known my mom and I were travelers before. I just hadn't known where until I saw this road, until I smelled it. This was where we had walked together, where we'd run together.

"Road's not safe at night, you know," I said, trying to sound casual. Jacob looked down at me, and I knew I hadn't pulled it off. "I'm not scared," I said. "I just heard some stuff about Route 7."

"We'll be fine," Jacob said, turning north. I went after him, trying not to look left or right. It didn't matter how dangerous Route 7 was, so long as Thomas and my mom were out ahead of me. I pressed my nose to the collar of my mom's coat, but all I smelled was smoke. Would I find her in New Rutland? Would she smell the same if I did?

For a while the only sounds were the chirping of crickets and the murmur of the wind. We passed by dark hills of kudzu that swallowed houses whole, wrapping around porches, roofs, and windows, and road signs bent and rusted along the roadside. My skin prickled as we walked, and I kept thinking I saw movement from the ruined houses. People could hide there. Anyone could be watching us.

Jacob walked a few steps ahead of me, and I followed as quietly as I could. His fist clenched and unclenched against his leg, and a few times he inhaled sharply, muttering something under his breath; once he shook his head hard, like he was trying to get rid of a bad thought. I knew he was hurting, but I couldn't think of anything I could do to help.

After a while, I don't know how long, we passed out of the trees and onto the floodplain where Otter Creek overflowed every few seasons. The moon slid into the sky. It'd been a long time since I'd seen the moon properly, since Bob and Denise made me stay inside and keep the shutters closed at night so the house didn't attract unwanted attention. The moon was a lopsided oval, like a river rock. I knew that the moon grew and shrank every month—I'd seen it as a full circle plenty of times when I was little. And I'd seen it as a little sliver, like a hangnail. But most of the time it was lopsided, not one thing or the other.

We climbed up a little hill, and far off in the night I saw the flickering lights of distant houses or cook fires. The thought of people out there in the dark made my mind wander in uncomfortable directions. Had Thomas even come this way or was I walking away from him? Maybe the circus hadn't taken him after all. Maybe he'd died, crushed by a falling tree in the storm, or been caught by whoever had murdered the girl under the maple tree.

"Probably the Greens killed that girl in the woods too," I said after a long silence.

"We don't know that the Greens killed anyone at all," Jacob said. His voice sounded tired, but he'd answered quickly enough. "That's what I'm going to find out."

"Who else could it be, though?"

"The circus, for one," he said. "They were in town, and that's enough to ask the question. And I've heard rumors. But rumors aren't proof of anything."

I thought of Alexandra, smiling and laughing with Thomas, and Sebastian, twirling his top hat on his finger. I thought of all the lights and color in the Big Apple. Jacob was crazy if he thought they'd murder three people.

"It had to be the Greens," I said. And that was all I said about it. I didn't have time to worry about the death of people I didn't even know. I had Thomas and my mom to find.

Soon after that I started to see shadows that looked like people. First, it was a hunched shape that turned out to be the handlebars of a motorcycle sinking into a ditch filled with stagnant water. Then it was a movement up ahead that disappeared before I got a good look. *Hide, Junie. Stay still.* I actually turned my head, because Mom's voice sounded clearer and closer than ever before.

"Jacob—" I started, and choked on my own voice because it was so loud in the night.

"Don't worry," he said, not stopping or even turning his head to me.

"Jacob, there's monsters on this road," I said, quieter this time.

He kept walking. "Monsters, huh?"

"Someone told me about them. Cannibals, I heard." I remembered it now: my mom had told me about them before she left me in a dark, damp hiding place. *Don't leave this shed. The monsters will eat you if you do.*

Jacob shook his head. "There are no monsters. Whoever said that lied to you."

I clenched my teeth but didn't answer.

Sometime in the next few hours Jacob turned off Route 7 and headed up a washed-out old side road. I was tired, more tired than I'd been in a long time, and my legs were walking without me by that time. I didn't notice we were on a new path until I tripped over a rock and stopped, looking around.

"Hey, where're we going?" I whisper-yelled. I hadn't seen any worrisome shadows in a long while, but I still felt like we were being watched.

"Got a place to stay for the night," he said over his shoulder.

"Stay? But we're going to New Rutland."

Jacob shook his head. "We can't make it there tonight. We'd be walking through till morning. We'll get a bit of sleep and go the rest of the way tomorrow."

"We can't stop," I said, louder this time. "The circus has horses—they'll be there already!"

"We'll catch up with them tomorrow."

"But Thomas—"

"I'm not going any farther tonight, and neither are you." And he kept walking up the path. I thought about just standing there, waiting till he came back for me, but the night was so big and dark and strange that I couldn't do it. I followed him, tripping over loose rocks in the path and clenching my jaw so tightly it hurt.

We walked until a building rose out of the darkness. It was an old sugarhouse, used for making maple syrup back before the Fall when sugar used to come out of trees. As far as I could tell, they cooked the syrup to make it hot, but I never knew why they wanted it hot, and right then making it seemed like a stupid waste of fuel. Jacob pulled the door open, tearing away the briars that had grown up in front of it, and we went in. Jacob lit his lantern, and I could see the room was full of old buckets and warped and twisted rubber tubes. I sat down near the door. I couldn't keep walking by myself, but I sure as heck wasn't going to sleep while Thomas was out there on his own, probably thinking I'd abandoned him.

Jacob barely seemed to notice me. He sighed as he sat down, mumbling something under his breath and shaking his head. I tried to ignore him as he settled in.

"Want some?" he asked eventually. I looked over before I could stop myself. He was holding out some jerky from his pack.

"No," I said, even though I was starving from all the walking we'd done and my legs hurt in ways I'd never known before. When Jacob tossed a strip of jerky to me anyway, I picked it up, turning away from him to eat it.

The night was quiet, apart from some bugs bouncing against the dirty windows. I worried someone might see the light and get suspicious about who was in the sugarhouse. I hoped Jacob knew what he was doing.

He finished his jerky and pulled something else out of his pack, something that rustled like paper. "What's that?" I asked, curiosity getting the better of me.

He was spreading a big square of paper onto the floor of the sugarhouse. I could tell even in the lamplight that it was old and fragile and covered in markings. It was a map.

I knew what maps were—I'd seen them plenty of times in magazines and books. They showed the world like a bird would see it, or like someone in an airplane might have seen it Before. I supposed that must've been how they made them—by sending artists up in airplanes and having them draw what they saw. But maps were hard for me to figure out—how was I supposed to match the ground I was on with what a bird was seeing? I usually just skipped over them to get to the stories.

So why did Jacob have a map? He couldn't read words. Surely that meant he couldn't read maps either.

"You want to take a look?" he asked. Part of me wanted to stay by the door, to be as restless as I could until we left again, but another part of me did want to take a look. I went and crouched beside him.

The map was all lines and words—no pictures or symbols like some maps had. It was from Before, that was for sure. The paper was ancient for one thing, and for another, the map was printed in blue and green and black, and so perfect it couldn't have been made by a person.

"Why are you looking at this?" I asked.

"I got it out to show you that it's okay for us to rest," Jacob said. "Look."

He laid his finger on a dot partway up the map with *Danby* printed next to it.

"That's the Borough," he said. He traced his finger up a line that led to another dot, labeled *Rutland.* "That's New Rutland."

"Thought you couldn't read," I said.

"I can read a map, even if I can't read the words. What's that say?"

"Rutland."

"There you go. Right now, we're just about here." He showed me a spot about halfway between the Borough and Rutland. "We've come far already. We'd walk ourselves dead if we tried to make it the rest of the way tonight, but this way we'll be fresh tomorrow."

"How d'you know where we are on a map?" I asked.

"Landmarks. We passed that intersection not too long ago, and these lines show the slope of the hill, so it's easy to follow."

He showed me a few more landmarks and I started to get it. I didn't understand the lines of the slope, but he said he'd show me in the morning. And just like that I could read maps—sort of.

Crouching over the map, I was concentrating so hard that I didn't notice my flannel shirt had dropped at the neck. I glanced up to ask a question and Jacob was staring at the scars on my chest, getting a closer look than anyone had in a long time. I pulled my shirt tight across my chest, but I wasn't as upset as I usually felt when anyone else saw my scars. The fire would've killed me if Jacob hadn't gotten me out.

"Sorry," Jacob muttered. I shook my head and tried to look at the map again.

"What's this say?" he asked, pointing at a little square of words on the corner of the map.

I was grateful for the distraction. I didn't know how to say some of the words, but I gave it my best shot. "It says *Visit www.stateatlas.com for printable expansions of dozens of tourist sites. Explore restaurants, entertainment, and lodging options on our digital dashboard and GO EXPLORE BETTER.*"

Jacob grunted. "Good skill, reading."

"That wasn't very helpful," I pointed out.

"Generally, though. Comes in useful."

"My mom taught me," I said, partly to see what he'd do and partly because all this walking and hoping had filled my mind up with her.

Something in Jacob's stance shifted. He didn't move or anything, but his shoulders got stiffer.

"That so," he said, folding up the map. "That was good of her."

"She was always good," I said. "It was just her and me. She'd do anything for me."

Jacob cleared his throat and slid the map back into his pack. He didn't say anything for so long that I thought I'd have to start prodding him again, to try to force him to reveal something. Then he rubbed his chin and looked at me, stared me right in the eyes.

"You sure she was always good? You remember everything?" he asked.

I blinked. He'd said that as if he knew the answer was no. "'Course I'm sure," I said, too quickly. "She's my mom."

"Well, sometimes we remember things differently than how they actually were," Jacob said finally. "Sometimes we want a memory to look a certain way, and that's how it becomes."

"What would you know about it?" I said. I didn't like what he was getting at. He'd said himself he didn't know my mom. Why did he keep trying to make me doubt her?

"I'm not saying anything," Jacob said. "Just think about it."

I went back to my spot by the door. "I'll ask her myself when I find her. I know she's in New Rutland," I said.

"How do you know that?" Jacob asked sharply.

I shrugged. "I just do."

"Let's find the circus first," Jacob said. I knew he was trying to get off the subject of my mom again.

"I still don't think it was the circus who killed your…Sarah and Wilson," I said. I was in a mood to disagree with him, but I also felt sure I was right. Plenty of people might've wanted the constable dead. And Jacob said himself that it was probably Lee, the dirty Green.

"Maybe," Jacob said, leaning back against his pack. He'd taken out the leather wallet I'd seen back in the quarry shaft. He held it gentle in his hands. "The circus left in a hurry right after it happened. And like I said, rumors… I've heard they might be American."

"Who cares if they're American?" I said, annoyed now. "Maybe they are American. Doesn't mean they're evil." I hadn't told Jacob that I knew for a fact they were American. He'd take it the wrong way, and the secret felt good in my chest.

"You think they kidnapped your brother, don't you?" Jacob raised his eyebrows at me, smiling as if I was being funny.

"It was probably a mistake, or he got confused. And anyway, plenty of folks in the Republic would kidnap someone; doesn't make them American." The word *kidnap* had made me mad, and I was tired of Jacob thinking the worst of Americans. "And anyway, you're one to talk about bad associations."

"Oh?" He sounded like he was humoring me.

"I heard you were in with the Alt-Zs."

I said it to be mean, just to get the smirk off his face. It's what the Green Mountain Boys had said about him, back in the Borough. But I didn't really believe it, so it took me by surprise when Jacob went still.

"Why do you say that?" he asked, and just like that the teasing side of him vanished.

I stared at him. I barely even remembered what the Greens had said, because I'd been so sure at the time that they'd been lying. But now I wasn't so sure. Had he been in with bandits?

"I didn't mean—" I started.

"Where did you hear that I'm in with the Alt-Zs?" He sounded wary now, and I wished I hadn't said anything.

"It was just something Lee and the Greens said. I heard them."

For some reason, that made him feel better. He relaxed, shook his head, and looked down at the wallet in his hands. "They're liars."

Now I was more uncertain than before. Who else would've told me about him and the Alt-Zs? I silently pondered that for a little while. Jacob shifted around some more, rearranging things in his pack, then he cleared his throat.

"Sorry," he said. "Don't mean to interrogate you. Deputy's habit, that's all."

I thought the talk was over then. Jacob rubbed the wallet between his fingers, and the bugs beat their bodies against the windows. I watched the wallet shifting around in Jacob's fingers, and eventually realized that he'd have turned out the lamp if he'd wanted to go to sleep. He was thinking on something.

"What's that thing?" I asked finally, tired of waiting. I didn't tell him I'd already snooped in it before.

He was quiet a minute longer, then he held the wallet out to me. I leaned over and took it, and opened it in the lamplight. The wallet was smooth and soft, and I realized his fingers had worn down all its rough edges. I looked at the portraits I'd first seen in the quarry shaft, the woman and the young girl. Then I moved the drawing aside and pulled out the other paper, the one with writing on it. It was handwritten in pencil, and the letters were so faded I could hardly make them out. The paper had gone soft too. It'd been unfolded and folded too many times.

"Can you read it?" Jacob asked, his voice light, like it didn't much matter to him one way or another.

"Yes," I said, hesitantly. I didn't much want to tell him what it said. I wasn't sure what Jacob was hoping for, but I was sure it wasn't this.

"Well? What is it?" he asked.

I swallowed. "It says, *Patch Leah's school socks. Sweep kitchen chimney. Put apples up. Remind J to pack lunch. Find lye recipe in almanac. Tax due Wednesday next.*"

I looked up at Jacob. He was staring at the paper in my hands, his eyes glassy and still. His fingers were bunched together in front of him, as if he'd forgotten what to do with his hands.

"Nothing else?" he asked finally.

"No," I said. "It's a list of chores."

He reached out his hand for the paper and held it up to the lamplight. "Show me where it says school socks," he asked. "There?"

"Yep, and that's apples. And that's lunch." I showed him each word. He watched me point them out, solemn and tight-jawed. I couldn't tell if he was disappointed or not. He'd carried that list around for a long time—he must've wanted it to say something important.

"Are you J?" I asked.

"I was J," he said. He folded the paper up and tucked it away in the wallet again.

"Who wrote it?" I asked.

"My wife," Jacob said, so quietly I almost couldn't hear him. He took the wallet and the papers back from me and tucked them away into his pack again. He cleared his throat. "She passed some years ago. My daughter, Leah, too."

I didn't know what to say to that. Jacob had just lost his friends today, and now it turned out he'd lost his wife and kid before that. I didn't know how he was still walking around, let alone caring about anything.

"What happened to them?" I asked finally.

"Flu," he muttered, rummaging around in his bag. "Long time ago."

"I'm sorry," I said. I didn't know what else to say. My problems felt small all of a sudden; getting Thomas back and finding my mom were easy compared with all that grieving. Whatever I'd gone through, Jacob had it worse.

"It was a long time ago," he said again.

"Is that why you became a deputy?" I asked. "Bob said you weren't a deputy before you saved me."

"Something like that. Now it's late," Jacob said. "Go to sleep." I curled up under my mom's coat, but I watched him out of the corner of my eye. Something else was itching in my memory. I remembered it just as Jacob blew out the lantern: *Leah.* That was the name he'd called me back in the jail. The name of his daughter.

The last thing I heard from him was a slow rattle, like he was slowly opening a pill bottle in secret.

14

Even though I'd been impatient as anything about stopping the night before, we had a slow start in the morning. Jacob took ages to wake up. He rolled over and over but couldn't seem to open his eyes, and when he did they looked but didn't see. He blinked at me and called me *Leah* again, and so I went outside for a while.

In the light of dawn I saw for the first time that the sugarhouse hugged the trees at the base of a hill. The morning was warm and sunlight streamed through the trees, waking the flies that buzzed around the muddy ground, mating and laying eggs in a hurry before they died.

It turned out I could barely take a step without my whole body hurting. My feet and legs hurt from the hard road. My shoulders, back, and arms hurt from the weight of my pack. I didn't know how I was going to walk another mile, let alone all the way to New Rutland.

I hadn't slept much, either. Something about the strange sounds around the sugarhouse, the rushing water from a nearby stream and unfamiliar bug chattering, had kept me awake at first. And then it was Jacob's pill bottle. I'd gotten to worrying about it, and pretty soon that was turning into something else, into a memory that came from way back, from when I was almost too little to have remembered much of anything:

Sunlight, warm and fuzzy, lighting up the orange plastic of a pill bottle. I held the bottle up to the sun and shook it. It rattled.

Later on, my mom's long hair fell across my arm and she swept me into her arms. Her hair smelled of her sweat and sharp, heady herbs. One little piggy, *she said, and she tucked a pill bottle into her sock.* Two little piggies, *another bottle slipped into my jacket pocket.* Three little piggies, *another in the other pocket. The rest of the bottles went back in her pack and rattled all together as we walked.*

She slept in the shade of a boulder, and behind her a trickle of water fell into a crack in the rocks, surrounded by green moss. I held one of the bottles from my pockets up to the light and shook it. This time, the lid opened and a hundred beautiful blue and orange tablets spilled onto the dirt. I picked one up, stroked it clean. I started to arrange them in a circle on the dirt, blue on the outside for the sky. Orange on the inside for the sun. Then a shadow rose up and my mom was awake, standing above me and screaming. She lunged for the tablets and knocked me aside, and my head hit the mossy rock behind me. I cried and cried but she had her back to me, hunched over the ground as she picked pill after pill from the dirt.

I looked around the sugarhouse and saw that Route 7 was a ways off, through some trees and across a stream. Closer by, a field swept up the hillside, and the roof of a house or barn just barely crested above the trees at the top.

Why hadn't I ever remembered those pill bottles before? Being with Jacob, being out on the road again after all this time, it was all forcing out memories I didn't much like. Between that and worrying about Thomas and wondering if he'd spent another night thinking I'd abandoned him, I barely noticed the bright sunlight and the breeze rippling the grass in the hillside field.

Finally I couldn't stand waiting around a minute longer, and I figured if we didn't get moving then I'd fall over and not be able to get up again. So I hobbled back into the sugarhouse to get Jacob. But he was finally up, packing his bag with his back to me.

"C'mon," I said. "We gotta get to New Rutland. Thomas is probably missing me bad by now."

"Thomas?" Jacob asked, turning to frown at me. His eyes still looked a little off, and his gray hair stuck up on one side.

"My brother." I tried to sound annoyed, to cover up the worry. Jacob was the only one helping me, and he was smart and resourceful, but he wasn't any of those things when he was high.

"Right," he said, hoisting his pack and pushing past me out the door and into the sun. "How could I forget."

The world looked different without the usual gray cloud cover. The shadows complicated everything, turning the mountains into patches of light and dark, throwing strips of brightness across the floodplains. We came out of the trees and the sun felt warm on my face. I took my mom's coat off—Jacob had seen my scars plenty, and no one else was on the road. I wasn't used to the feel of the air on my neck. I thought of Alexandra, dancing in her red dress. Was this what that felt like? If my body hadn't been so tired, I might've thought so.

But the feel of the breeze and the sunlight couldn't loosen the dark tangle of doubt I'd stepped into on Route 7. I didn't want to think about my mom knocking me into a rock, or the little plastic bottles she'd had in her possession. I walked carefully, like the memory was a balanced knife hanging above my head that would cut me if it fell. To distract myself, I took note of the landscape around me. My mom and I had traveled all over. Maybe I'd seen that tree before, or that turned-over car. But all I remembered clearly were stories, and my mom's voice as she walked. She'd talked to me about *Vermont Life*, saying that the things from that magazine were under our feet, tucked into the hills, hiding behind the next bend.

The Republic we were walking through now wasn't *Vermont Life*, but it wasn't the apocalypse I'd read about in books, either. The Fall was everywhere—in the burnt husks of buildings and the giant wind turbines still as statues on the mountains, in the strangling kudzu and diseased trees. Even so, the landscape was dappled with life, just like it was dappled with sunlight. The hills rose up on either side of the valley, and some of the things I saw weren't so bad. We walked past a barn high up in a mountain meadow, sturdy and new. A white horse grazed in the field with a little colt. Farther on, someone had built a huge mill of stone and wood over a rushing stream, the water wheel turning in the current.

Every time we rounded a bend or came over a hill, I looked for the circus. I imagined that they'd spent the night on the road, maybe taken a long breakfast, broken an axle or lost track of one of their horses—anything to let us catch up, to let me see Thomas coming out from between the carts, running to me with his corncob pipe and an adventure to tell.

But we didn't see them. We didn't see anyone, which I started to think strange. The world was still alive. So where were the people? Were the bandits so fearsome that no one dared get close to the road? But we hadn't seen any Alt-Z sentries either. Jacob didn't speak, hadn't said anything since the sugarhouse. He didn't look left or right, even when the sun made a lake to our left shimmer with a thousand spots of light.

About an hour after we'd started walking, we passed by a sheer rock face that rose up from the roadside. I could see marks in the stone where some kind of machine had sliced it, making way for Route 7. That was something people did before the Fall—they just tunneled through hillsides instead of going around them. I looked back as we passed and saw there was an American flag painted on the northern side of the rock wall.

I stopped, wincing as I felt a blister pop. The painting was rough, with long drips of red and blue, and looked a few years old—bits of it were faded or scraped away. Someone had painted a shiny black X over the flag, and beside it they'd written BUZZ ALL AMERICANS.

"What's it say?" Jacob asked, breaking the long silence.

I told him. He grunted and turned away again. Buzzing was what happened to the worst criminals in the Republic—death by electricity.

Jacob trudged on, but I couldn't tear my eyes from the rock wall. Someone had painted that flag, someone who'd supported Americans. And someone else had wanted to kill them. The picture made me hopeful and terrified all at once. What if my mom had painted the flag? And what if whoever painted over it had found her too?

I finally made myself start walking again and caught up to Jacob. "Why does everyone hate Americans?" I asked.

"They're enemies of the Republic," Jacob said, squinting ahead at the road.

"They can't all be bad, though," I insisted. "That's like saying everyone in the Republic is good."

"Sure," he said.

"I think Vermonters are prejudiced," I said, thinking of Bob's assumption that anything bad must've come from America. "Most of us haven't ever met an American, but people hate them anyway. It's not fair."

Jacob didn't say anything for a little while. We passed by a car-charging station, the kind that used to run on electricity. Someone had detached all the wiring and tried to burn the place down, by the looks of it. The metal casing on the charging ports was scorched.

"You've never been outside the Republic, so you don't really know how bad the Fall was," Jacob said finally. "No one really does, but America remembers better than us. Big cities had it the worst. Millions of people lived in them, and there wasn't any food."

"But that was the Fall. It was ages ago." The Fall had never felt particularly real to me. It was like the Mississippi River—something from so long ago that it might as well be fiction as history.

"Things are better now, sure," Jacob said. "And the Republic still keeps up with some of the old ways and laws. But out in America, the rules are different. Even good and bad don't mean the same thing there as here."

"What does that mean?" I asked.

"It means folks are right to be afraid of Americans. They're dangerous now, doesn't matter whether or not they used to be. People do what they have to to survive."

I thought about that for a little while.

"Have you been to America?" I asked.

"Yes," he said.

"Why?"

Jacob didn't answer. He was squinting ahead at where the road wound into a thick stand of fir trees.

"Why—" I said again, but just then he stopped, his whole

body going still. I followed his gaze, a spike of fear rising in my throat.

Something lay on the road up ahead—a mounded pile of what looked like clothes, lying in the dirt. I tried to tell myself that it might be lost baggage fallen off the back of a cart. But my body didn't believe me—I shivered, stopping in my tracks.

The things on the ground were people. I knew it before I saw a hand, then a leg. I knew it before I heard the flies buzzing over their bodies.

The dead people had been thrown to the ground, arms and legs spread and twisted and crushed under their bodies. We were close enough to see fingers, ears, the face of a woman whose expression was like a bad dream. A path of blackened blood meandered from her body and pooled in a rut near her hip. She wore a bracelet of twisted grass on one wrist, and her fingers were wrapped around the hilt of a knife.

Nothing moved except my chest, rising and falling.

Then Jacob started forward, and I followed him without thinking. I'd almost forgotten he was there.

There were three bodies, and I couldn't see two of their faces. A warm rush of fear came over me—what if one of them was Thomas?

I ran past Jacob then and circled around, getting a look at the others. I didn't recognize any of them. They wore clothes that anyone might wear—faded jackets, old jeans, homespun shirts. I don't know why this was my first question—who they were, instead of who'd killed them. I wasn't thinking straight. Jacob was, though. While I looked at their faces he stared around into the trees, spinning in a slow circle. He'd pulled the knife from his belt. Too late, I looked around too. If anyone had been waiting to attack us, I'd probably have been dead by now. My breathing came heavy and the flies buzzed loudly. I stumbled back and turned away, just as Jacob brushed past me and knelt down next to the closest body, feeling its neck for a pulse.

"Who's killing everyone?" I whispered, my voice sounding like it came from far away.

Jacob walked over and pulled me into a one-armed hug. I was so surprised I didn't step away. His jacket was rough and smelled of rain.

"It's okay," he said gently. "Nothing we could've done."

"But who—"

"Let's keep moving. Don't want to be here when their people come to collect them."

We started walking again, Jacob's arm still around my shoulders. I leaned against him, grateful for his solid warmth, and for a minute I didn't think of anything at all. Glancing over my shoulder, I couldn't see anything but the trees close and dark around the road.

"Shouldn't we have buried them or something?" I asked shakily.

"They were Alt-Zs," Jacob said. "The others will come for them soon. They don't leave their dead behind."

"How d'you know they were Alt-Zs?"

"Recognized one of them," he said shortly.

We came out of the forest and the valley opened up before us, slung between mountains. The ruins of a little town stood off to our left, and on the right a long-rusted freight train sat dead on its tracks.

"Why'd you recognize Alt-Zs?" I asked suddenly. My mind was moving slowly, every thought interrupted by what we'd seen.

"Those three were an ambush party. The Alt-Zs do that—someone doesn't pay the tax at a checkpoint, they meet an ambush over the next hill."

"They got killed trying to ambush someone?"

"Might be." Jacob paused. "The circus have weapons, as far as you could tell?"

I thought about the giant strong man, and the knife thrower, and the tinker with his shining eyes. The dead woman on the road with the grass bracelet might have had a knife in her back, or a bullet. And the man beside her, whose arms were twisted under his body in a way that made me queasy…

"Probably," I said, and my stomach clenched as I thought about Thomas. What if it had been them who'd done this? Maybe it'd been self-defense. I didn't want to even imagine it.

"The Greens came through this way too," Jacob said, thoughtful.

I pulled free of his arm and stared up at him. "Yeah, I heard them talking about the Alt-Zs! Said they wouldn't let the Alt-Zs stop them getting to Middlebury for Town Meeting." My breathing eased—surely the Greens had killed that ambush party, not the circus. That had to be it. Thomas wasn't mixed up with murderers, after all.

Jacob didn't answer me. "Lee and the others did it!" I said, trying to get his attention. He shook his head, his eyes fixed on something in the distance.

"You need to be more careful on this road, June," he whispered, and jerked his chin. "Twice now I've seen things you don't. This isn't the Hollow."

I followed his gaze down the road. He was right—I'd been so busy thinking about Thomas and the circus that I hadn't seen the dangers that were right in front of me. Route 7 curved down a hill and then up the next slope, skimming by Otter Creek and the floodplain. On the next hill I could see two people riding toward us on bicycles.

"Don't say anything to them," Jacob said when the pair were about fifty yards away. "They're trouble." He looked grim before, but now he seemed nervous too. Something about the two biking toward us, the first living people we'd seen since we left the Borough, worried him more than the dead bodies behind us.

"You know them?" I asked.

"Alt-Zs," Jacob said. "Let me handle this."

It was then that I remembered he hadn't answered my question before—the one about how he came to know the faces of Alt-Zs. Come to think of it, I wasn't sure how he knew these strangers on bikes were Alt-Zs from fifty feet away. I watched them come, but out of the corner of my eye I watched him too.

"'Sup, Jacob," the woman on the first bike said, coasting to a stop and planting her feet on the ground. She had dark hair pulled back in a braid that rested on her shoulder and ended in a silver clasp. A bright beaded necklace was just visible inside her coat, and I knew it meant she was Abenaki. I'd seen an Abenaki family at market day in the Borough wearing similar beaded clothes and jewelry. Folks loved the cane sugar they sold, but no one stuck around long to talk with them. I wondered if all Abenakis were in the Alt-Zs, or if this woman just happened to be one.

"Nice day for it," Jacob replied calmly; but I noticed his hands were clenched at his sides.

"Nice day for what, exactly?" the woman asked, grinning. She looked at the other biker, a boy a few years older than me, and raised her eyebrows. "What d'you think Jacob here's trying to sell us, Rick?"

The boy shrugged. He had reddish hair and freckles and wore a deer-hide vest over a faded red shirt from Before. "Looks like a deputy to me," he said, nodding at the tarnished star on Jacob's shirt. "Not selling anything I want to buy."

"Ah, Rick, you haven't met our comrade before, have you?" the woman said. "Well, I remember him well enough. Never sold me his product, so I never got around to forgetting."

She laughed again, but the boy still didn't seem to get it.

"Where you headed, Medusa?" Jacob asked sharply. I hadn't noticed until now, but he'd shifted until he was standing a little in front of me, making it so Medusa and Rick couldn't see me properly. I moved a little to the side, but Jacob moved right along with me. He was hiding me.

"Could ask you the same thing," Medusa replied, leaning her forearms on her bike handles. "Haven't seen you on our road since the old days. Chasing criminals now, are you? Enforcing *laws*?"

Jacob nodded. "Looking for a circus come through here. Got some questions for them."

He didn't mention the Greens, but then I guess he wouldn't

talk bad about law enforcement to a bandit, not even law enforcement as crooked as Lee.

"Might've seen a circus," Medusa said breezily. "Hard to keep track."

"Did they have a boy with them?" Jacob asked.

Medusa smiled sweetly. "Like I said, hard to keep track."

Jacob sighed. "Protein?" he said. I didn't know what that meant, until Medusa smiled wider and Jacob pulled his packet of jerky out of his pack. He handed a few strips over to Medusa, who passed one to the boy beside her.

"Hmm, I do seem to remember a caravan of weirdos coming through. Passed an hour or so ago, little while after a crew of low-life Greens came by." She spat casually on the ground. "Didn't see any boy."

"Did they say anything?"

Medusa ripped a bite of jerky off her strip and chewed thoughtfully. I wanted to scream, but Jacob just watched her, expressionless.

Finally she swallowed. "Might've, but it's hard to keep—" Jacob didn't even let her finish. He tossed another strip of jerky her way. She caught it.

"Guess I do remember! Talked to a woman in a red dress. She wanted to know if we'd been in contact with an American 'round these parts."

I tried to step forward, but Jacob held a hand out to block me.

"Why?" he asked, calm as ever.

Medusa shrugged. "Didn't say. And I told them the truth: Alt-Zs don't work with Americans anymore. Got our own trade routes set up." She made a little bow to Jacob, pretending to tip a hat.

"Did they say which American they were looking for?" I asked, pushing Jacob's arm aside and stepping out from behind him before he could stop me.

Medusa looked at me properly now. At first she just threw a glance at me, but then her eyes locked onto my face and something shifted in her smile. Her eyes were shining and I realized she wasn't quite as old as I'd thought. Closer to my age than Jacob's. She sucked in air between her teeth.

"Who've you got here, Jay?" she asked.

"Don't—" Jacob said, his voice low and threatening.

"Holy crum! First the mother, then the daughter…It's her, right?" Medusa laughed. My whole body went cold and then hot, and I felt my face grow heated. What mother? What daughter?

"Medusa—" Jacob said.

"It *is* her!" Medusa crowed. "I can't believe it. Jacob, you're one of a kind. Is she *yours*? Holy crum, I knew you two hung around, but not—"

"Your ambush party is dead," Jacob interrupted.

Medusa's laughter faded. She looked at the boy named Rick, then back at Jacob.

"What are you talking about?"

"The ambush party at the fir stand, couple miles south," he said. "They're dead. We passed them a little while ago."

"Feck," Rick said. Medusa looked like she didn't know what to do. I was totally forgotten.

"But how—?"

"They were dead when we found them. Don't know anything else," Jacob said flatly.

"They— Dammit, why didn't you tell us right off?"

Jacob shrugged.

"Once a snake, always a snake," Medusa snarled. "Best you stay off this road from now on. Out of the way."

She put her foot on her bike pedal and rolled forward, forcing Jacob out of the way. Without another word, she and the boy pedaled off, picking up speed and heading in the direction we'd come from.

"Wait!" I yelled after them. "What about my mom?"

Medusa didn't even look back. I started to follow her, even though I knew I wouldn't be able to run as fast as their bikes. But Jacob caught me by the arm.

"Don't," he said.

I turned on him. "What was she talking about?"

Jacob didn't answer. He was watching Medusa go, stuffing his hands in his pockets and then pulling them out again, looking everywhere but at me.

"Jacob, why'd she say 'mother and daughter'?"

"She doesn't know what she's talking about. Let's go," Jacob finally said. He turned back toward New Rutland, hitched up his pack, and started to walk.

"But—"

"You need to act your age, Le—June. This road's too dangerous for you to go running off after every Alt-Z you see," Jacob said sharply, turning on me. He was sweating, a sheen on his forehead that hadn't been there before. His gray eyes were sharp in his weathered face.

"She was talking about my mom," I said. "That's what she meant. And she asked if I'm yours."

I couldn't move. The weight of all the guessing was too heavy.

Part of me wanted to laugh it off, to move my feet and forget whatever Medusa had said. But I couldn't. Whatever was coming, there wasn't any stopping it now.

"Are you…?" I asked, not quite able to say the word. I'd never even thought about having a dad before. I'd never known one.

Jacob stopped, shaking his head hard. "I'm not your father."

I breathed in and then out. "Then what? Why won't you tell me?" A cloud wall was coming in from the west, and a shadow slid down the road, covering us.

"Jacob!" I said again.

"I knew your mother, before. Worked with her," he snapped finally. His voice came out tight and hard, as if the words hurt to say.

I sat down then. My knees bent first, and then I lowered myself the rest of the way down so I wouldn't fall. It was easier than standing, and I was so tired all of a sudden. Jacob stood back, looking over my head at the road.

It might've been a happy moment—he knew her! He could bring me to her! But I was terrified. He'd lied from the first time I saw him. He'd been lying this whole time.

"Why didn't you tell me?" I asked. But then I thought of something else, something more important. He'd saved me from the barn fire, and he'd known who my mom was.

"Why didn't you bring me back to her?" I gasped, and I looked up and saw that he still couldn't meet my eyes. My heart was shuddering in my chest. I could barely breathe.

"You didn't bring me back to her," I said again. He'd brought me to Bob and Denise instead. The ground rocked under me.

"She's dead," I choked out.

Jacob crouched down beside me then. "No," he said. "Not as far as I know."

A breeze lifted my hair and I brushed it away, and it was amazing I could still do something as normal as that.

"So…why am I not with her?" I asked.

"I took you to Bob and Denise instead."

"But—" I couldn't figure out what he meant. Why would he have taken me away from her on purpose?

"I knew when she came back to the barn and saw it burned she'd think you were dead. So I took you to the Hollow."

"You stole me from her." The terror was fading, but something just as hot and powerful was building up in its place. I glared at him, tried to make him look at me.

"I didn't steal you. I saved you."

"I've been stuck at the Hollow, not knowing if she's alive or dead. I've been all alone."

He flushed. "You've had food, and a warm bed, and work."

"I had those things before. You kidnapped me."

He opened his mouth, closed it again.

"It's not that simple," he said, his voice rough and defiant. He sat back on his heels and hung his head, still refusing to meet my gaze.

"Where is my mother?" I asked. "You know, don't you?"

"No, I don't know," he said.

"You're lying."

He paused. "I'm not. She moved around a lot. She could be anywhere."

I stood up, the hardest thing I'd done all day, and heaved my pack back onto my aching shoulders. "Don't follow me," I said.

He looked up at me, his face tight and worried. "Where are you—"

"I'm going to get Thomas, and then we're going to find my mom."

"You can't go alone," he said.

I turned away from him. I didn't want to be around him one second longer. For all I knew, he was going to kidnap me again. I started walking.

"June, you need to be careful," he called after me. "She's not the mother you thought she was. She left you."

I spun to face him. I didn't want him to say another word, didn't want to hear whatever he was about to say about her. "I don't believe you. You've wanted to keep me from her this whole time."

"I've been trying to protect you—"

"Don't follow me," I said again.

"June, the road isn't safe, and the circus might be dangerous." He struggled to his feet and started after me. "Let me take you the rest of the way. I want to explain—"

"No," I said.

"You can't go alone. Someone's killing people."

"I don't care."

"I have to question the Greens anyway, and the circus." Jacob sounded desperate now. "I'll take you to New Rutland, and then we can—"

I was walking again, holding my hands over my ears. I couldn't hear another word without exploding. He was lying, trying to turn me against my mom. I didn't want to spend another second in his presence.

"Just let me explain, Le—"

"Don't call me Leah," I shouted to the road. "I'm not your daughter. And don't come near me again."

I ran, barely feeling my feet on the ground, ignoring my burning muscles. The whole sky was obscured in gray clouds again—exactly the weather I was used to. No sun to burn my skin and confuse the landscape. I was on the next hillside before I finally looked back. Route 7 snaked south behind me, and Jacob stood still on the road where I'd left him, looking very small. I felt small too. I turned away and kept walking, too tired to run anymore.

15

At first I was too angry to be scared. Every step was a step away from Jacob and his lies, and that was good enough for me. Route 7 widened around me, then split in two lanes. One lane was choked with trees and puckerbush, but the other was clear and even. It took me a while to realize that if the road was clear, it had to be because someone was clearing it. And that reminded me of the Alt-Zs, who ambushed anyone who couldn't pay the road toll.

And then I was too scared to be angry anymore.

I was alone. I was alone and I didn't know where I was going. I'd seen Jacob's map, but he'd been leading the way; he knew how to get to New Rutland. Heck, I wasn't even sure I'd be able to get back to the Borough if I turned around. As the afternoon light started to fade, the mountains seemed farther away on either side. And stretching out in all directions was the puckerbush and the scraggly trees, old buildings and piles of junk—a thousand places to hide an ambush. Soon every muscle in my body was tense.

And all the while I kept turning Jacob over in my mind, pondering everything he'd ever said to me and wondering if any scrap of it was true. If he'd known my mother, he must've hated her or been jealous of her. And so he'd lied about her. Maybe he'd wanted me to be his new Leah, and he figured I'd only stay with him if I gave up on my mom.

I edged through a dark, tree-covered section of road, my knife in my hand and my fingers shaking. My stomach was an empty pit, and my legs were starting to feel like jelly. I knew I wouldn't be able to go much farther, but I didn't want to think about what would happen when the last of the daylight faded.

I came out of the trees and found myself at an intersection between Route 7 and another big road, this one all overgrown except for a path just wide enough for a few people to walk side by side. Off in the distance I caught a glimpse of three or four church steeples and even more buildings around them, taller than any I'd ever seen before, weathered and empty-windowed against the sky.

I recognized those buildings: New Rutland. And I recognized the intersection too.

I stopped right in the intersection, fear bubbling in my belly, and looked up. I didn't know what I'd see, but I knew something was there. I remembered.

Above me, metal scaffolding stretched over the road, decorated with three-colored lamps every few feet. A tattered noose hung from the scaffolding, swinging in the breeze and empty.

What I remembered was this: my mom's cool palm on my cheek, leading me under this scaffolding and keeping me from looking up at whatever was hanging from the noose.

What is it? I'd asked.

It's just an ugly bird, she'd said, her hand slipping from my cheek.

I'd had that memory before, back in the Hollow. The feel of her soft hand on my face, the sound of her voice. But now that I was standing here, I remembered more. We'd sat down against the concrete blocks heaped on the side of the road, right over there. We'd been waiting for something. She took out *Vermont Life* and read to me about the colors of autumn. I stared hard at the pages, wishing we could wait anywhere else. Her voice was hoarse and she kept clearing her throat.

See the ugly bird? she said finally, putting *Vermont Life* away. I was playing with a row of pebbles and didn't want to look. I shook my head.

Look at it, Junie. It's an American bird. She pushed my chin up so I had to see. The thing hanging from the noose was a person, or it had been a long time ago. Most of its skin was gone, and what was left had gone black. It swung slowly around and I caught a glimpse of its grinning skeletal face, and I looked away.

Bastards, all of them, my mom said. *This is why they have to burn.*

Alone under the scaffolding and the swinging noose, I clenched my eyes shut so hard they hurt. I didn't want to see these things. Jacob had filled my head up with doubt.

My vision was all foggy when I opened my eyes, probably from being so hungry and tired. I stumbled and made my way over to the side of the road to find a place to sit down.

I stepped off the road and down a steep path toward Otter Creek, looking for a soft spot where I could curl up and rest. The brush was thick and thorny, but I pushed my way through anyway, my feet heavy in their boots.

I didn't hear the voices up ahead, and I didn't smell the smoke. When I fought my way out into the clearing by the river's edge, two people were already standing there, watching me.

"You are very loud," the woman said. I froze, remembering what Jacob had said. *You need to be more careful...this isn't the Hollow.*

The woman held a knife in her hand, and I recognized her, but my mind wasn't working fast enough for me to remember why. The knife glinted in the dull afternoon light.

"Jailbird," the man behind her said. He was massive, with huge muscles and a tiny mustache. I knew him too.

"You're—you're with the circus," I said.

They were. Sebastian had called them the knife thrower and the strongman. And now here they were, on the bank of Otter Creek, with their horses tied to a knotty tree and a sack of wet clothes dripping down the strongman's back, a little fire dying at their feet.

"And *you're* our jailbird friend!" the knife thrower said. She flourished her blade and slid it into a sheath at her hip. "You've flown far, little bird!" She wore all black, and her hair was thick and black, but her skin was pale, almost blue.

"What are you doing here? Where's the circus?" I asked. My heart was racing, and I was almost starting to feel a little swell of hope.

"Alas, laundry duty," the knife thrower sighed, gesturing to the strongman. Suddenly she had a knife in her hand again, a smaller one. She twirled it between her fingers. "And the circus—well, it is near enough for us to find." Behind her, the strongman said nothing.

"Is my brother with them?" I asked. "Thomas?"

The knife thrower narrowed her eyes. "Thomas…Thomas. You think he ran away with the circus? Is that why you're here too? Want to join us?" She grinned.

"No, I—" I started.

"You could be my lovely assistant," the knife thrower interrupted. "Here, stand still."

Before I could do anything, the knife thrower flicked her wrist and the small knife flew at me. I blinked, and it was gone. A lock of my hair drifted down to the ground.

"Ta-da!" she said. Then she dropped to the ground, did a somersault, skipped past me to the knotty tree, and pulled the little knife from its bark. The strongman grunted, which I thought must be his way of laughing.

"But my brother—" I said. They were so full of energy, these two, but I could barely stand anymore. Why was this so hard?

"We don't have your brother, jailbird," the knife thrower said. She flicked a finger at the strongman, who lumbered over and tossed the laundry over one of the horse's backs. They untied the leads and started climbing back up the thin trail toward the road.

"Wait!" I followed after them. "Are you sure? He was there the night of the storm."

"Too many storms to keep track of, don't you think?" the knife thrower called back to me.

I followed them out onto the road again. It was darker now than before, the air thick with evening.

"Can you take me with you?" I asked, hating how my voice quivered.

The strongman and the knife thrower climbed onto their horses. The strongman leaned over, pulling something out of his saddlebag, but the knife thrower just smiled down at me. "It's getting late," she said. "You should go home."

"But—"

"It was good to see you, jailbird," she said, and kicked her horse into a trot.

The strongman raised his head from his saddlebag. He had a pipe clenched in his teeth now, and he smiled at me. My stomach dropped and my heart leapt. It was Thomas's corncob pipe.

"Wait," I said again, but he turned and followed the knife thrower.

I thought about running after them. They had Thomas, and they wouldn't admit it. Instead they were trying to shake me off, just like Jacob had tried to stop me looking for my mom. What did they want with Thomas? And why didn't they want me coming with them?

By that time, the performers had disappeared around a bend. I couldn't catch them. I wanted to kick something, to scream, but I didn't. My muscles were too tired to kick, and I was too scared to make a noise.

I had to get to New Rutland. My need to get to Thomas and my mom was like a shard of glass under my skin now—painful, fragile, unavoidable. I was so close. I could see Old Rutland. But without the knife thrower and the strongman, and without Jacob, I didn't know where to go. There were side roads all along Route 7, and only one of them would take me to Thomas and the circus.

I looked back down Route 7. The highway disappeared into darkness. Somewhere out there the Alt-Zs were carrying their dead home, angry and armed.

I started down the road again, through the settling dust left by the hooves of the knife thrower and the strongman's horses. It was all I could do. I walked slowly, my knees stabbing with pain and my muscles aching. Darkness fell around me.

I would've passed right by the turnoff to New Rutland if it hadn't been for the U-Haul.

I was walking slowly, stopping every time I heard a rustle in the brush or the call of a far-off animal, when I heard something new behind me—a rumbling. I turned back and saw a light swaying toward me, far off down the road. I limped off the road and lay down in a mound of kudzu between two rusted-out cars. The rumbling got louder, the light swayed closer and closer, and I wrapped my fingers around the handle of my knife.

Two horses came out of the darkness, pulling a gutted truck that read *U-Haul* on its side. Its roof and sides were held together with scavenged metal, and its wheels were wooden with sheet metal wrapped around them and big nails driven in to make treads. A lamp hung from the front window, but I couldn't see who was driving.

I was so exhausted I couldn't decide if I should stay put or run—but before I could make a decision the van slowed down and then turned, the horses straining up an unmarked side road. I heard someone holler at the horses, urging them up the hill. Then the truck disappeared into the trees.

I stood up, swaying a little. That was the first sign of life I'd seen since the knife thrower and the strongman, and it was headed up a side road near Old Rutland. It seemed the best clue I'd get.

It wasn't hard to catch the U-Haul, since it was struggling up such a steep hill. I sneaked up behind it in the dark, though its wheels made such a clatter I doubt anyone would have heard me. The back of the truck was covered by a threadbare plastic tarp. Hoisting myself up into the truck, I clambered underneath the tarp. The truck was full of boxes and bags, stuffed full. I wriggled into a little space between two heavy boxes and sat back, my arms wrapped around my knees in the darkness.

I was probably headed into New Rutland, I figured. Thomas had to be there, no matter what the knife thrower said, and I'd been wrong about the circus. I'd defended them to Jacob, but in the meantime they'd taken Thomas and tried to hide it from me.

A whisper in the back of my mind wondered if whatever they were up to had something to do with my mom.

But that didn't matter. I was done trying to get the circus to help me. I'd get Thomas back, and then we'd find my mom together. My stomach rolled at the thought. Would I be able to feel it if she were close? All I felt right then was tired.

The U-Haul creaked and shuddered up the road, and the rocking made me sleepy. But I was too scared to sleep. I didn't want to be caught unawares, and I didn't want to have bad dreams.

Finally, the U-Haul rattled to a stop and I caught a glimpse of firelight beyond the tarp. I shuffled further back, tucking my feet in. If someone pulled back the tarp, they'd see me.

"Hey, Yoder," a voice said. "You're late." Gravel crunched as the speaker walked up to the cab.

The driver said something I couldn't hear, low and gruff.

"Gotcha. Same haul as usual?" the first voice said.

Low growling again. I was holding my breath.

"Constable reckons we ought to do more inspections, you know."

I was guessing the voice had to be a guard, like the ones posted outside the Borough. I closed my eyes, willing him not to do an inspection.

"That'd take all night," a new voice said—a woman. "The truck's so full of junk—I mean, valuable products, Yoder."

Yoder grumbled something I couldn't hear. The two guards laughed.

"Park it in your usual spot. See you at Al's later," the first guard said. I let out my breath as the U-Haul started forward again. It climbed a little farther up the gravel path, then shuddered over a big bump and leveled out. I peered under the tarp and saw an open gate we'd just passed through, cut out of a high wall made of tree trunks. Another guard was there, looking the other way. I pulled my pack on, and when the U-Haul rounded a bend, I slipped out of the back and onto the road.

And just like that, I was in New Rutland.

16

The U-Haul rattled off down the street, and I stood still, trying to look at everything all at once. New Rutland wasn't like anywhere I'd been before. A long row of window lights lined the street. Some were lanterns and candles, but I could tell most of them were electric. The street was paved with gravel. And even though it was night, voices came through windows and doors, dogs barked, and some kind of music played far off. I smelled fires and cooking food and manure all in one breath.

Maybe it was because of the night, but New Rutland felt like a real city, like something from a book. Everywhere I looked there were more lights, more buildings, more people.

I took a step, and then another, the lights and noise washing my weariness away. But I'd hardly gone a few feet when a group of people came out of a side passage between two houses and nearly ran into me. They were wearing town clothes—collared shirts with neat woven jackets—and all of them were laughing. I shied away, but they didn't even look at me, didn't say hello or ask who I was or what I thought I was doing there. I felt mousy and clunky again, something I hadn't felt when it'd just been me and Jacob on the road. My mom's coat hung heavy and ratty from my shoulders, and I wished it weren't so stained and old.

After they passed, I walked on. I saw more people, sitting on their porches or hurrying past me like they had somewhere important to get to. Any of the women could've been my mom, though in the dark and the confusion I couldn't even think what her face might have looked like. I didn't see any boys Thomas's age, or anyone from the circus. The buildings closed in around me, and I couldn't think what to do.

The circus—and Thomas—had to be here somewhere. But the town was big, and in the dark everything was confusing and mysterious. I could walk for hours, walk till I dropped, and maybe I still wouldn't find them.

I came to a stop at an intersection and looked both ways. Each direction had a row of buildings, each lit by a row of electric lights. It was impossible to avoid getting the electric light in my eyes. My bones started to ache again.

To my left I heard someone whistling in the looming shadow between two houses. It was a boy, leaning against a stack of firewood and staring down the road at a group of men gathered up under one of the electric lights. He was about my age, with a wisp of hair on his lip and a cap that didn't stop his hair from flopping into his face. Something about his gangly arms and legs reminded me of Cyrus.

"Hey," I said.

The boy jumped and looked around at me. He had big, earnest eyes that looked me up and down while he thought through his answer. "Hey," he said, finally.

"You know if there's a circus around here somewhere?" I asked. I kept my distance, just in case, but he didn't worry me. And I was too tired to be embarrassed about talking to a stranger.

The boy blinked, then grinned. "Circus? Wait, you with the circus?" He straightened up, staring at me like he thought I might be hiding a white rabbit or something.

"What? No. I'm *looking* for them."

"Oh," the boy said, with a frown. "But I mean...you're not from here, are you?"

"No," I said, glancing down at myself, wondering if I was wearing something wrong for this town. My pants were caked with dust from the road, and my mom's coat was frayed as always. I guessed I must have looked like I'd come a long way.

"Where you from?" the boy asked. He was a fair bit taller than me, now that I saw him up close.

I shrugged. "South a ways. I'm just looking for the circus." I looked both ways down the road again, hoping he'd get the hint.

He didn't get the hint. "But how'd you get here?" he asked.

"I walked."

"Damn." He looked amazed. "Run into any Alt-Zs?"

"Yeah, a few."

"Damn." He looked even more amazed than before, his eyebrows disappearing under his flop of hair. Then he seemed to catch himself. He cleared his throat. "I mean, I seen 'em too, plenty of times. Nothing I can't handle."

"They weren't so bad," I agreed. That deflated him a bit, even though I wasn't trying to outdo him. "So that circus?" I said again.

The boy looked up and down the road, like he might spot them. "I know they're in town. Not sure where they set up. I could look with you."

I would've laughed if I hadn't been so tired and nervous. Instead, I just shook my head. "Is there someone else I could ask?"

The boy stepped back, clearing his throat again and rubbing his nose to cover up the flash of disappointment I'd seen. He leaned against the woodpile again. "Al's. Go to Al's. Someone in there'll know. I'm heading there later, soon as my shift's over."

I wasn't sure what kind of shift he was on, but I didn't much care right then. "Okay. Where is Al's?"

The boy jutted his chin toward the road I'd just walked down. "That way, take the second right and you'll see it."

"Thanks," I said, and then turned before he could say anything else. I hurried down the road, hearing wind high up in the dark sky. I thought of Jacob, how he'd said I couldn't do this on my own. But I hadn't needed him to get me into New Rutland, and now I was going to find Thomas without him too.

I turned at the second right and started down the street, a little bloom of hope rising in me. But then I stopped dead.

Up ahead, a building shone out of the darkness, lit up by more electricity than I'd ever seen in my life. Its windows were blinding squares, and big signs made of colored light hung from the walls. I didn't want to look too closely, but I saw the word *Coke* before I could tear my eyes away. Worse still, I saw the name lit up over the door: AL'S FUN SHACK.

I felt sick just looking at it.

Two women came out of the door and into the street. Electricity flooded out the door behind them, lighting up a crowd of people in brown robes standing in front of the building. Music came dancing out the door, too, something tinny and recorded.

I didn't want to go into Al's Fun Shack. I wanted to go anywhere else. I looked around, and New Rutland spread out into the darkness on all sides. Someone darted across the road down a cross-street, someone whose face I couldn't see. I'd already almost forgotten the way back to the boy, and the way back to the gated entrance. There wasn't anywhere else for me to go. Much as I didn't want to, I pressed my lips together, trained my eyes on the dark ground, and walked forward.

As I got closer, the crowd in front of the bar flickered in the electric light. I'd seen people in that kind of brown robe before—Millerites. They believed the same thing as my mom—that electricity came from the devil. Difference was, the Millerites were trying to do something about it.

"Don't go in," one of them said when I got close enough to see their faces. He had big, sad eyes and a harelip. I ignored him.

"Don't go in," the man said again, and I wanted to turn around and run back into the cool darkness. None of the Millerites touched me or said anything mean, but every single one had something to say about Al's Fun Shack. "Stay away," "The light burns," "The devil lives in fluorescence." I kept walking, right up to the front door. It was hard, though—I don't know how to explain it, but I could *hear* the lights. They buzzed as if they were alive. I ducked my head when I went under them, and then the noise of the bar overtook the whispers of the light.

Al's Fun Shack was full of people, packed tighter than the Millerites. In one corner, an old man with a big belly and skinny arms was playing a fiddle. On the other side of the room a dusty machine screeched something that might've been music out of busted speakers. Between the two of them I could barely hear anything.

And electricity was everywhere. The walls were covered in more lit-up signs: *Bud Light*, *Corona*, and an image of a woman with long legs and a short skirt. The electric lights flickered as if they all had the same beating heart, and the only steady glow came from oil lamps on the bar and tables. I blinked, and blinked some more. The flickering made me feel dizzy, but I didn't want to look like an ignorant hill person now that I was inside.

I made my way up to the bar, trying to see the faces around me without meeting their eyes. My mom could be here, I thought. But instead of a warm glow, I felt sick at the thought. Jacob had filled my head with doubt, and I could never forgive him for that. He was a liar, I told myself for the hundredth time. Everything he'd said had been a lie. I just needed to talk to my mom, to hear her explain what had really happened. I'd find Thomas, and then I'd find her, and then everything would make sense.

But all the faces in the room belonged to strangers. And I'd never seen so many strangers, and so many who didn't look like me. I was the only one wearing sheepskin, the only one not in town clothes. In the thirty seconds it took me to walk across the room, I saw a nose piercing for the first time in real life, and faces both paler and darker than mine. I inched up to the bar and found an empty seat.

The bartender was a big man wearing a shirt that I knew from books was called "Hawaiian," though I didn't know what the word meant. It was covered in flowers, and must've been very colorful once upon a time.

"Excuse me," I said to his back. The noise of the crowd swept my voice away, and the bartender didn't answer, didn't look around. He finished pouring beer from a glass jug into a battered plastic cup, then strode off to the other end of the bar to deliver it.

I waited, worrying the edge of my mom's coat between my

fingers. It was too hot, weighing heavy on me and making me sweat, but I didn't take it off.

When the bartender came back, I said, "Excuse me" again. This time he glanced at me before he walked past and went into the back room behind the bar. I looked at the old man beside me, but he just sucked on his beer.

"Hey," I shouted when the bartender came back out again. Finally he stopped and squinted at me through one eye, keeping the other screwed shut.

"Quit nagging," he said. "Heard you the first time."

"Oh," I said, and felt my face getting red.

"Well, what you want?" he asked, sounding impatient even though no one else at the bar was asking for anything.

"Do you know where the circus is?" I asked.

"Fuck're you talking about?" he snapped. "I look like a god-durned elephant to you? Or like a—a lion? A clown?"

"No—" I said, but he kept going, sounding like he was enjoying himself now.

"I look like one of those folks who rides a bike with one wheel? Like a juggler?"

The man sitting beside me hacked out a few laughs, and that seemed to satisfy the bartender. I waited till they'd both stopped laughing.

"There's a traveling circus came into town today," I said. "I want to find them."

"Yeah, I know the one you're talking about," the bartender said, barely letting me finish.

"Then why—" I started, but then stopped myself. "So you know where they are?"

"Nope," he said. "Heard they're doing a show tomorrow, though. So you can just wait like the rest of us."

He turned and walked away before I could say anything else. I thought about what he'd said while I waited for him to come back. The circus was somewhere in New Rutland, but I wasn't any closer to finding them in the dark.

"Hey," I said as the bartender walked back down the bar. He ignored me.

"Al," the man next to me croaked. "She's talking again."

"I know," the bartender named Al called from the back room. "Think I'm deaf?" He came back out, taking his time. "What now?"

"I need a place to stay for the night," I said.

Al squinted down at me through his one open eye again, looking over my burned coat and messy braids. "Who you with, kid?"

"No one," I said. "I'm in town to get my brother."

"Hmm." Al glanced at the man next to me, who shrugged as if he had something to do with it. "Got any way to pay for a room?"

I hadn't thought of that. The lights and the music from the machine and all the people talking all at once were distracting me, and I couldn't think straight. I just wanted to get somewhere quiet, to be alone for a minute. But I made myself sit up straight and look Al in the eye.

"I can work for it," I said.

Al shook his head, getting ready to turn away again. "Nothing you can do that I need, kid. This ain't that kind of establishment."

"Well, I could trade—" I put a hand on my pack, trying to remember what I had. I didn't think Al would want any of the books I'd brought to trade with the circus. My fingers brushed against the sock that hid my mom's American money. I wasn't sure if American money was allowed in here, not to mention whether I could trade it without getting into trouble. And that reminded me of how little I knew, and how alone I was.

"I've got books," I said weakly.

"Comic books?" Al asked, raising his eyebrows and leaning his elbows on the counter.

"No—book books," I said. Comic books were hard to come by. Too fragile to last long after the Fall.

"Got any with good pictures in 'em?" Al asked, a little doubtful now. "I'm a collector, see." He gestured vaguely around at the electric signs on the walls and plucked at his Hawaiian shirt. "Anything from Before, anything *authentic* and *visually appealing*."

"What about..." I felt awkward, but I leaned forward and whispered so the man next to me wouldn't hear. "What about American stuff?"

Al leaned back and laughed. "Kid, everything from Before is American. Whole world was America before the Fall." Then he looked down the bar and spotted an empty glass. He lumbered off to get more beer, still chuckling to himself.

When he came back, I had my mom's American money out on the bar. He didn't walk past me this time. His eye bulged out with excitement—the good one, not the squinty one. He dropped the jug he was carrying and leaned over the bar again.

"Where'd you get this?" he whispered.

"Found it," I said.

Al fumbled under the bar and came up with a glass jar full of metal pieces. He dumped them out onto the bar next to my money, and I saw they were coins from Before. I'd come across coins every once in a while, beside roads or in old houses. The Republic burned all the American money it could find, but metal didn't burn easy.

"I got about seventy—" I started, but Al shook his hands at me to get me to shut up.

"Shhhh, let me do it," he said. He hitched up his pants and spread the money on the bar, mixing my paper with his coins. A few of the people sitting nearby watched him, but most just glanced over and then kept drinking. Maybe they were used to seeing American stuff in Al's collection.

"Seventy, then another five is seventy-five, and a one for seventy-six, that's the easy part," Al said, pushing the faded green paper all into a pile. "Now watch this. I've counted the coins before, but it gets harder when it's added to a higher number. So two pennies, that's two, and that's a—a nickel, and here's the two quarters, look at that." He held one of the silver coins up to me so quickly I jerked back.

"Look, that's a New York one. Got the woman with a torch on it." He put it carefully back on the bar and picked up the last quarter. "Don't know where this other one's from. Look at those big fucking bulls."

"It says North Dakota, and those are buffalo," I said, since I could read the little words on the quarter upside down.

"Whu?" he said, still looking at the quarter.

"Those animals are called buffalo. Different animal from cows."

"The fuck is she talking about?" Al asked the old man beside me. The man shrugged and took another slurp of his beer.

"I'll give you a room for the money," Al said to me, after waiting for an answer he didn't get.

I looked down at the money. It had been my mom's. I'd kept it hidden in my room in the Hollow for as long as I'd been there. Some nights, I'd taken a bill out and rubbed it between my fingers, because her fingers had touched it too.

"Okay," I told Al.

Al tapped the table with a knuckle and then scooped up the rest of the money and folded it up careful in his shirt pocket.

"Your room's last on the left, up the back stairs," he said. "And you can have some food too." So I guessed we were friends now. He brought me over a plate of soggy rice and spicy beans, and I suddenly remembered just how hungry I was. The old man beside me slurped the last of his beer and then stood up a little unsteadily.

"Live long 'n' prosper," he said to me, and shuffled away to join a table where a group of other men were playing a game that involved a stack of old iPhones and a power cord.

The warm food in my stomach was the first good feeling I'd had in a long while. I ate steady and silent, and I didn't think about my mom or Thomas or the circus or anything except the food and the bed upstairs.

I was just finishing the last of my rice when the front door opened again, sending a gust of wind against my back. It stayed open a long time, letting in a whole group of people. I didn't really notice them at first, I just kept chasing the last grains of rice around the plate, trying to finish it all as quickly as I could. I wanted to get upstairs to my room, to get away from the noise and people and the electricity so I could think in peace. But then I heard a familiar laugh, and the rice turned to sand in my mouth.

I didn't move, didn't turn around. Behind me, the group scraped chairs on the wooden floor as they jostled around a table. The skipping machine stopped, as if someone had pulled its cord out of the electricity port, and the room went quiet for a moment before voices filled it again. I listened closely, trying to hear what the newcomers were saying.

"—Larry and them won't care. Captain's messenger said the fifth day, and that's not for another two days. We've got time," said a gravelly voice I couldn't quite place.

"But we've been delayed—" a woman replied, and I pictured braids, the scared whites of brown eyes.

"This ain't up for discussion. I say we spend the night here, we spend the night here. And we'll stay tomorrow if I feel like it."

And then I was sure, because that voice belonged to Lee. The Green Mountain Boys were with me in Al's Fun Shack, the very same ones who'd told me to go home, and who I was pretty sure had killed the constable and Wilson and the Alt-Z ambush party. I'd forgotten that they were passing through New Rutland on the way to Town Meeting.

The last grains of rice sat on my plate, my hunger totally wiped away by fear. I had to get out without them seeing me. They'd wonder why I was in New Rutland, and they'd have questions no matter what I told them. They might think I suspected them and would try to send me back. Or they might kill me, if that was how they took care of matters they didn't much like.

Someone sidled up beside me, leaned against the bar. I glanced up and saw that it was the woman Green, the one called McMillan. I looked back down at my plate as quickly as I could and didn't move, hoping she wouldn't look down and see me.

"Food for that table?" she asked as Al shuffled along the bar. He didn't pass her by like he had me. He nodded and grunted. McMillan turned to go, brushing my arm as she did. I couldn't help it—I looked up again. Our eyes met, and I saw her recognize me. She blinked, then walked back to the table with the others. Nothing more than that.

It took me a minute to breathe again. I wanted so badly to bolt. But if I did that, the rest of them would see me for sure. So I didn't move. Behind me, the fiddler was playing a song I recognized. Gemma had played that song on the old fiddle she'd inherited from her grandmother. Thinking of Gemma was like thinking of a story from a book. Just a few days ago I'd been kneeling in the mud, digging poison parsnip roots, but now I was someone entirely different, someone who hunched over bars in strange towns, hiding from the law.

The fluorescent lights on the walls buzzed, a constant sound I'd almost stopped hearing altogether. I waited, but no hand landed on my shoulder, no shadow fell across my plate. My heartbeat slowed.

I was just about to get up, to try and edge my way to the stairs and up to wherever my room was, when another shoulder pushed against me and squeezed up to the bar. I knew it was Lee by his sour smell, even before I saw the green brim of his hat. He hadn't taken it off, even though we were inside.

"Al!" he bellowed. "Drinks!"

Al was at the other end of the bar, but he came over right away. "I'll bring them to the table," he said to Lee, not grousing at all.

"Why you got all this electricity in here still?" Lee asked. "Told you to get rid of it. It's bad luck."

Al laughed, a little too loud. "Yeah, between you and the damned Millerites you'd think I'd learn my lesson. But it's my luck, not yours, eh?"

Lee grunted and turned to leave, and just like McMillan his eyes landed on me as he went. He took another step toward the table, and I thought maybe he hadn't recognized me, but then his head whipped back around.

"You're that girl," he said, looking confused, like he didn't think it was physically possible for me to be there. Then he came back and planted himself in front of me, smiling. He was glad to see me, glad at how worried I looked. I tried to sit up straight. But something about his expression—just like in the Borough—frightened me into stillness.

"What the hell are you doing in New Rutland?" he asked, sweet and low. Behind him, the rest of the Greens were eating and taking drinks from Al.

"I'm getting my brother," I said, not quite meeting his eyes. Now that he'd seen me, I couldn't think of a reason to lie. Plus, I wanted him to know I wasn't a coward. "You said you wouldn't, so I came myself."

Lee squinted as if he was trying to remember something unpleasant. "But how'd you get here?"

"I walked."

"Who helped you?"

I didn't say anything to that. My head was filling up with the things he could do to me on account of his being a Green. He could arrest me right now, for starters. Al wouldn't stop him, and no one else would, either. I realized my fingers were curled into my palms below the bar.

"Your brother took a job with the circus," Lee said abruptly. "No one's taken him, and even if you try to get him back he won't come."

I blinked. "You don't know what happened," I said. "He didn't want to go."

"He left of his own free will. The whole world don't just stay or go on account of what you want, so you best get used to not getting your way. You go bothering that circus, I'll arrest you."

I opened my mouth to talk back, but something in Lee's expression made me stop. He wasn't making fun of me now. He was staring hard into my eyes, his lips pressed against his teeth and cocked in a little smile. He wanted to hurt me.

He stared at me for a minute longer, but I couldn't think of anything to say and wasn't sure I could talk if I wanted to, anyway. Finally he winked, patted my shoulder hard, and walked away. I waited until he was sitting down, his back to me like he didn't even care what I did next, and then I slid off the bar stool and ran for it.

The stairway up to the second floor was dark except for one candle at the top. Soon as I was out of sight of the bar room below, I stopped to let out a big breath I'd been holding for too long. Then I pictured Lee following me, coming up the stairs, and so I ran down the dark hallway and felt my way to the last door on the left. It opened easily and I went in and closed the door. The whole second floor was quiet.

When my eyes had become accustomed to the dim light coming through the one window, I found a lamp and lit it. No electricity in the room, thank goodness. The bedroom door had a deadbolt from Before, still shiny and sturdy. I locked it and then went and sat on the bed, too scared to do more than watch the door.

Why had Lee said that Thomas took a job with the circus? I couldn't think why Lee would know a thing about it.

I don't know how long I'd been sitting there in the dim light when I heard footsteps on the stairs, lots of them. I recognized Lee's voice again. I looked around, trying to think where to hide if they tried to get through my door—but instead I heard other doors opening and shutting, and the voices went low and muffled. So the Greens were spending the night at Al's Fun Shack too.

I hurried over to the window and looked out. There was no way to climb down, and it was too far to jump. I looked around the room and didn't see any other way out, so I went and crouched on the ground on the far side of the bed.

I listened until all the voices faded away, and then I listened a while more until I heard snoring. Then, finally, I took off my pack and coat and crawled on the bed and blew out the lamp. I knew I'd have to wait until the Greens left before I did anything else. Hopefully they'd be gone by morning, and I'd be able to sleep until then and wake up ready to find the circus.

I stared at the dark heap of my mom's coat, lying beside the bed, and wondered again if she was nearby. The thought should've made me feel good, but it didn't. What would she be doing when I finally found her? What had she been doing all these years? Whatever it was, I couldn't imagine it. So I burrowed under the covers of the bed, which smelled clean enough, and tried to make my aching muscles relax. In the end, it was the questions swirling through my head that kept me awake late into the night.

17

I dreamed that I found her. I was walking down the street in New Rutland, floating really, and calling her name. She came out of a doorway and smiled at me. She was beautiful, her hair long and wavy, wearing a clean blue dress.

How nice to see you! she said. I ran to her and wrapped my arms around her, but my arms closed around nothing. I looked up to see her a few feet away, still smiling. *Come in!* she said and led me into the house. The kitchen was clean and shining, set up like pictures I'd seen of kitchens from Before.

I searched for you, I said. She smiled again, but when I reached out for her, I found there was a table between us, and I couldn't get to her. I looked down at the table and saw a girl sitting there. She was a little younger than me.

This is my daughter, my mom said. *It's so nice that you get to meet her.*

I'm your daughter! I shouted. *I'm your daughter!*

I jerked awake to the sound of breaking glass. A dull, watery light streamed through the dusty window, so I stumbled off the bed and wiped a hole in the sticky dust on one of the windowpanes. Daylight was breaking through a light misty rain. Down below, a man was throwing glass bottles at the wall of a shed. He kept toppling sideways, like the world was shifting out from under him. He got another bottle and threw it.

Once I saw he wasn't harming anything but beer bottles, I turned and checked the door to make sure it was still bolted. For the first time, I realized my room was set up to look like a bedroom from Before. A carpet stretched from wall to wall, dusty and stained. A big blanket on the bed was decorated with a picture of a red car. The walls were hung with posters, all of them faded to mud and spooky in the dim light. And a television sat against a wall. Someone had glued a cartoon of a yellow, square-shaped person on the front, with the words *Spongebob Squarepants* over their head. I guessed this was more of Al's collection, and I figured the other rooms, where the Greens were sleeping, must be full of stuff from Before too.

The lock was still bolted tight. I listened at the door, wondering if the Greens had left yet. I needed to go outside and keep looking for Thomas, but if they were still in the rooms across the way then I didn't want to risk it. My stomach was already twisted up with knots of worry, and I'd only just woken up.

I looked around while I listened for any sounds from the other rooms. A shelf on one wall was full of trinkets from Before: dusty cloth animals, dolls with rubber faces, plastic trucks and sunglasses and bottles. I read somewhere that before the Fall, there was so much plastic that it got in everyone's blood, and their lungs, and birds would die and decompose but you'd know the spot where they died because of the piles of plastic they'd left behind. Or maybe my mom had told me that. I was having a hard time keeping straight what was what.

Someone shouted outside my window. Looking outside, I saw Al, the bartender, picking the drunk man up off the ground and shaking him by the shoulders.

Then someone knocked on my door.

I jumped and whirled around, ready for the door to smash in and for Lee to come attack me. He must know I was in here, and he'd decided to arrest me after all. But nothing else happened, and for a second of ringing silence I thought maybe I'd imagined the noise.

Then the knock came again. I leapt back, even though I'd been listening for it. There was nowhere for me to hide.

"Who's there?" I whispered. Down in the yard, the drunk man was moaning something profane at Al.

"It's me," said a hoarse voice. For a second I couldn't place it, because it was the last one I'd expected to hear. It was Jacob's voice.

I didn't move. Jacob was standing right outside the Greens' rooms, and he probably didn't even know they were there. And they'd accused him of murder.

"What do you want?" I asked, going right up to the door and hissing through the crack.

"Got someone here who wants to see you," Jacob said. My heart jumped at that. Who'd want me? It was either my mom or Thomas—there wasn't anyone else. I slid back the deadbolt with shaking fingers and opened the door.

Jacob was standing there in the dark hall, his gray hair wet with rain and his oilskin coat hanging limply off his shoulders. I thought he'd fooled me again, got me to open the door with a lie. But then the shadow next to him moved, and Jacob pulled the shape forward by the arm.

It was Thomas, whole and unhurt and rubbing tears from his eyes.

"Thomas!" I reached out and grabbed him by the shoulders, and for a minute everything fell away—the Greens across the hall, the circus, Jacob and his sad eyes…just like that, it was all gone. I held Thomas tight and breathed in the smell of him. I wouldn't have to sneak out past the Greens, or even find the circus. I wouldn't have to do anything.

"Are you okay?" I asked Thomas finally, trying to look in his face. He smelled like smoke and his clothes were dirty and wrinkled, but he wasn't hurt. He wasn't happy, either.

"Fine," he said, and he let me pull him into another hug.

Jacob just stood there in the hallway, watching me and Thomas like he was waiting for something. "How'd you find him?" I asked over Thomas's shoulder. I couldn't think what else to say.

"Circus is down in a field close to New Rutland's solar array, just like they were in the Borough. Looks to me like they're tapping into the system to power their camp up. Didn't take long to find." Jacob shifted a little, rubbed his chin with the heel of his hand. He still didn't make a move to leave.

My eyes drifted to the hallway behind him. A pair of muddy

boots sat outside the opposite doorway, one leaning against the other. They must belong to one of the Greens. I glanced back at Jacob, but I didn't say anything about it. I didn't say anything to Jacob at all.

I turned to Thomas instead. "The circus let you go, just like that?" I tried to pull him away from me so I could see him, but he kept his face down.

"They didn't let him go," Jacob said before Thomas could answer. "I took him in the night. Kid bites, by the way."

"You scared him," I said.

"He struggled the whole way, June," he said. "Wanted to go back."

I felt Thomas's body shaking and I held him closer. He didn't seem like he wanted to go back. "You scared him," I said again, harder this time.

Jacob opened his mouth to argue but when I looked him in the eye he closed his mouth and backed up a step.

"You can go back to the Borough now," he said instead. "Here—" He reached into his pack and pulled out his package of jerky. "Should be enough to barter a ride home on the trade caravan. One's coming through tomorrow." He held the jerky out to me.

I looked down at the packet of meat and felt the anger boiling up so hot and fast I couldn't stop it.

"We're not going back. How many times do I have to say it?" I spat, cold as I could and not even bothering to keep my voice down.

"I figured you might've changed your mind about your—" Jacob started, but I made to close the door and he put up his hands. "I won't stop you. Just let me explain myself, now I'm here. Explain why I took you away after the barn fire."

I took you. I felt his hand pulling me out of the flames, smelled my skin burning. I couldn't go back there again. I shook my head.

"Your daughter died so you figured you'd kidnap me instead," I said, louder than I ought to. Behind Jacob, I thought

I saw a shadow shift under one of the doors across the way. I raised my voice a little higher. "Then you thought it'd be more fun to play deputy, so you dumped me at an orphan farm. That it?"

"No, that's not it. Your mother—" Jacob sounded tense, desperate. I tried to close the door again but he held it open. Behind me, Thomas sniffled.

"She wasn't caring for you right," Jacob continued, talking fast now. "I saw it. I worked with her, saw you going hungry and left alone and worse than that."

"It was none of your business," I said, but weaker this time. Because in a flash of clear memory, I saw his face, young and haloed by gray-brown hair. He was looking over my head at someone. And I felt the hunger eating at my belly, and I heard her yelling something, and—

"I couldn't just watch—" Jacob continued.

"She was working on it! She had a plan—she only had to leave that one last time," I blurted, almost shouting now. That stopped him. It stopped me too. I didn't remember that, did I? Because it wasn't true; because he was a liar. We stared at each other for a long second.

And then the door behind Jacob swung open and hit the wall with a bang.

"Hello, deputy," Lee drawled, filling up the doorframe with his belly and his grin. He was half dressed, a green jacket pulled over his bare chest and his flat-brimmed hat perched on his head as always. The next door down opened, too, and the red-haired Green Mountain Boy poked his head out, saw Jacob, and swore.

Jacob turned to both of them, his hand still on my door.

"Lee," he said. "Didn't know you were staying here too."

"Lucky coincidence, I guess," Lee said, glancing at me. "Not every day we catch a murderer in our sleep."

Jacob didn't say anything to that. He glanced over his shoulder at me. I didn't move—I felt like I couldn't. Jacob knew what I'd done; I could see it in his gray eyes. I'd let him hang around,

I'd shouted so the Greens woke up, and now I was going to let them arrest him for a murder he didn't commit. I stared down at Lee's boots across the way.

"Don't hurt him," I said, just loud enough for Lee to hear. "I'll tell if you do."

Jacob turned back to the Greens and gently pushed my door. He was trying to close it, I realized. I held my hand against it, almost mad at him for trying to protect me even now. And I half wanted the Greens to arrest me too. Maybe I deserved it.

"We won't hurt him 'less he resists," Lee said. "But it's a long walk to the jail, lot could happen."

Jacob pushed harder on my door. I held it open another few seconds, not knowing what to do. But then I remembered that Thomas was with me, and I let the door swing shut.

I stared at the closed door and listened while the other Greens came out of their rooms. I listened while Lee knocked Jacob to the ground and told him he was a murdering pig. I held Thomas tight while they lifted Jacob up again and marched him down the stairs. Then I listened a while longer, but the only sound was Thomas, whispering for me to let go of his arm. Something terrible was happening inside me, an aching desperate hurt that got worse when I thought of what Jacob had told me and what he hadn't, and then got worse again when I pictured him with the Greens on the long walk to the New Rutland jail.

"June, let go," Thomas said, pulling me back to the quiet bedroom.

"Sorry," I said finally, blinking down at him and loosening my fingers. Surely the New Rutland constable would know Jacob was innocent. They'd let him go, and they'd figure out that it was really the Greens who should be locked up. And anyway, I had half of my family back again. I tried to focus on that, instead of on Jacob and what I'd done to him.

"How come you're here?" Thomas said. I noticed that his voice was different, strange. He sounded a little like Sebastian, with sharp edges on his vowels and a bounce in his tone. He didn't have his corncob pipe, of course. He didn't have the top hat, either.

"I came to get you," I said, sinking onto the bed with its red car design.

Thomas sat down on the bed beside me. "He hurt me," he said.

"Who hurt you? Sebastian?"

"No—Jacob." He showed me his wrist, which had a red ring around it where Jacob had been holding him. I felt a weak tug of anger—Jacob had dragged Thomas by the wrist. But the anger didn't quite fill the hollow pit in my stomach that had opened up when I let Jacob shut the door.

"He won't hurt you anymore," I said, and my voice was hollow too.

"Sebastian will kill him if he tries," Thomas said.

"Sebastian? No, we aren't going back to the circus." I heard myself say it like I was in a dream and someone else was talking. "My mom's here, somewhere close by." I couldn't imagine finding her, standing in front of her and asking where she'd been. The flash of memory came again, of a whisper: the smell of dusty hay. *Just this last time, I promise.* I pushed the thought away, tried to smile up at Thomas.

"I don't want to find your mom." Thomas was getting that flat hardness in his voice that meant he was digging in his heels. "I want to go back to the circus."

My breath caught in my throat at that. I turned to look at him. "The circus isn't where you belong. You're my family, my brother," I snapped, almost grateful that I could be angry at Thomas instead of thinking about anything else.

Thomas blinked at me, like I was saying something crazy. "They're gonna adopt me. You can come too, if you want a family so bad."

"What? No, Thomas." This was just what Lee had said about Thomas and the circus, just what I'd been afraid of. "They just wanted to…I dunno…make you work for them or something! They had no right to take you, and I had to come all this way just to save you!" I wanted to shake him by the shoulders, but I knew it'd make him start to cry. He looked on the edge of it already.

"No," he said, stubborn as ever. "They had a daughter. Only families have daughters. But she died and now I'm going to be their son."

"What daughter?" He wasn't making any sense.

Thomas shrugged and slid off the bed, and I could tell he was satisfied he'd gotten my full attention. He wandered over to the shelves with the plastic toys, picked up a green car, and rolled it on the wall. "When can I go back?"

"You're not going back." I walked over and pulled the green car out of his hand. "You and I are gonna stick together." I didn't know how else to convince him, except by saying the truth over and over. I had enough to worry about without Thomas being so stupid. I slammed the toy car back onto the shelf so hard that one of its wheels broke off and fell to the floor.

Thomas's face pinched and his eyes followed the car wheel as it rolled across the carpet. He looked so upset that I felt mean for what I'd said. He'd been through a terrible time too, I remembered.

"I'm sorry," I said. "Come sit down." I went back to the bed and patted the space beside me. He grimaced but came over, dragging his feet like a little kid. All I could think of was to get *Vermont Life* out of my pack and read to him. That way he'd be quiet and I could think what to do next. I pulled it out, flattening the wrinkled cover as best I could.

"What pictures you wanna look at?" I thought he maybe wouldn't answer, or that he'd say he didn't want to read with me anymore, and that made my heart crack a little bit. But his face cleared when he saw the magazine and he sat on the edge of the bed, like we used to do in my bedroom at Bob and Denise's.

"The 'Mericans," Thomas said. I turned to the story called "Our Civil War Veterans," with the picture of an American flag below the title.

"Why this one?" I asked. He'd never asked for this story before.

"I wanna be an American," Thomas said. "Like Sebastian and Alexandra."

I looked down at the picture of the flag in the magazine, and felt a dull ache of worry, the kind you get when you know something bad's about to happen and you can't stop it.

"They told you they're Americans?" I asked. I'd thought that was supposed to be a secret, something only I knew about. The worry was shifting, coming closer, almost like a memory. I suddenly didn't want Thomas to answer.

"Yep," he said, looking up at me.

"I thought you hated Americans." He'd been all excited to become a Green Mountain Boy and catch American spies. But now he shrugged, and I knew he was telling the truth. The circus had told him they were Americans.

"I like Americans now," he said. "I'm gonna be an American."

I didn't know what to say to that, so I started to read. "'A mere century ago, so many of our state's brave youth took up arms and marched, perhaps never to return, to join the Union army.'"

"That's gonna be me," Thomas said. He mimed holding up a gun, shooting at the ceiling. "Cut out the disease!"

The phrase jangled something in my memory, something I had almost forgotten. I'd been so excited to see my mom's name in Alexandra's cart, everything before it had faded away. But I'd read Thomas's words before, in the book called *Manifesto of Unity.*

I closed the magazine, but I couldn't hide from what he'd said. Things were coming clear for the first time, things that I should've seen before but didn't.

"What does that mean, cut out the disease?" I asked, trying to keep my voice light.

Thomas shrugged. "Thought you didn't care about the circus."

"Tell me, Thomas," I said, pulling him around to face me. "And tell me why you think you're going to be American."

Thomas wriggled in my grip, but I didn't let go. "Jeez, fine," he said. "They're gonna make the Republic a part of America again. That's why they're here."

My skin prickled, but I let him go and tried to laugh. "How're they gonna make us part of America, huh?"

"Town Meeting," he said. "They're gonna get rid of all the bad leaders, and then more Americans are gonna come help us."

"Get rid of all the bad leaders? What does that mean?" My face felt hot, and the hollow emptiness inside me got deeper.

Thomas shrugged again, but I didn't need him to say anything else. Jacob had suspected the circus, and now I realized that he'd been right. I'd been so busy thinking the Greens were up to no good, I hadn't seen the obvious. Now my memories shifted, and I saw all that had happened in the Borough in another way: the circus had arrived right before the constable and Wilson died. They'd even seen the plant that killed them. They might've heard me reading what it did to anyone who ate it.

I'd stuck up for the circus all this time, even though they'd taken Thomas. I'd been so sure that everyone else was prejudiced, that Americans didn't mean any harm. And I hadn't even told Jacob that they were Americans. If I had, they could've been arrested already.

Then I thought of something else, and grabbed Thomas's shoulder again.

"How did their daughter die?" I asked.

Thomas sighed like I was being stupid. "I dunno… She ran away and died. She was the one we saw in the woods, remember? They were glad we found her."

I stood up. The room felt very small all of a sudden. The circus had killed the girl in the woods, too, or at least she died trying to run from them. And they'd killed the constable and Wilson. And no one else knew what I knew.

I tried to think what to do, while Thomas settled back on the bed and started leafing through *Vermont Life.* My first thought, though I wasn't proud of it, was that I didn't have to do anything. I could pretend I hadn't heard what Thomas had said. I wasn't a deputy, and probably the real law enforcement would figure it out sooner or later.

But Jacob still haunted me. I'd kept the truth about the circus from him. Maybe if I hadn't, he would've arrested them already and the Greens would've had nothing on him. He hadn't deserved what I'd just done to him, no matter what he'd done to me. Every choice I'd made on this trip had been the wrong one.

I took a deep breath. "We have to tell Jacob about the circus. And whoever the constable in this town is." I took *Vermont Life* from Thomas and stuffed it back in my pack, wrinkling the pages.

"What? No!" Thomas sprang up from the bed. "We can't get them in trouble."

"Don't be stupid. They're *killing* people. They aren't your friends." I slung my pack over my back.

"Let's go find your mom, isn't that what you wanted to do?" Thomas asked.

I paused. For a second, I felt the way I had when I'd first found her name in Alexandra's book—excited and hopeful, sure that wherever my mom was, she'd solve all my problems. If there was ever a time I needed my mom, it was now. But it lasted only a second, and then all the doubt and worry came back again, all the bad memories that had haunted me since I left the Hollow, since Jacob had started making me remember.

"We have to do this first," I said. It was a relief, because it meant I didn't need to really answer his question.

Before Thomas could do more than groan, I took him by the hand and pulled him out of the bedroom from Before.

18

The morning's mist was lifting out of the streets when we left Al's Fun Shack, and the town was waking up. In the daylight New Rutland looked shabbier. The houses were big, but held together with plastic and plywood, just like in the Borough. The one big difference was the electric lines that crisscrossed over the road.

I held Thomas's hand tight, tried not to look at the lines, and started walking as if I knew where I was going, as if I was supposed to be there. Thomas didn't want to go, though. He looked all around, tried to make me stop to watch a man fiddling with a big tangle of wires on the side of his house. Even so, no one gave us a second glance. I guessed that strangers were normal in a town this big.

I steered us toward the center of town, 'cause that's where the jail was in the Borough, and the more folks we saw the more I wondered what was up. People were standing in the road in little clumps now, hands on their hips, shaking their heads. Seemed as if they all had something to talk about.

We passed another person fussing around with the wires on the side of a house that looked like three houses nailed together, and I couldn't help watching. It made me shudder, just seeing the woman touch the wires with her bare fingers. Then I remembered that the only reason I hated electricity was because of what my mom had told me. It was one of the things I'd always remembered clearly about her, even when everything else was hazy. But I didn't want to think about her just now. So I kept walking.

Thomas dragged his feet behind me, moaning that he wanted to sleep, but I just pulled him along. It didn't take us long to find the jail. The building had a sign over the door that read *County Jail*, though that could've been a coincidence. Clearly no one cared much what words said—a big plastic slab propping up a wall on the building next door said *New York, New York*, and that sure wasn't true. What made me certain about the jail was the man sitting on the porch with a mug of steaming tea in his hand and a star pinned to his overalls.

"Approach, young strangers," the man said when he noticed us hesitating at the foot of the stairs. He was leaning back in a rickety chair, his eyes just slits. He had a scruffy beard and gray hair held back in a bandanna, faded like the flannel shirt he wore over a pair of overalls. I thought he'd look more at home drinking in Al's bar than running the town's law enforcement.

I pulled Thomas up the steps onto the porch. "We got some information for you," I said, and because the man didn't know me and no one knew me around here, it was easy to pretend I wasn't nervous.

"Hmmm," the constable said, finally opening his eyes. They were blue, a blue like I hadn't expected to see. Too young for his old face.

He looked me up and down and then back out at the road. "Your information wouldn't happen to regard the electricity outage, now would it?"

"The what?" I asked, watching him watch a woman who was setting up a little portable solar panel across the way.

"I suppose not, then." He didn't sound disappointed, just thoughtful. "Power's out, you know. The whole town grid is down."

"This isn't about that," I said. "You've got Jacob in there, right? I gotta talk to him. I think I know who killed his boss."

That made the constable pay attention to me again. He stood up, barely as tall as me. "Why don't you come inside?" he said, and went through the shadowy doorway, gesturing at us to follow.

I took a step, but Thomas plucked at my mom's coat. "I don't want to," he said. "Come on, let's go find your m—"

"It'll be an adventure, okay?" I said, cutting him off. "We're going to stop some bad guys, just like in the stories."

"I'm not a baby," Thomas said. "You just want to get the circus in trouble because you're jealous."

I turned on him. "Why would I be jealous?" I hissed.

"Because I found a family before you did, that's why!" Thomas said, his eyes filling up with angry tears again. I didn't know what to say to that, but just then the constable poked his head back out the door and cleared his throat delicately.

"Come in if you've got something to say," he said. I gave Thomas one last look and then followed the constable in, still pulling Thomas by the arm.

The room we walked into was dark. One oil lamp shone on a table in the corner and another hung over the middle of the room, but both together were still barely enough to see by. It took me a few blinks to notice two other people sitting in front of a big wood stove on the far side of the room. I couldn't see their faces, even when they turned to watch me.

"I'm constable Larry Greer," the constable said, gesturing us over toward a big wooden desk. "You can call me Larry."

"I'm June, and this is Thomas. Why's it so dark?" I asked Larry.

"Like I said, electricity's out. You're not from here, or you'd know most of the town buildings run on full electricity."

He didn't sound impatient or anything, even though we were strangers and I'd just told him that we knew an accused murderer. He seemed like nothing could possibly upset him, like he could walk through a hurricane and come out the other side looking no more or less scruffy than he already did. But I couldn't wait any longer.

"Where's Jacob?" I asked. "I know the Greens brought him in, but he's innocent, and the people who actually killed his constable are here in town, right now."

"He's here," Larry said, sinking into the chair behind the wooden desk and resting his chin on his folded fingers. "But this sounds like something you better tell me. Start at the beginning."

I opened my mouth, but he held up a hand. "I can see you're

fixing to drop me right in the middle of whatever you've got to say, and I'll tell you now that folks listen better if they understand what they're hearing."

He was right. I swallowed and tried to think where the beginning was.

"There's this traveling circus, and I went to…to trade books with them when they came through my town—" I started.

"Trade books? What do you want with books?" Larry asked.

"I read them," I said, just as the man and woman by the stove wandered over. They wore deputy badges on their chests, just like Jacob's. They stood on either side of Larry, both taller than him and younger too. I blushed, not wanting to talk to a whole crowd.

"Start from the start," Larry said, holding up a hand to stop the other two saying anything. Then he looked at me expectantly.

I told them everything I could remember. I told them about finding the dead girl and stumbling onto the constable and Wilson's bodies, about the circus keeping American propaganda, about the dead Alt-Zs on Route 7. Then I tried to get Thomas to say what he'd heard from the circus, but he just scowled at the floor and wouldn't say anything at all. So I told the constable and his deputies how the circus had something planned for Town Meeting, and how they wanted to make us all Americans. Thomas glared at me, as if I'd betrayed his deepest secret, but I knew he was just being dramatic, trying to act like people do in stories.

"And the Greens arrested Jacob just now, even though they knew he didn't do it, and he couldn't have done it because he was with me that night." I didn't tell them about how I'd let the Greens take him. About how I'd practically handed him to them. I didn't tell them about my mom, either.

While I talked, the male deputy pulled a carrot out of his pocket, and it disappeared bit by bit into his mouth. The woman stared at me like I was a complicated puzzle, like every word

I said might unlock some kind of code. And Larry hooked his thumbs in his pockets, nodding encouragingly.

Finally I was finished, and I swallowed and looked at the floor.

"Sheeeyit," the deputy with the carrot said into the silence. He looked at the others. "Sounds a little…I mean…well…" He trailed off, but I could hear in his voice that he didn't believe me one bit. I shifted my weight, feeling my mom's coat scratch against my scars.

"Sounds like some bad stuff's happened to you," the other deputy said, and I knew from how nice and gentle her voice was that she didn't believe me either.

"Doesn't matter that bad stuff's happened to me," I said, talking to the floor because I couldn't quite meet her eyes. "What I said's still true. You gotta let Jacob go." I was starting to feel mad now. No one made me and Thomas come here, to spill our guts to the law. We'd done it because it was right, and we didn't deserve to get laughed at now. This was why my mom hadn't trusted law enforcement. Maybe she'd been right after all.

"Where's Jacob?" I said again. "I want to talk to him."

"That might be difficult at the moment," Larry said. "But you were right to tell us. I know Jacob, and it's clear to me he didn't kill anyone. Truth told, I'm much more inclined to believe your story."

"Will you arrest the circus?" I said quickly.

"You can't," Thomas piped up. "They're not gonna do anything bad."

Larry looked between us. "We'll see what they have to say. I believe we gave them leave to set up in one of the perimeter fields, right, Sheila?"

Sheila nodded, still looking skeptical. "We got this electricity problem to deal with, don't forget," she said.

Larry nodded, pushing his lips out and staring past me out the door to the street. "Electricity can wait. We'll pay this circus a visit, then swing by the solar panels and see what we can see, won't we?"

I realized I was hunched down and forced myself to stand up straighter. My heart was fluttering in my throat. Larry made everything sound so easy, like the problem was already fixed. It was too easy, actually. If they arrested the circus, if they let Jacob go, then what was left? I knew the answer, of course. I had one more thing to do in New Rutland. I just didn't want to think about it right now.

Before anyone could say anything else, a boy came running into the jail. He had a deputy pin on his chest, too, but he was younger than the other two—barely older than me. It took me a second to recognize him; he was the one who'd directed me to Al's last night.

"Whoa, Benny," Larry said, holding out his hands. "No galloping in my jail!"

"'Pologies, sir," Benny said. In the light of day, I saw he had freckles and blotchy red cheeks. His hair still flopped in his face. He didn't even look at me, he was so eager to get his news out.

"Sir, we've got some Millerites putting up a fight down in the solar field. Looks like it's them sabotaged the solar array."

"Damn zealots," Larry said, standing up with a groan and stretching his back again. "How many?"

"Just three…zealots, sir."

"Quit using words you don't know. Just three took down the whole array?"

"I guess so, sir. They say they did."

I was bursting to get a word in, but the constable was firing off questions so fast I couldn't get the rhythm. So I was glad he looked at me and said, "Spit it out, already."

"The circus," I said, trying hard to say the right thing. It was difficult being asked to talk so fast and keep the words straight in my head. "I bet they broke your panels. Back in the Borough, I saw the solar panels fall off their posts in a storm, like they never did before, right after the circus came to town."

Benny looked at me finally, tightening his hat down further on his head when he recognized me.

"You—whoa. Hi. I didn't see you at Al's last—"

"Catch up later, kid, we got important actions to consider," Larry interrupted. He put his thumbs in his pockets and walked past us all, ambling out onto the porch again. The deputies all followed him, Benny glancing over his shoulder at me. I followed, too, and for a brief second we were all walking in stride, our feet falling at the exact same time. I wished the distance to the porch were farther, so I could stay in that moment a little longer. It felt good to pretend I was part of their team.

"What'll we do, sir?" Benny asked.

Larry squinted out at the street, looking for something he couldn't see.

"Well, if there are Millerites trying to start a crusade, we had better tend to that first. I'll talk them down, more likely than not. Then we'll pay a call to this circus, see if we can nip that one in the bud before they murder us all."

He started down the stairs, and the others followed.

"Wait!" I said. "What about Jacob? Will you let him go?"

"He's not under arrest. Clear as day that the Greens just wanted someone to beat. But he's not going anywhere till he's... dried out, shall we say."

"But—"

"Benny, you stay here," Larry said, turning away from me. "Hold down the fort, as it were. See if Jacob's awake yet. See if he needs water, and tell him I'm going to have a few choice words with him when I get back." Then he set off down the road, the two deputies beside him taking one step for every two of his.

The hollowness in my stomach opened up again.

"Why's Jacob not awake?" I asked Benny, who was looking sore at getting left behind, standing on the porch with his thumbs hooked in his belt loops. He rolled his eyes at me.

"He's stoned. Ate three 'tabs soon as the Greens dumped

him, 'fore we got a chance to confiscate it." Benny looked like he wanted to say something else, but thought better of it. He turned and stumped back into the jail.

Jacob must've wanted to forget what I'd done to him, I thought. That's why people took LoTabs, wasn't it? To stop the present from hurting so much. I took a deep breath of misty air and followed Benny back inside.

Thomas hadn't come out with us—he was still standing in the main room with his arms crossed, a sour look on his face.

"C'mon, let's go," he said. "Didn't you want to go find your mom?"

I swallowed. "Yeah, but just hold on a minute."

"June—" he started, so I took him by the shoulders again.

"I know this isn't what you want to be doing, but I promise it's almost over," I said. "I need to do one more thing, and then we can go find my mom." My stomach lurched. I wasn't ready yet. I didn't know enough; I hadn't remembered enough to see her again, even if we could find her. But I tried to smile, and tried to look like I wasn't worried. Thomas wrinkled his nose, but then shrugged. My arms slipped off his shoulders, and Thomas stalked over to Larry's desk and flopped onto the chair.

Benny was trying to pretend he was inspecting a knife over by the wood stove, but he was glancing at us out of the corner of his eye. I went over to him.

"Can I see Jacob?" I asked. Behind me Thomas made a barfing noise that almost made me smile for real, except that I was so nervous about what I had to do. I had to tell Jacob I was sorry, and that I knew who'd really killed his friends.

Benny eyed me, pulled his hat down a little tighter, then sheathed his knife again. "Sorry, can't. It's against the rules: *No civil-yins shall be allowed in the un-authorized areas of the jail, except if they're accused of a crime and got to be locked up*. Deputy policy." He blushed as he said it, like he wasn't used to telling folks what to do.

"C'mon. It'll only be a minute. You're in charge, right?" I said. "It's not like he's an Alt-Z."

Benny glanced out the door, then back at me. "Fine. Just this once, and just 'cause I trust you," he whispered in a voice that was somehow louder than just talking normal. He heaved himself out of his chair, pushed open the door to the back room, and gestured me in, keeping an eye on the front door.

I looked back at Thomas. "Can you stay here? I'll be right out."

Thomas nodded, flashing a smile. And for some reason I didn't think that was odd. I just smiled back.

The back room was dim and long, dark even compared to the front room. Benny paused and flapped his hand along the wall beside the door for a little while, and I didn't know what he was doing until he said, "Shit, keep forgetting, power's out." Then he pulled an oil lamp off a hook, fumbled with the wick, and raised the flame so high it jumped all the way up the lamp's glass chimney.

"There you go. Jacob probably won't say anything, you know. He's LoTab dreaming," he said, and handed me the lamp. Then he went back out into the front room, closing the door behind him a little reluctantly. I heard him say something in muffled tones to Thomas.

The flame threw its shadowy light through the back room. The jail cells looked just like the ones in the Borough, but this room had more of them—lots more. The lamplight didn't reach the back of the room, so it was easy enough to imagine that the cells kept going further and further, full of shadowy people who'd been there since the Fall.

Jacob was sitting in the cell closest to the door, hunched over with his head resting on his hands. His clothes were dirty, as if he'd been rolling in the street, and he didn't have his coat with him anymore. He looked like someone who belonged in a jail cell. The door was shut, but its lock hung open.

"Jacob?" I said, because he hadn't looked up or moved when Benny and I came in, or when the lamp lit up the room. He ignored me. When I walked closer I saw that one of his eyes was swollen shut, the opening just a tight slit with a wet line of lashes. The Greens had made sure the walk to the jail was long, just as Lee had said.

"Jacob?" I said again. He jumped a little and looked up at me. His good eye was unfocused, and his face looked wrong, too limp. It was as if he wasn't there. I knew he'd taken LoTabs, but I hadn't expected this—I'd thought he'd just be sleepy and forgetful, like he'd been on the road. But this was different. He reminded me of the people Thomas and I had seen in the outskirts of the Borough, staring at nothing and smiling.

I looked into his blank eyes and realized I'd been stupid to think I should talk to him. High or not, he wouldn't want to talk to me after what I'd done. I turned to leave.

"Water?" Jacob said. I looked back around and he was staring at me harder, his brows furrowed.

I took my bottle out of my pack and handed it through the bars to him. He drank and that seemed to help him. When he handed the bottle back to me, he met my eyes.

"You came back," he said, smiling a little.

"Yeah, well, we got interrupted before," I said, but then I broke off, remembering again how I'd shut the door in his face, let the Greens have him. I put the lamp down on the ground, trying to hide my face. "I just wanted to say, you know, I'm sorry. I should've..." I didn't know what I should've done.

Jacob just looked at me. I didn't know if he'd even heard me.

"Larry's going after the circus," I said. "They're the ones who killed Sarah and Wilson. Thomas told me."

Jacob's brows knit together. "The circus?"

"They're American, and they're trying to make us American," I said, digging my fingernails into my palms. "I guess they're killing anyone in charge. They're planning something bad for Town Meeting." I didn't tell him that I'd known that they were American all along.

"So it wasn't the Greens after all," Jacob said, leaning his head back against the wall and closing his good eye. He sat there for so long that I thought maybe he'd gone to sleep. But then his head jerked upright again.

"Where is your mother?"

"I—I don't know." Her name on his lips hurt to hear. I should've guessed he'd want to finish what he started saying before. But I didn't know if I could hear it. I didn't know if I could tell him how scared I was to find her, how much my flashes of memory frightened me.

"She might be out at the stream," Jacob said. I felt my stomach clench up again, and part of me wanted to run away before he could tell me for sure where she was. If I knew, then I'd have to face her. What if she didn't even want to see me? What if I didn't want to see her?

"What's the matter, Leah?" Jacob asked then.

He stood up and came over to the bars of the cell, but I backed away before he could reach out for me. He looked at me with such soft concern that I wanted to cry. I wanted to cry even without the look on his face. He wasn't talking to me at all.

"You mean your wife is at the stream?" I asked. I felt so stupid. Jacob put a hand on the bars of the cell, steadying himself. I backed away a few more steps. He thought I was his daughter again. He didn't know what he was saying. I watched his face harden, watched him blink at me through the dim lamplight.

"No…she isn't," he said slowly. And then I watched him remember that his wife was dead, and that Leah was dead, and that he was stuck in a jail cell because I'd let the Greens catch him. He slumped back down on the seat, put his head back in his hands.

"I should go," I said.

"Wait," he said, looking up again. I could see that the LoTabs were still there behind his eyes. He had to work to keep himself in this dark jail with me. "I want to tell you about her. About Leah."

"I don't…" I said, but I couldn't finish. I couldn't leave, either.

He sat up straighter and looked off into some part of the past I couldn't see. "The LoTabs, they…" He gestured at his head. "They take you where you want to go. Everything is… vivid."

That was different from how Old Bill explained LoTabs. He said they made you forget. But I didn't much care what exactly LoTabs did right then. I wanted to get out of there, to hide from all Jacob's sadness and loss. But he started talking, and I couldn't leave him there to remember her alone.

"Leah didn't come home one night, when she was about seven," Jacob said, the crease between his brows deepening. "I went out looking for her, found her out in the woods. She had a plastic bucket I'd brought home for her from a scavenging trip, and she was carrying water. I asked her what she was doing, why she hadn't come home." His brows softened again.

"Turns out she'd found a bunch of frog eggs in a little pool, but that spring was dry and the pool was almost gone. So she was hauling water to save them. She'd already walked back and forth so many times she'd beaten a path through the pucker-bush. I told her that even if she saved the eggs, the frogs would die of the dryness. There wasn't anywhere for them to go. But the next morning, she was out there again with her bucket. I don't know what happened to the eggs. But her bucket was yellow, and her shirt that day was yellow too."

Jacob smiled, and his eyes darted up and down, like she was standing right in front of him. Then he glanced at me again.

"She was a lot like you. Smart and tough. It was so easy to look at you and see her, after she was gone. I think that's why I took the work with your mother."

"What work?" I asked.

"Running LoTabs across the Yorker border."

"Is that what she's doing now? Is that where she's been?"

Jacob frowned, then winced as if the movement hurt his bruised face. "I don't know. I stopped running with her, the last few years before the barn fire. Didn't see you two much, 'cept when our paths crossed by chance. I think she got into something more serious, but I don't know what."

"I don't know if I can look for her anymore," I said. My real mother wasn't the person who'd given me hope all these years. She was a mystery, just a half-forgotten face and a handful of painful memories.

Jacob shook his head. "I didn't have a right to take you away from her. I thought I was saving you, like I couldn't save Leah. She died of the flu, and I couldn't do anything to stop it." He turned his head and looked down the dark line of cells. "I wouldn't have let anyone stop me looking for Leah, if she'd still been alive. And I shouldn't have tried to stop you finding your mom, either."

I wiped my face. "Do you think she wants me?"

"I can't imagine any parent wouldn't want you," Jacob said, his voice rough. "Can you forgive me for what I did?" He said it so low, so open that I wanted to tell him yes, I wanted to say whatever would make him feel better. I hadn't known how much he cared about me. But I had to tell him the truth.

"I don't know. But I'm sorry, too. I—" I gestured at his bruised face, his dirty clothes.

Jacob nodded, took a deep breath, and then scrabbled in his pocket. He came up empty. He frowned, glanced at his hand, and then reached down into his boot, wincing as he bent. He pulled out a little twist of plastic with two blue pills wrapped inside it.

"Take them," he said, thrusting his hand out through the bars at me. "Otherwise I will. I gotta stop. I got things to do."

I hesitated, remembering what had happened to me the last time I touched pills like that. But I saw how desperate he was, and I pulled the plastic out of his fingers. I slipped the pills into my pants pocket, figuring I could dump them in the nearest sump pit.

Jacob nodded at me, and I could see him drifting away again, like whatever the LoTabs in his body were offering was too sweet to refuse any longer. He blinked one more time and settled back on the bench.

"Your mom used to hang around the old train station, June. That's not so far from here. She used to do that, at least."

And then he lowered his head, and I knew he wouldn't say anything else until he got sober.

I wiped my eyes again, but the tears kept coming.

"I know where the train station is."

I jumped. Thomas was standing in the doorway, watching me and Jacob. I wondered how long he'd been there, what all he'd heard.

"You what?"

"The train station. I know where it is. We can find your mom now."

19

I stepped into the watery light of the street, holding on to Thomas. The sky was brighter now, glimmering on the rusty metal roofs and plastic siding of the buildings around us. My stomach was aching from what I was about to do. There was only one way forward. Find my mom or…or nothing. It was what we'd come here for, and I didn't have another plan. Jacob was dreaming, and Larry was probably arresting the circus now. And Jacob was right. I couldn't stop looking for her, not when there was a chance she still wanted me. Not when I didn't know for sure.

"This way," Thomas said, starting off along a street I hadn't been down before. I followed him, trying to steady my breathing. She probably wasn't there anyway. Just because she used to hang out at the train station six years ago didn't mean she'd be there today. Even so, I was already trying to figure out what to say to her. *Hello, Mom. It's me, June. I came to find you.*

I barely looked where we were going, barely saw the people still fiddling with their electricity, or sitting out on their cluttered porches with gloomy looks on their faces. Soon the houses got smaller and older, and the center of town shrank away behind us.

"Is it close?" I asked. It was happening too fast. I figured the train station had to be on the edge of the town, where the train tracks used to run. But it couldn't be too far from New Rutland, or why would Thomas have seen it?

"It's close," Thomas said. We were passing by empty lots now, crowded with puckerbush. Thomas had plucked a dead rod of poison parsnip from the roadside and was twirling it like a baton or a sword. He walked quickly. I remembered that he didn't know any of the things about my mom that were making my feet drag.

"Slow down," I said as he started skipping, getting way ahead of me. He looked back and grinned, and that was the moment when I started to wonder what he was up to. But before I could say anything else, he turned off the main road all of a sudden, skipping down what looked like a sheep path through the brambles on the roadside.

"Hey!" I shouted. I ran after him, but when I turned onto the path it was already too late. He was out in the field on the other side of the brambles, running to meet a man who was striding toward him through the tall grass.

I recognized Sebastian from halfway across the field. Behind him, the carts and carriages of the circus were circled up in the middle of the field. It was just like the Borough.

I stumbled to a stop, my heart pounding in my throat. Way ahead in the field, Thomas said something to Sebastian, and Sebastian glanced over Thomas's shoulder at me. He looked surprised, a little wary. But then his face smoothed and he waved at me.

"Thomas," I said, probably too quiet for either of them to hear. I didn't understand what was happening. The field was lower than the road, out of sight of town, and the train station wasn't anywhere in sight. So why would Thomas have led us here?

Thomas came jogging back over to me through the grass.

"C'mon, he wants to see you," he said, like he thought I'd be happy.

And then I understood. Thomas had known right where the circus was camped. He'd lied to get me here. He took my hand and started trying to pull me toward Sebastian, who was smiling at both of us.

"What are you doing?" I hissed at Thomas, gripping his hand tight. "You know the circus is dangerous!"

"No, they aren't!" Thomas said. "I told you, they're my friends. You'll see once you talk to them—come on!"

"June!" Sebastian called, waving again. As Thomas pulled me

forward I thought of Wilson, his face ashy white and pressed against the floor, and of Sarah the constable, dead at her desk.

Sebastian wasn't in his American flag suit today. Instead he wore blue jeans that were still blue, and a checkered shirt tucked into a belt with a big silver buckle. He still had his top hat, though. He grinned as we got close, chuckling a little.

"You couldn't stay away, eh?" he said. "Thomas says you came all this way to find us. Welcome, welcome!"

He hooked one arm around my waist and slung the other over Thomas's shoulder, and pulled us toward the nearest carts. My legs felt numb under me. I didn't know what to do. I glanced at the circus. The rest of them were there, watching us come. The musicians crouched around a little fire, cooking something in a pot. The contortionist, behind them, was packing supplies into a box. Thomas waved at each of them, and they waved back, grinning. The Big Apple wasn't set up, so I guessed they weren't doing a show after all. Just stopping to rest, or who knew what.

"We were so worried about you, Tommy," Sebastian said, ruffling Thomas's hair. "We woke up and you were gone. Thought we might be in trouble!" He laughed, and the sound of it echoed off the tall trees lining the field. Of course they hadn't wanted Thomas to leave—they were afraid of what he'd tell the world about them.

Sebastian steered us to a cart with one open wall, like a stage. It had a table and chairs, a little chest of drawers and a curtain pulled to one side of the open wall. Sebastian swept his hat off his head and gestured me up the stairs, smiling like he didn't see the scowl on my face. But what could I do? Run away? Leave Thomas after I'd just gotten him back? I walked up the steps with Thomas, too angry with him to say anything. Probably too scared anyway.

Sebastian rang a little bell sitting on the table. Over by the fire, one of the musicians sprang to her feet. She came over with three bowls of whatever they'd been cooking on the fire.

It turned out to be oatmeal, but a kind I'd never seen before. It was creamy white and smooth, not sticky and lumpy like the stuff we ate at Bob and Denise's.

"Tommy, I hope this means you left to persuade your sister to join us, and that she's the newest member of our merry family," Sebastian said, still smiling.

Thomas nodded, his mouth full of oatmeal. I didn't take a bite. I'd just noticed the strongman, who was walking slowly out of the woods behind Sebastian's cart, rolling up a thick wire as he went. Something about the wire, the way it moved, made the hairs on my arm stand up.

"So, June, you came all this way just because you wanted to be a circus hand?" Sebastian asked, his voice light and friendly. "It's a long way to travel all by yourself—and so quickly!" He trailed off there, looking at me all wide-eyed and expectant.

"I came to get Thomas," I said, steady as I could.

We were eating oatmeal in a field, and Sebastian hadn't said anything threatening, but my heart was pounding like he was pointing a gun at me. I didn't know if it was a coincidence, but it seemed that no matter which direction I looked, someone from the circus was there, watching. The only one I hadn't seen was Alexandra.

"Ah, well, now you've got him…and we've got you!" Sebastian laughed and lifted his top hat off his head again, twirling it on a finger before dropping it back in place. Thomas copied him with an invisible hat. I was almost too furious to look at him. He was being so foolish, and I'd been foolish too, for not noticing what he was doing until it was too late. I should've known he was lying to me. He was still trying to be like a character in *Huckleberry Finn*, to have an adventure.

"We gotta leave," he suddenly announced to Sebastian.

"Why's that, sport?" Sebastian asked.

"Don't—" I started, but—

"The constable said he's gonna arrest us, because he thinks we killed some people."

Three seconds of ringing silence.

The breeze rustled the tablecloth.

"The constable, hmm?" Sebastian said. His eyes flicked to me, back to Thomas. *He's gonna arrest us. Us.* The air felt too thick to breathe.

"Yeah, so we gotta leave," Thomas chirped into the silence.

"How did the constable get that idea in his head?" Sebastian asked, and in his mouth every word was sharp.

Thomas's smile faded a little. He looked at me. I met his eyes, and in that second I felt a wave of vertigo. He was going to give me up.

But he looked back at Sebastian and shrugged. "Dunno," he said, his voice small now.

Sebastian wasn't fooled, of course. I could tell from the way he smiled at me that he knew what I'd done. I glanced around. There was no direction I could run without being caught. The circus was everywhere.

"It's okay," Thomas said, anxious now. "They won't catch us. The ambush didn't catch us, right?"

Sebastian's careful smile turned into a flash of anger for a quick second.

"Shut up, Tommy," he said. "Your tongue will get you into trouble."

Thomas shut his mouth tight, and I remembered the dead Alt-Zs on the road, their blood pooling underneath them. My heart was pounding so hard now I couldn't focus right. If Thomas and I could get a second alone, maybe we could sneak away before anyone noticed. But otherwise we were stuck.

Sebastian sighed, hitched a smile back on his face, and then winked, tweaking Thomas's cheek. "Boys, so spirited. I forget how young you are, Tommy." The tension broke like a storm. Thomas frowned a little.

"Sorry," he said, bashful.

"Well, we need to hurry if we're going to beat the constable out of this town!" Sebastian said, clapping his hands together. "Tommy, you'll find Alexandra in her cart. Tell her what's happened, and help her start packing."

Thomas stood up.

"No!" I said, standing up too. "Thomas, stay here with me."

Sebastian pushed his own chair back and rose up, taller than me by far. "Tommy can't help Alexandra from here," he said, looking around at the empty platform and frowning, pretending to be confused. "I think you'll have to let him go, June."

Thomas started down the stairs. "It's okay, June," he said. "I'll be right over there!"

"Thomas, come back!" I shouted. My voice was unsteady. They were going to kill me, and they were probably going to kill Thomas too. I could see it in Sebastian's stupid smile. I started after Thomas, but Sebastian grabbed me by the arm.

"You let him go, and nothing bad happens to him," he whispered, so low that only I could hear. "Tommy's a valued member of our group as long as he stays useful. You wouldn't want him to lose his place like his predecessor, would you? I expect you know who she was by now."

I remembered the girl in the woods, the ants crawling across her face. My breath caught in my throat, and I felt bile rising up again. Thomas hopped off the stairs and ran away through the cook-fire smoke, heading for a cart on the far side of camp, waving once. He didn't look back after that.

"Now, what to do with you?" Sebastian said, looking down at me without taking his hand off my arm. I felt the old bruise where Lee had held me in the same place, back in the Borough.

"Let us go," I said, trying to keep my voice steady. "The constable is coming, so there's no point trying to run." But I agreed with Thomas. If they'd gotten through an Alt-Z ambush, I didn't think Larry and his two deputies would stand much of a chance.

Sebastian thought the same. "Forgive me for not believing you," he said. Then his smile widened and he glanced after Thomas. "And I don't think there's any 'us' left, you know. At least not one that includes you."

He straightened up, pulling me forward by the arm. "Come along now. Don't fuss, or I might have to call Tommy back."

He pulled me down the stairs and across the grass. My legs were still numb, and I stumbled to keep my body upright. I felt sure that if I opened my mouth I'd throw up, so I kept it closed and breathed quick and shallow through my nose. The world blurred around me. I was going to die, just like the girl in the woods.

We walked away from where Thomas had gone, toward the only tent standing among the carts. It was red, like the Big Apple, and only as big as one of Bob's greenhouses. Sebastian pushed me through the closed flap, never letting go of my arm.

The tent was full of circus equipment, ropes and platforms and juggling clubs piled along the walls. In the back of the tent, a nest of electrical wires twisted around a huge black box that looked like a machine of some kind. The grass in the center of the tent had been flattened by footprints, so I guessed this was where they practiced their acts. For now, though, the place was empty.

"So, Junie," Sebastian said, letting go of my arm so hard that I stumbled back. The tent flaps hung limp behind him, but he kept himself between me and the entrance. "You've tried to be a little hero, hmm?"

"The constable's coming," I said again. My voice sounded young and awkward, like a hill person's voice.

"I do hope he comes soon," Sebastian said. "If we finish packing before he arrives, we won't have the chance to kill him."

I took a few steps back. Sebastian let me take them. He pulled his top hat off, twirled it casually for a moment. Then he put it carefully on his head again.

"What exactly do you know, and who did you tell it to?" he asked, his voice calm and reasonable. "I'm truly curious, but it's also important so we can plan accordingly."

"I don't know anything," I said. "I didn't say anything." The red light was making me sweat, and the air felt close and heavy in the tent. I didn't want this to be the last air I breathed. I wanted to feel the mountain wind on my neck, like I had on the road with Jacob.

"You know, we may still be able to fix this," Sebastian said, gentler still. "You did what you thought was right when you told the constable about us. You were looking for your brother, and that's admirable. Well, now you have him, and you can help us. We aren't evil. We aren't here to hurt people."

"What about Sarah and Wilson?" I said.

"Some casualties are unavoidable," Sebastian said, shrugging.

"What about the girl in the woods?" I wasn't trying to be brave. I wasn't trying to talk back. The last question came out pleading.

Sebastian shrugged. "She tried to leave us, lost sight of the mission. The mission is too important for weakness. You have no idea, tucked away here in this Republic. Things are happening outside these borders. You can't escape it much longer. Join us and you'll be joining the strongest province in the new world."

I shook my head, not understanding. He clicked his tongue impatiently. "Consider the alternative: the New Mainers! Now there is a group of hateful hoarders who would love to break down your delicate borders. Annexation is coming either way. York would give you many benefits, just as your resources will benefit us."

I didn't know what he was saying. I wasn't sure what *annexation* meant, for one, and for another I didn't really know the difference between New Mainers and Yorkers. They were all Americans, and I hadn't known there was more than one kind.

"You're here to hurt people," I said. "That's what Thomas told me. You're going to kill the leaders at Town Meeting."

Sebastian sighed. "A narrow view of our goal. I can see this isn't going to work." He stepped forward and I backed up again, even though there was nowhere for me to go.

"It's a shame," he continued. "I thought that you'd be more like your mother." His lips twitched at the look on my face.

"What—" I gasped. I'd almost forgotten that her name had been written in the book in Alexandra's tent. And that they'd asked Medusa, the Alt-Z on the road, about American spies. "What do you know about my mom?"

"Thomas told us you were looking for her. Too bad you didn't join us, or you could have seen her again."

I felt my head shaking back and forth. The red walls of the tent felt closer, as if they were sagging in toward me. "You don't know where she is."

"Indeed, we do. We collected her report just a few days ago. She didn't mention you."

My vision tunneled and all of a sudden the walls of the tent felt too close. "A few days ago?" I said, my voice choked. I hadn't really believed that she was alive and well, I realized. Not until just now. Until this moment, I'd thought that if I found her, she'd be stoned or blind or broken too badly to search for me. Or dead. Dead would have been better than this.

Sebastian clicked his tongue again, this time pretending to be sympathetic. But his eyes were shining and crinkled at the corners, like he couldn't stop himself smiling just a little.

"It's a shame," he said again. "You don't have her intelligence, or you could have seen the benefit of working with us." He turned on his toes, light and floaty like a dancer. Then he left the tent.

I stood there, sweating in my mom's coat, suffocating. My mother's coat.

I didn't have time to do more than take a few shallow breaths before the tent flap whipped aside again.

It was the strongman, the one I'd seen rolling the electric cable out of the woods.

"I don't—" I started, but he walked straight to me and hit me across the side of the head. I fell hard, rolling on the grass. My ears rang and the whole side of my face went numb. I turned over and he was standing over me, looking at me with empty eyes that didn't quite meet mine.

I tried to scream, but he kicked out at me, knocking all the wind out of my lungs. I crawled away, gasping. He grabbed the back of my mom's coat and I wriggled out of it, jumping away, leaving him holding the empty coat. I tried to get around him to the tent flap, but he lunged at me again and I leapt aside, bouncing off the canvas tent wall and tripping over a pile of juggling equipment.

My only thought was to get out of the tent. I tugged at the base of the canvas tent wall, digging into the dirt, but the wall was staked down and I didn't have time to get under it. The strongman grabbed my ankle and pulled me toward him, and I dug my fingers into the ground, felt my fingernails tearing. I kicked out at him with my free leg and he let go for an instant, snarling. I scrambled up and stumbled to the back of the tent, clambering over the coiled electrical wires with the strongman right behind me.

I still don't know exactly what happened next. I tripped hard and fell. A wire looped around my calf and cut into my skin, and then tugged tight as I heard the strongman grunt and trip behind me.

And then the air exploded with electricity.

I was on the ground, tangled in wires, and my whole body went stiff as I heard the buzzing crackle and smelled burning. I thought I'd been electrocuted, that the wires were flowing with it, but after a few heartbeats I realized my body was stiff with fear, not electricity. I scrambled out of the tangle and looked back.

The strongman had half fallen onto the boxy black machine I'd noticed before. He must've tripped over the same wire I had. One of his fingers had stuck deep in a socket on the side of the machine, and his hand was encased in blue electricity that sparked and burned. His whole body smoked, and his face was a kind of red that meant death. In the second I watched, his shirt caught fire. The room was filling with smoke.

I heard shouting from far away. I turned to the tent wall and pressed myself to the ground, wriggling inch by inch under the taut canvas and out into the cold, damp air. I didn't know where I was, but I saw a tree line up ahead. I ran for it, not looking back, the smell of the strongman's flesh still burning in my nose.

20

I didn't make it far into the trees before my knees quit working and sent me sprawling onto the ground. Wincing, I pulled myself into a damp hollow between a mound of kudzu and a rotting log. Then I covered my head with my arms and listened for running feet.

Soon the side of my face where the strongman had hit me was pounding with pain, and a sharp, deep pain stuck in my ribs whenever I breathed. I felt blood dripping down my leg from where the electric cord had cut into my shin. I couldn't get straight what had happened—the cord had tripped the strongman, and he'd reached for the black box to steady himself, and somehow it had been full of electricity? I was sure he was dead, and sure the others would be coming for me, and all I could do was lie there and try to stay quiet.

It was hard. My whole body hurt, and I couldn't shift into a more comfortable position. And even when the pain backed off a bit, my mind was still on fire. Thomas let this happen to me. He'd chosen them over me. And worse—I could barely even think it—Sebastian said he'd seen my mom, that she was somewhere near the Borough, as if she'd been waiting for them the same way I'd been waiting for her.

No one came running. I stayed there until my heart slowed, until the pain in my side got so bad I had to roll over. I kept thinking Sebastian was there in the woods, silent, waiting for me to make the slightest move and show him where I was. But no one came. Every once in a while I caught a breath of voices on the air, coming from far away. Wouldn't they follow me? Wouldn't they want to kill me even more after what had happened to the strongman?

Finally my fear of waiting got worse than the hurt all over my body. I pushed myself up and groaned at the pounding in my head, then got my feet under me. Out through the trees, I could just see the red of the practice tent and the edge of a cart in the field. I caught a glimpse of movement, too far away to be sure about. I turned fast as I could and ran through the trees, limping on my hurt leg and gritting my teeth through the headache.

The light changed as I fled, half-running and half-walking. The woods darkened, and the sky overhead looked white through the tree branches. My whole side was wet from lying in the damp leaves. I looked back and couldn't see the field at all, or the circus. I kept going because I didn't know what else to do.

When I stumbled out of the woods, dusk was lowering over the hills. I squinted out and saw solar panels stretching away in both directions. I was in a solar field three or four times bigger than the one in the Borough. This must be where New Rutland got so much electricity. Sure enough, way down the hill I saw rooftops and glowing windows.

I stopped at the tree line. The last thing I wanted was to go back to that town. It hurt just to think about it. Was the circus down there, looking for me? Or what if they'd left? The constable might be dead by now, if he'd confronted them. And even if he wasn't dead, if I saw him I'd have to explain where Thomas had gone. I couldn't bear to think about Jacob, either—if he was sober, he'd want to know why I wasn't looking for my mom anymore.

I didn't have anyone left, really. I didn't have anywhere to go, either. All of my possible futures had been cut off, except the ones that I'd already walked away from.

I sat down, even though the ground was damp and cold. I was thirsty, but my pack had come off in the red tent, along with my mom's coat. I didn't have anything. I shifted my weight to take some of the pressure off my side and heard a crinkling of plastic.

That wasn't true. I did have one thing left.

I slipped the twist of plastic out of my pants pocket and stared at the little blue pills Jacob had handed me through the bars of his cell. I thought of Old Bill, so long ago in the Borough... *We could forget together... You got plenty you want to forget, right?* Was that what the LoTabs would do? Jacob had said they made things vivid, that *they take you where you want to go.* And then he'd told me a memory. So which was it?

I wasn't sure, but I didn't much care.

The LoTabs went down too easily. Once I'd swallowed, I had a moment of panic when I regretted what I'd done. I even put my hand on my throat, like I wanted to reach in and snatch them back. But I didn't. I curled up smaller and closed my eyes and tried to think of my favorite memory. I didn't even know what it was, but I pictured it hidden away somewhere in my mind, about to unfold and wrap me up in its arms.

Instead, my thoughts drifted. Small things rustled through the brush around me, and a cool breeze whispered in the leaves above. I thought I might sleep. I was so tired, and I felt so far from everything I knew. I wondered what Bob and Denise were doing. I wondered what Cyrus and Gemma were up to. They seemed like bits of my imagination now. They were so far away from me, so different from the person I'd become in the days since I'd left.

Cyrus and Gemma would be helping in the Hastings' field soon, probably. Every year the whole Hollow came together to mow that huge field, and to haul the hay. An old tractor sat rusting into the dirt in one corner of the field, and Bob said that Before, that one machine would've done the work of a dozen people in half the time.

They'd been haying when I built my search house. I'd almost forgotten about it. That was the first summer after I'd come to Bob and Denise. I felt myself drifting.

What you doing with that scrap wood? Bob asked. I looked up and saw the sun behind him, glinting through swaying tree branches.

Making a fort, I said. He grunted and turned back to his broken-down old car. His arms disappeared into its engine.

The sun shone while I built the search house. I remembered that.

I felt my body lying against the hard, wet ground, aching. I felt my fingers clutched around my knees and heard the breeze and a whisper of voices of the leaves. But I wasn't there in the New Rutland solar field anymore, I realized. Not really. I was in my search house, and the sun was shining.

From where I sat I could see down the Hollow road all the way to the Hastings' field, and a little farther than that. I saw Cyrus swinging a scythe as tall as he was. My scars were red and tender still, but the search house kept them hidden from the sun and kept me hidden from everyone. I'd piled scrap wood against a low concrete foundation, then hidden in the empty space inside. No one notices scrap wood beside a road.

My stomach tingled with warm excitement. I'd be able to sit here every day, every hour, and watch the road. When my mom came, I'd see her before anyone else. I could even hide from her if I wanted, and then jump out at the last minute when she was right next to the search house.

Got you! I'd say, like she used to say to me when she found me in hide and seek.

I shifted, folding my legs underneath me so I'd be ready to jump when she came. Old Bill biked up the road, but he didn't see me, and the warm tingle surged in my stomach. No one saw me unless I wanted them to.

I shifted my legs again and felt a chill dampness pressing into my knees. I wondered what it was—my search house was warm and dry. I looked down and saw my arms wrapped around my legs in darkness, and then I remembered I didn't want to think about that anymore.

I squinted down the sunlit road and saw someone new walking up it. She had long, dark hair, and she looked like she was flying because the valley opened up behind her. I'd planned to wait but I couldn't; I ran out of the search house to meet her. My bare feet were light on the road, each toe just barely touching down before I leapt away again. The Hollow blurred around me, I was running so fast. Up ahead, my mom changed directions. She was walking away from me now, and I ran and ran. The mountains rose up around us, and the path narrowed, and then we were walking through a forest so full of kudzu that the road became a leafy tunnel.

Mama, I said, and she turned and smiled at me. I saw her face clearly, and that's what made me remember that I was dreaming. I hadn't seen her face, not even in my memory, in six years. I ran again, stretching my little legs as far as they would reach, and held my hand up to meet hers.

Come on, baby, she said. We walked together through the leafy kudzu. I was dreaming, I knew it, but her big hand was warm around mine and my bare feet stung every few steps from twigs and prickers and stones. My skin was smooth and scarless.

Carry me, I said, and then I was on her back, my nose pressed against her long hair, breathing in the smell of woodsmoke.

The kudzu faded into darkness, night falling while I half-slept with my arms wrapped around my mom. The woodsmoke smell grew, and then we were sitting at a fire. Around us night noises blended with the crackling of the fire and my mom's humming. She had her hands in my hair, braiding and unbraiding strand after strand. I leaned against her thighs, played with pebbles on the ground in the light of the flames. My knees felt cold and wet again, and my hip, too, so I shimmied them closer to the fire.

On the other side of the flames, a face watched me. It flickered in the firelight, but I could see warm gray eyes, a dark beard flecked with gray, a half-smile.

Jacob? I said. He looked younger, stronger than the Jacob I knew. His hands clasped in front of him, scarless.

Hello, Junie, he said. *How many pebbles have you got?*

Seven, I said, holding up a spread hand to show him. He smiled, but his eyes looked sad.

Six, my mom said, taking one of the rocks from my hand and tossing it in the fire.

I reached out my hand for it, but Jacob leaned over the fire and pushed me gently back. *Careful*, he said. I started to cry.

It was just a joke, my mom said. *Quiet down.*

Don't tease her, Jacob said. I looked up at him and he'd grown older. His beard was gray, his skin lined, and his hands mottled by scars. His gray eyes met mine.

This is my memory. You can't be here, I said. Suddenly my whole side was wet from the forest floor, and I felt the cold biting into the cut on my shin.

The LoTabs, they take you where you want to go, he said, his voice echoing and strange. The fire was burning low now. I turned away from him and looked at my mom. She was staring into the fire at my pebble, smiling like she didn't notice I was crying. Then I couldn't see her through the tears anymore.

Shhh, she said, and I opened my eyes and felt her brushing tears from my cheeks with a soft thumb. *Don't cry, baby.*

She was holding me in her arms, and we were leaning together against an old counter in a half-collapsed electric car charging station. Dusty shelves leaned against each other in the shadows, and glass glittered on the old linoleum. Rain poured down outside. Thunder rolled overhead. But my mom was warm, and so was I.

Want me to read to you? she asked. I nodded. She pulled her pack over to us and took out *Vermont Life*. Its cover was whole, and I could see the picture of the little boy walking along a road in autumn. I'd forgotten what it looked like.

What do you want to hear?

Colors of Time, I said. She opened the magazine and read the words to me, and I drifted almost to sleep while I stared at the pictures of a world where everything was whole and perfect, where kids stood in the sun outside brilliant red barns. I opened my eyes and saw her rolling a pill bottle back and forth between her fingers. The little blue pills glowed in the candlelight.

Someone knocked on the door. My mom kept reading, but I stood and went to the barricade and pulled it open. Jacob walked in out of the storm and stood dripping on the floor of the charging station. He pulled back his hood.

I thought I was saving you, like I couldn't save Leah, he said, looking intently at me. One eye was swollen shut. I stepped back, looked to my mom to tell me what to do. She smiled up at me and then kept reading.

The days shorten, the autumn air turns clear and crisp, and the sun hangs lower in the sky. Gradually, the look of everything changes: the light, the forested hills, the colors that define a suddenly limited world.

The charging station darkened and then lit up again, and she was sleeping on the floor, *Vermont Life* crumpled at her side and the pill bottle lying a few inches from her hand. I was thirsty, but I wasn't allowed to drink water that pooled in metal and everything around us was metal.

Mama, I said, shaking her shoulder. She didn't move.

A while later, I tried again. She didn't move. I was cold and hungry now too. I was crying. Then the door opened behind me and I turned and there was Jacob, young and tired and anxious. I ran to him.

She won't wake up, I said.

Let's get you some breakfast, he said. *She'll wake when she's ready.* He led me away by the hand. We picked our way through the broken-down cars outside the gas station, but when we got to the road Jacob stopped. I felt scars on his hand and pulled mine away. He was old again, the Jacob I'd left behind in the jail cell.

I didn't have a right to take you away from her, he said. But I looked back and the charging station was a wreck, ready to fall in.

Suddenly I was alone and hiding, and my stomach was an empty fist. I was under a tanglerose bush in a scraped-out hollow. I'd counted all the pebbles, I'd named every root, and still my mom hadn't come back. I blinked, and for a moment I was June who'd taken LoTabs, June who was dreaming. And this wasn't where I'd wanted to be. These were supposed to be good memories. Where were the good memories?

June? A woman's voice, not my mom's, came from close by. I was little again, cold and hungry again, hiding under the tanglerose.

You under there? The tanglerose was shaking, someone hacking away at the branches, and then a hand grabbed my arm and pulled me out into the cold air. *Hell, you're a mess.* The woman was young like my mom, but her face was longer and a beaded necklace swung through the air as she leaned over me, brushing the dirt off. *Effie's gonna owe me when she gets back. C'mon.*

I wanted my mom. But the woman pulled me behind her through the woods, and my mom wasn't there. I closed my eyes, wishing for her.

The hand on my arm changed, and when I opened my eyes it was my mom's hand. My arm hurt from being pulled.

Can we—I whispered, but she cut me off with a *shhhh.*

I looked around. We were by an old highway, a huge berm of pavement and abandoned cars. Electric lights lined the old road, but we were hiding in a dark shadow. Someone else was with us now—a man, tall and faceless in the dark void under a metal bridge that held up the highway. I was scared—what if it fell? Could something that big fall?

We gave you ten, you brought back eight, he said. I couldn't see his face in the shadows. I wrapped my fingers in my mom's jacket, hid behind her legs. I didn't understand what she said back to him, something angry that I didn't want to hear. I wrapped my arms around her leg. *Can we...*

She didn't hear me. *Can't take that many,* she was saying. *The kid slows me down.*

We can take the kid off your hands if it's too difficult, the shadowy face said.

Screw you, my mom said, a swear she'd told me not to say.

You're a runner in debt. Run faster or we'll take her. And next time you steal a Tab, we'll take one of her fingers.

I closed my hands into fists so the man couldn't see my fingers at all. A new voice laughed—another man came stalking out of the shadows behind the first. I saw a green uniform, a black mustache under a flat-brimmed hat.

You can't hide your little piggies like that, the newcomer said, and he pushed back his hat so I could see his face.

It was Lee. Younger, thinner, but definitely Lee. I took a step back, feeling the pain in my side and the throbbing of my head.

What was Lee doing in my memory? What was he doing here, with an American drug trader and my mother?

Just keep her quiet, and we'll turn a blind eye, Lee said to my mom. *What's good for the Yorkers is good for us, right?* He turned back to the other man, and the two of them walked off under the bridge, disappearing in the shadows.

Then my mom took me by the arm and dragged me away again.

We were running. The rain poured down, so cold it was almost frozen. I was wailing, my throat raw from crying, but my mom couldn't hear me over the thundering rain. She was dragging me along, looking over her shoulder with wide, fearful eyes. And someone was chasing us. Someone who wanted to hurt us.

Run faster, my mom snarled at me. *Border's just up there!* But then she tripped and we both fell, and her pack flew off her back and down the gully. She let go of me and dove after it, disappearing into the dark. And then I was alone.

Mom! I stood up, looked behind me. They were coming. I could see someone on the road, heard shouting. I turned and ran through the darkness, the rain blinding me. I ran until I couldn't run anymore, and then I stumbled off the road and huddled under a half-fallen tree. I closed my eyes and felt the dampness on my knees and hip, and a breeze that didn't belong to the rainstorm, a breeze that whispered in leaves from another time and place.

Jacob was next to me when I opened my eyes again. The rain was still coming down, and out on the road a man was walking up and down, searching for my mom and me. I didn't know where she was.

Jacob was warm and dry, even in the rain. His lined face was swollen from where the Green Mountain Boys had beat him. His hands were wrapped around each other, scarred and shaking.

I know I didn't have a right, he said. *And I shouldn't have tried to stop you finding your mom, either.*

I leaned against him, like I'd done on Route 7 when we saw the bodies of the Alt-Zs the circus had killed. He put an arm around me and I felt warmer.

Who were those men chasing us? And the one under the bridge with Lee? And why was Lee helping the Americans? I asked. My body felt light, like I was going to float away.

It's your memory, June, he said. *I don't know anything more than you.*

They were Americans. You said you and my mom worked for them, smuggling drugs with the Alt-Zs.

Jacob nodded.

So it's them I should blame, not you, I said. *You tried to help me.*

Jacob lowered his head, breathed out a sigh so long I could feel his body shaking with it. *I can't imagine any parent wouldn't want you*, he said. Then he was gone.

Quit whining or the cannibals will hear you, my mom's voice said. We were walking along a dirt road in twilight, and I was crying again. My ankle ached and my stomach was empty and we'd been walking too long.

Be quiet or I'll leave you, she said again. She had an empty pack slung over her back, so I knew we were going to the border. I didn't think I could walk that far. I told her I couldn't do it.

Fine, just shut up, she said finally. She pulled me by the hand off the road, into an old barn with red paint peeling off its walls in strips.

Stay here, she said, pushing me down into a dusty pile of hay and pulling her coat off, tossing it on me.

I'm scared, I said. She sighed, then took *Vermont Life* and a candle stub out of her limp pack.

Just be quiet until I get back, she said, lighting the candle. Then, before I could say anything else, she'd turned and disappeared, closing the barn door behind her. I was alone with a flicker of candlelight. I was still scared, but the candle and the magazine helped. Before long, I was drifting. Then I smelled smoke. When I looked again, the barn was on fire around me.

Don't stay here, Jacob said, his face orange and sweaty in the firelight. *You can go anywhere.*

So I closed my eyes, and when I opened them I was smaller and warmer, wrapped in my mom's arms. She was reading *Vermont Life* to me, and as she read I looked at the pictures: a valley from high up, filled with mists in the twilight. Five little kids jumping rope beside a set of big red doors. *But there are other colors to savor now as well. An ordinary red barn glows with a richer hue in the late October sunlight. On clear autumn days ponds look up at a sky turned impossibly blue, and give the color back again, in seasonal affirmation.*

I drifted to sleep like that, in her arms, with the words from that one perfect day echoing in my ears.

21

The sky was painful white. I could barely open my eyes to slits before they burned. My body ached like I'd just fallen down a mountain, bouncing on every rock and stick. My whole right side was still wet and cold.

"Daughter, wake up now," a voice said somewhere over my head. A dark shape came closer, blocking out most of the sky. I tried opening my eyes again and saw a face hovering above me, a face I'd never seen before.

I sat up, groaning. Gentle hands touched my shoulders, helping me up. I was on the edge of New Rutland's solar field. In the bright white daylight, I saw that the panels were fancier than the Borough's, and bigger too.

The woman who had helped me stood back. She was with two others, and they all wore brown robes and had short, cropped hair. They were Millerites, like the ones I'd seen the other night outside Al's Fun Shack.

"Why..." I croaked, my voice tearing at my dry throat. I turned and looked around, searching for my pack. Then I remembered that it was gone, along with my mom's coat.

"Here," the first woman said, taking a canteen slung over her shoulder and handing it to me. I drank. My head felt heavy, full of fog. Images bounced around my mind—my mom's face and Jacob's, a red barn and a campfire... I'd taken LoTabs, and now I was back. My head still ached but my leg felt a little better than before.

"You were asleep, and we couldn't wake you," one of the other women said. "Did the electricity strike you down?"

"No..." It took me a moment to figure out what she was talking about. Then, finally, a memory came into focus: Benny had said that the electricity was out, that the Millerites had done it. And then the constable had gone to question them.

Remembering that made me remember the smell of the strongman's skin burning. I shuddered. "Is the electricity back on?"

"The devil has returned, yes," the first woman said solemnly. "He is many-headed. Cut one cord, another appears. And his anger intensifies." She looked behind her, which I figured was the direction of New Rutland. I saw a haze of smoke over the trees—too much.

"What's happened?" I tried to stretch to see what was burning, then winced. My side still hurt, and my body was wet from lying in the dewy grass. Balance felt strange, and I couldn't be sure how long I'd being dreaming. Hours? Days? I was still trying to get my head around what had happened. But the more I remembered, the worse I felt.

"The devil ran along the electric lines," the second woman said, her voice cold and angry. "We let our guard down for one moment and he struck with his blue dagger. Sometime in the night, the electricity reignited and burst its shackles, and now the town is burning."

"They promised it would never return," hissed the third woman, the youngest. "They promised they would destroy the grid."

"They lied. Where are they now? Their camp is gone, their promise broken," the woman who had helped me replied, slow and sad.

"Who? What are you talking about?" I asked.

"Those circus folk. They told us they'd eradicate the town's electricity, that they'd do it for free if we took responsibility for the attack. They said they had the means, and were sympathetic to our cause." She touched each of her shoulders with three fingers and shook her head.

"Perhaps they tried, but—" the second woman said.

"They didn't try. They stole the electricity, and then turned it back on us when they'd had their fill of the devil. I saw the cord leading to their camp!" said the third woman.

"You cannot say for certain what you saw. Scripture tells

us that all men are innocent until proven guilty, sister. Do not forget."

I remembered the strongman rolling a cord up from the woods, back at the circus camp. I wondered if that's what they were talking about. I opened my mouth to tell them, but then shut it again. I didn't want to get wrapped up in whatever the Millerites were doing out here.

"Did you say the town is burning?" I asked.

"Yes, though they've doused many of the flames. The constable was able to turn off the electricity again, with the help of our Lord. We have come to make sure the lines never run with devilry again. We should have done this years ago, with the town's approval or not. Be well, daughter."

The women turned and headed toward the solar panels, their shoulders squared. I wasn't sure what they intended to do, since there had to be a hundred panels, twenty feet tall each. I didn't plan to stick around to find out.

Instead, I breathed in and out through my nose, trying to think through the pounding of my head. I touched the side of my face and found it swollen and tender. My fingers were stiff too. I made a fist, hiding my fingers in my palm, and looked down at my hand. *Little piggies.* Another part of my dream came back to me then.

I turned and stumbled toward town.

The smell of smoke brought me back to myself more than all the bickering of the Millerite sisters. It came in strong when the wind changed directions, an acidy scent that meant all kinds of things were burning that shouldn't be. I sped up. Surely the circus had left, and surely they were on their way to Town Meeting. But they weren't the only criminals in town. Because I knew now why Lee had been in my memory. And I knew how the circus had been able to do so much damage without anyone catching on.

I came through the tree line that separated the solar field from New Rutland proper and stepped into a crowd. Everyone was out in the street like it was market day. But instead of bartering and music, the air was full of serious, low discussions. People had piled everything they owned outside in the streets. Little kids huddled together while their parents carried water or slumped beside them. Thomas came to my mind. What he'd done to me was an ache worse than all the pains in my body. But I couldn't think about that, or I wouldn't be able to keep going.

Every house in New Rutland was damaged. Some were piles of rubble, still smoking. I saw scorch marks where the electric wires attached to walls of houses, as if the fire had come from the electricity. I didn't understand how it had happened, but I was sure the black box in the red tent had something to do with it. A different kind of devil.

I pressed through the crowds, coughing and trying to get my bearings. The things I'd seen in my LoTab dream were with me, too, every step I took. I didn't think about finding my mom. I didn't think about her at all. I made sure of that. But I did think about Jacob, and all he'd said to me in my dreams. I had to get to him, and that thought was strong enough to keep all the other thoughts away. He needed to know what I'd seen. He needed to know that Lee was working with the Americans.

The building with the sign that read *New York, New York*, had burned to the ground. Electric cables lay tangled in the muck in front of the rubble like sleeping snakes. Everything looked so different I might've walked right past the scorched jail if I hadn't seen the rocking chair. It sat on the porch right where it had the day before, looking just as unruffled as I imagined Larry must look. I walked carefully up the steps.

"Jacob?" I said, peering in the door of the jail. "Larry?"

"Jeezum hell!" a voice rang out of the dark, and I heard a thump and a stumble like someone had stood up too fast and knocked a chair over.

I stepped inside and blinked in the dark. The room smelled acrid. Someone came hurrying through the gloom and leapt on me before I could see his face, wrapping me up in a hug like I hadn't known in a long time.

"You're alive!" Benny said, letting go of me and then grabbing my arm again when I stumbled from the force of his hug.

"'Course I'm alive," I muttered, though it was a little surprising to me, too, if I was honest with myself.

"Where you been—Jeezum hell, what happened to your face?" he yelped, pointing at my swollen cheek. But my head was still spinning from everything that had happened and I couldn't answer. I looked around instead. The room was just the same as before, apart from the smell and a blackened scorch mark where the electric wires snaked into the room. They must've gotten the fire out quickly here.

"Where—" Benny started again.

"I been around," I said, not even trying to lie. Benny looked me up and down in the light from the door, his eyes sticking on the scars on my neck and chest. No coat to cover me anymore.

"Sit down, let me— I got a med kit here somewhere, I—"

"What happened? Where is everyone?" I asked, ignoring him.

"Well…well, the electricity came back, but it blew everything," Benny said, scrabbling around in a row of lockers, looking for a med kit. "Larry thought it was a accident, but then those Millerites that we'd rounded up for breaking the grid told us. They said it was the *circus* that shut off the power, and the *circus* that turned it back on again. By that time, everything was burning and we didn't have time to piss our own pants 'fore we had to get out in the water lines. Then when we got most of the fires out, Larry went and checked and the circus was *gone*. He reckons they fiddled with the electricity on purpose."

"Jacob still back there?" I asked, leaning against Larry's desk to stop my legs shaking. My head was feeling woozy again from the pain and the smell of burning.

"Nope, he's with Larry," Benny said, gesturing off in some vague direction. "Off to rescue you and arrest the circus. Just arrest the circus now, I guess."

"Rescue me?"

"Yup. Jacob said the circus must've got you, and that you knew so much they might want to kill you. He was in a state."

I tried to say something, but I didn't manage it on the first try. Jacob had gone to save me, again. I cleared my throat. "So they're following the circus? To Town Meeting?"

"Yep. They're probably in Middlebury by now. Took the fast horses." Benny shook his head, grimacing. "I always wanted to go to Middlebury, and now they all go and leave me? It ain't fair, and I got work up to my ears trying to sort out all the fires."

"But—just Jacob and Larry alone?" The circus was too big, and Jacob was hurt. But Benny shook his head.

"No, they sure ain't. They're gonna render-vous with the Green Mountain Boys camp up there, get their help arresting 'em."

My breath caught in my throat. I thought of Lee's face when he saw Jacob in the hallway at Al's Fun Shack, and wondered how I ever could've thought he was anything but a criminal. Then I remembered the constable in the Borough, her head resting on the desk, her eyes empty and staring. And the way Lee had called my fingers *little piggies* all those years ago.

"You okay?" Benny asked, studying my face awkwardly. "You gonna cry or something?"

"You gotta get word to Jacob and Larry," I said. "They can't talk to the Greens. They're working with the Americans."

"Who's working with the Americans?" Benny asked, frowning.

"The Greens! You gotta get word to Larry and Jacob."

"June, ain't no way to get word to 'em. They took our fast horses, they're probably up there already. But I don't get what you're saying. The Greens—"

"Lee's been helping the circus this whole time!" I said. It was clear as day, but I didn't have time to explain to Benny how Lee and his crew had arrived and left the Borough at the same time as the circus. How he'd blamed the deaths on Jacob so no one would suspect the circus. All the times he'd tried to get me to leave the circus alone. And he'd probably been the one to get rid of the girl's body, after the circus had realized Thomas and I knew about her.

"He's working with them," I repeated, steady as I could. "And he'll stop Larry and Jacob when they get to Town Meeting."

Benny pulled his hat off and ran his fingers through his hair. He looked like a little kid all of a sudden. "I don't—but that don't make sense… Greens are there to stop attackers, not help 'em."

I barely heard him. I'd never felt so stuck in my life, not even in the Hollow. That had been a slow, sad kind of stuck, but this feeling was terrible, urgent. I couldn't be here. I had to be in Middlebury, to warn Jacob. Benny was shifting his hat around on his head, pulling it off and putting it back on again, glancing out the door.

"Benny—"

"I don't know, June. We can…when Sheila and Eugene get back, we can ask them, but—I'm supposed to get the med kits and go back to the town center, and I dunno what…" He was babbling now, trying to talk until he hit on the right thing. There wasn't any time.

"I need a ride to Middlebury. Now," I said.

"Well, you could…we've got a mule, but she's lame, and—"

"Now," I said again. "Or I'll have to walk." Which I knew I wouldn't be able to do. I didn't know the way, and Middlebury was twice as far as the distance from the Borough to New Rutland. By the time I got there, Lee might've killed Jacob, all because I hadn't been brave enough to remember him until now. All because I hadn't been straight with Jacob about the circus, and he hadn't been straight with me.

"Isn't there anyone going that way anyway? Any traders?" I asked.

"Yes! Yoder's U-Haul!" Benny actually ran to the door of the jail and looked out. "He was here this morning! Just passed out the gates when I was coming back to get the med kits. Heading north!"

"Which way?" I said.

Fifteen minutes later, I was standing in front of the same truck I'd hitched into town on the night I arrived, and Benny was arguing with the old walnut of a man sitting in the cab. Benny was carrying an armful of med kits, and he kept losing his grip on one or another. The old man, whose name was Yoder, didn't want to take me with him.

"Mowr weight, mowr trouble," he'd muttered three or four times already. I didn't have anything to offer him.

"I order you, by order of—I'm deputizing you, I mean—" Benny said, struggling to get the words out while looking over his shoulder at town, juggling five or six med packs, and pushing his hair out of his face.

"Here," I finally said, when I couldn't stand it anymore. I plucked one of the med kits out of Benny's arms and pushed it up into Yoder's cab. "Will you take me if we give you this?"

"I can't give that away," Benny said, though he looked relieved to have one less box to carry.

I glared at him, and he shrugged, still glancing over his shoulder.

"Go back to town," I said. "They need you. But I need that med kit."

Benny hissed out a long breath. "Larry's gonna kill me for this," he said.

"He'll be happy if it saves his life," I snapped back.

"C'mon," Yoder said. "Get going 'fore the crap catches fire." I guessed that meant I'd earned a spot in his truck.

"Thank you," I said to Benny, then I ran around the front of the truck and climbed into the cab. I felt strange, too light, without my pack or my mom's coat. But I didn't have time to think about it.

"Don't get killed," Benny said weakly, watching me go. By the time the two horses pulling the U-Haul had broken into a halfhearted trot, I'd lost sight of him in the smoking streets of New Rutland.

22

Middlebury was big and mysterious in the rain. From miles away we'd been able to see the church spires and huge square buildings rising out of the valley. Yoder said the town hadn't been abandoned after the Fall, which made it different from most towns. The buildings were relics from Before, made out of marble and brick, and the Republic had just grown over them all like kudzu.

Yoder talked most of the seven-hour journey. I didn't listen to all of it, didn't understand some of it, and still learned more about him than I knew about most other people. He'd spent his life crisscrossing the Republic, picking up supplies in one town and selling them in the next. All the stuff he had in the back of the truck was *quality building material, quality produce, quality tools.* He'd told me that about a dozen times, enough for me to start doubting him.

But most of the trip I spent staring ahead, my back stiff and my fingers bunched together in my lap, letting Yoder's stories wash over me without catching a word. Yoder gave me a few flat biscuits to eat, but I could barely swallow them. I didn't notice the landscape, or the ghost towns we drove through. We passed a few folks, all heading in the direction of Town Meeting, but I didn't recognize any of them. No sign of Lee and his crew. No sign of the circus or Thomas. No sign of Jacob. No sign of my mom, but then I wasn't looking for her anymore.

It felt like something had come loose in me in the night I'd spent LoTab dreaming. All the years I'd forgotten had come flooding back, washing away all my questions and doubt and leaving nothing behind but certainty. I finally knew who my mom was. I finally knew who I was.

I had time, while Yoder droned on and the landscape shifted around me, to change my mind. I had time to jump down from the U-Haul and start walking back. But I stayed. I couldn't let Jacob face Lee alone, not again. If I could, I wanted to save him, like he'd saved me all those times when my mom hadn't been able to. And I wanted to stop the circus. Not just for Thomas. For me too. I was too tired to be scared. I didn't have the energy to doubt myself anymore.

The road into Middlebury was backed up on account of Town Meeting, and all the traffic had left it a rutted smear of gray. Even though most of the day had passed, there were still people everywhere. Up ahead a woman was unhitching a horse from a wagon stuck wheel-deep in the mud. Another wagon had already been abandoned just a few feet farther into the muck. Other folks were taking the road on foot, edging along planks that'd been laid out to float on what used to be solid ground. I stayed in Yoder's U-Haul as long as I could stand it, then I thanked him and jumped out into the mud to walk.

"Good luck!" he called after me, and then I heard him start telling a story again, even though no one was in the truck with him anymore.

Middlebury didn't have a wall around it, or a gate. Instead, three Green Mountain Boys stood alongside the road, watching people pass without saying much. I was sure they must sense my jangling nerves. I tried to walk fast, but not too fast, and to keep my head down. I didn't breathe at all until I was well past them, and then I had to take a gasp and my legs went to jelly for a second. I didn't look back to see if they were watching me, but my skin prickled all the same as I hurried on into the shadows of Middlebury's tall buildings.

Before I'd gone far into town, the whole road was jam-packed with people. I couldn't take a step without getting in someone's way. What's more, I could tell most of the folks in the streets weren't from Middlebury at all. They were all dressed in their best clothes: suits, ties, beaded vests, buckskin jackets, even some dresses from Before with long skirts trailing in the muck. The rain was falling gently, but no one seemed to mind. And no one seemed quite sure where they were headed, so traffic was slow and meandering. A banner hung between two brick buildings and showed a picture of a group of people sitting in a circle, the symbol for Town Meeting.

I looked around. How was I supposed to find Jacob in all this mess? I hadn't thought past getting here. I'd assumed if I could do that, the next step would just happen. And now I was in the middle of Town Meeting without a coat or a pack, trying to rescue Jacob and Larry from an international conspiracy. 'Course I didn't know what to do.

I decided to keep walking toward the center of things. I figured that was the best way to get the lay of the land. But that meant going where the crowds were, and each step made my chest feel tighter and my head lighter. I kept trying to pull my coat closed, kept realizing that it was gone, and anyone who looked could see my scars.

Up ahead someone was yelling from the middle of the crowd. "Wind power is the future! Think of the storms—think of the wind! Every gust a lightbulb!"

"For shame!" a chorus of voices answered. Through the crowd I saw a gaggle of Millerites facing down a man wearing a three-piece suit and a bright-pink scarf bunched under his huge beard. He poked out his tongue and blew a raspberry at the Millerites. Everyone laughed, even a few of the Millerites.

"Your logic is astounding!" one of the Millerites yelled, and the crowd laughed again. I slipped over to a wall and slid along it, trying to get out of the crush of people. Everyone seemed excited, even though nothing was happening. It was like a big party, and I didn't have time for it. I came to a set of stairs squeezed between two shacks built against a tall brick building. I climbed up them just to get out of the fray. The glass in the brick window frames was gone, replaced by wooden shutters, but the doorway at the top was open. The crowd roared so loudly behind me that I couldn't think. I slipped inside, out of the rain and noise.

"Close the door behind you if you're coming in!" a sharp voice said. I blinked—it was a lot darker in this room behind the wooden shutters. But I closed the door, and the shouting and laughing from outside faded a bit.

"Are you the Upper Valley delegate?" someone else asked.

"Um…" I slowly turned around while my eyes adjusted to the light. The room was long and narrow, and had so many tables and chairs in it that I figured it must've been a restaurant once upon a time. In the dim light coming through cracks at the tops of the windows, I saw a circle of four people.

"Oh, certainly not, she can't be a delegate," said the sharp voice I'd heard first. It came from a tall woman wearing an enormous knitted smock that looked more like a tent than a piece of clothing. She wore a matching knitted hat on her head. She did look warm, at least.

"Come into the light," said a man sitting next to her. He was wearing a knitted vest and a hat that matched hers, so I figured they must be together.

"I just wanted to get out of the crowd," I said. I shuffled a few steps forward but tried to keep my swollen face in shadow.

"We're in session!" said another woman, who crinkled a bit as she turned to look at me, on account of a strange jacket she was wearing, woven out of what looked like greenish plastic.

"Sorry," I said, and took a few steps back again. "I just need—" I stopped, because the woman's eyes reminded me of Bob's, and I knew I had to slow down. I swallowed.

"That's a nice jacket."

The woman smiled, and turned to look at the other three. "See? She likes it."

"She's being polite!" said the fourth man, who was very old and whose jacket was made of beautiful gray felt. "Whose jacket do you like better—hers or mine?" he shot at me.

"What are you…in session about?" I asked.

"Fibers, child. Production and distribution of wool and cotton—not as exciting as *electricity*, of course, but our work is just as important! More important, some would say. Electricity is flashy but does it keep you warm? Does it?"

"Well…it can in some—" said the knitted woman, but the

man in the gray felt cut her off: "I was speaking rhetorically!"

"Have you seen..." I wasn't sure how to ask for what I wanted without seeming crazy, but I had to find Jacob quick. "Have there been any problems around here today or yesterday? Any crimes?"

"We really are in session," said the woman with the plastic vest.

The man in the felt raised his bushy eyebrows up and bobbed his head like an owl. "We're much too busy to concern ourselves with gossip, you know."

It was a dead end and I knew it. I needed to keep moving.

"Thanks anyway," I said. "I like all your fibers."

But as I said it, I noticed for the first time that the noise outside had changed. The fiber committee knew it too. The man in the knitted hat stood up, looking over my shoulder toward the door. "What's going on?" he said.

The crowd outside had gone quiet. Now the only sounds were the voices of a few men, yelling over each other. They sounded angry. The woman in the plastic stood, too, and brushed past me to look out a crack in the wooden shutters. "Goodness!" she said.

I turned and opened the door to peek out, thinking maybe the Millerites had started a real fight. The other committee members crowded around behind me so I almost fell onto the stoop before I could get a good look.

It wasn't the Millerites making a fuss in the street.

The crowd was still there, pressed together tight on either side of the road. An opening had cleared out through their middle, though, a space no one seemed to want to fill. And in the middle of that space, five men struggled in the mud. Three of them wore the flat-brimmed hats of the Green Mountain Boys. The other two were Jacob and Larry.

"My heavens," said the wool representative, his voice right in my ear because he was hanging on my shoulder to see out the door.

Down below, the Greens struggled to their feet, pulling

Jacob and Larry up. They both looked a mess—covered in mud and blood, their jackets hanging off them and their arms pinned behind their backs. Larry spat out a mouthful of blood.

"Unhand me—" I heard him start, before one of the Greens kneed him in the stomach. A few folks in the crowd gasped. Jacob didn't say anything at all. He was bent over as if something in his side was hurt bad. He kept his head down so I couldn't see his face.

"These men have been detained on account of their intent to commit a terrorist act," said the tallest Green, loud enough that the whole crowd could hear. I saw his face as he pushed back his hat, and I ducked to avoid being seen. It was Lee, of course.

The crowd murmured at that. A few even applauded a little. Lee took Jacob by the elbow and started dragging him down the road. The second Green took Jacob's other arm, and the last one followed with Larry.

I started out the door. I didn't know what I was going to do—attack the Greens? Maybe. I was mad enough to do it, even if it would've ended with me face down in the mud. But I never got to find out, because three or four hands grabbed me by the flannel and hauled me back into the old restaurant.

"What are you *doing*?" the knitted woman asked.

"Those Greens just stopped a *terrorist* plot," cut in the plastic woman. "You can't go disturbing them."

I pulled myself free of the committee. They all looked at me like I was a wild animal they'd trapped by accident.

"They aren't terrorists!" I shouted. "They were set up!" I whipped back around, looked out the door. The crowd was following Lee and the others, watching them drag Jacob and Larry along. Larry wasn't trying to object anymore. I had to do something.

"You know those criminals?" the knitted man asked, taking a little half-step away from me.

"Not criminals. The Greens are the criminals. They—"

"No matter who's at fault, you won't help anyone by interfering with that arrest," the man in the wool vest said, gentle enough that I actually stopped to listen. "The Greens have jurisdiction here. Their word's the last word."

"But they're wrong. Lee— I don't have time to explain."

"You want to get this sorted out, you best go talk to the Greens' captain. He'll hear you out."

I started to tell him that I didn't think anyone would take my word over Lee's, but I stopped myself. I didn't have time to argue. I had to go.

"Where're the Greens taking them?" I asked.

The committee blinked up at me.

"Where?"

"Out to the old school, I suppose, dear," said the plastic woman, getting a few nods from the others. "It's their garrison now."

"I'm going," I said.

"Careful. Don't cross those Greens we just saw, child," the knitted woman whispered.

"Follow this road down the hill, then take a left at the river," the wool man said over her. "You'll find the captain there."

I turned and burst out the door, but as I went I heard the plastic woman saying, "Poor dear. See how wet she was? Plastic weave would be perfect in weather like this."

The crowd was packed into the streets again, and it took me too long to push my way in the direction Lee had taken Jacob and Larry. Everyone was talking about the arrest.

"I heard they had a *bomb*—"

"No, a new strain of flu—"

"Greens ought to get a medal for that—"

I pushed past them all, my heart pounding. Lee had Jacob and Larry. That meant no one was left to stop the circus. And something terrible was probably going to happen to Jacob and Larry too. People buzzed for a lot less than being labeled terrorists.

And the worst part was, I was the only one in this town who knew what was happening. It was just me.

I was worrying so hard, I didn't pay attention to the singing until it was almost too late. It came over the crowd and everyone went quiet and looked around. When I finally noticed it, I stopped so suddenly that a man shouldering his way through with an armful of rope knocked into me. He grumbled something, but I barely even noticed him.

The voice was getting closer. "Come one, come all, to see the Greatest Show on Earth! Forget your woes, come see the circus!"

I knew that voice.

"The world's over, but the show must go on! The spectacular, the strange, the lost secrets of the Before Times!"

I ducked down beside the man with the rope, trying to keep him between me and Sebastian, who was making his way closer through the crowd. I couldn't let him see me. I wriggled through the crowd and managed to slip down a side alley between the old brick building and a new straw bale house. When I looked back, I saw Sebastian's horse struggling through the mud, its stripes running off in the rain. Sebastian was smiling and waving his top hat.

"Come one, come all! Mayors and town officials watch for free! A special show to honor Town Meeting Day! Come celebrate the season at the Big Apple on the college green!"

He passed out of sight.

A trickle of rain slid cold and quick down my neck and into my shirt. For a long while, I couldn't make myself move for fear of Sebastian coming back. But finally I thought of Jacob, of how he'd held his hurt body, and how the Greens had hit Larry. And I made myself move. I pushed my way back out of the crowd and down the hill to the river. It was swollen and roaring from all the rain, but I barely heard it.

The old school was huge: flat and wide and surrounded by fields of poison parsnip. But the real giveaway was the twenty or so square tents set up in what used to be a parking lot, like a Civil War camp I'd seen pictures of in *Vermont Life*. That had to be the Green Mountain Boys.

I watched the garrison from the road for a few minutes, but then figured I should get out of sight. So I made my way into the scraggle of trees between the road and the school, and found a downed log with space enough under it for me to stay out of the rain and still see the garrison.

I waited to catch my breath for a little while, but then I started to get scared again. There had to be fifty or so Greens at the garrison, based on the crowd of tents. And maybe there were more inside. How would I find Jacob and Larry, and then how would I get them free? I was just one damp, tired kid, hiding under a log in the woods. The Greens were an army.

My breathing had calmed down, but it started to pick up again as my mind turned itself around in circles. Was Lee the only one working with the circus? Or were there more Greens in on it? Could it be all of them?

The rain was coming down harder now.

I tried to focus. I just had to find Jacob and Larry and then it'd get easier from there. I just had to do this one thing. Just this one impossible thing.

The leaves were slick and wet under my legs. The log over my head was covered in a fine green moss, the kind that grows everywhere during the stormy seasons. I didn't have a plan. I didn't know what to do. I wondered what my mom would do, and then I remembered that the mother I had in my head didn't exist. She wouldn't do anything. So I tried to think what Jacob would do. Disguise himself? Sneak in under cover of night? It all sounded like a stupid story from some kid's book.

While I thought, my eyes watched the garrison without really seeing it. A few Greens walked in and out of the school's big, dark doors, small and distant from where I lay, barely real.

Then another man walked out of the school, and it took me a second to realize that it was Lee.

He was swaggering. I could see his mustache pull back as he

grinned at a few Greens going in the other direction. One of them patted Lee on the shoulder as he went by. Lee pulled his flat-brimmed hat down against the rain, jogged down the line of tents, and disappeared into the tent at the end.

My heart thundered in my chest. Before I could stop to think about it, I jumped up and headed out onto the old paved driveway.

As I walked past the first tents I tried to keep my head down, to avoid eye contact like I'd done with the Green Mountain Boys at the edge of town. I kept waiting for someone to call out to me, or grab me by the scruff of my shirt, but no one did. No one gave me more than a glance. I passed by the tent that Lee had gone into and sped up a little, feeling uneasy with him behind me where I couldn't see him. The open doorway to the school loomed up and swallowed me.

The rain and the sounds of the camp faded away as I walked inside. The school was in bad shape. Big panels from the ceiling had fallen in and been kicked to the side of the hallway. Overhead in the gloom I could see a creepy mess of wires and pipes and dust. The walls hadn't fared much better—they were covered in water marks and mold.

No one was waiting for me inside. My eyes caught on a poster hung on the far wall. It read *Apply to Community College of Vermont Today* over a picture of a smiling girl holding a book. She wore a backpack and a tight pink shirt that had faded to brown like the rest of the poster.

A rumble of voices distracted me from the smiling girl. A little ways down the hall, a glass-walled room was lit up by a row of sharp electric lights, and inside, a whole herd of Greens was circled up, talking in low voices. I recognized one of them—the brown-braided woman from Lee's crew, McMillan.

As soon as I saw her I heard footsteps coming down the hallway from the other direction and backed against the wall, into a little nook beside an empty glass-fronted case. Two more Greens came out of the gloom, talking in low voices.

"No way I'm switching with you. Crew seven's hosting tonight. You think I want to miss that to guard some stinking prisoners?"

"I took your night duty last week! You owe me," said the other Green, a short woman with a round face.

"I don't owe you nothing. Now get going—you'll be late for the terrorists."

The woman snorted and walked past me down the hallway, while the man turned and went out the front doors. Neither of them saw me.

I waited until the woman went around the corner at the end of the hallway and then started to follow her. If she was guarding Jacob and the others, she'd lead me right to them.

"Hey! What're you doing here?"

I whipped around. McMillan, the woman from Lee's crew, was standing in the hallway outside the glass room, looking like she was trying to decide whether to come grab me.

The other Greens in the glass room looked around all at once, like cows noticing a coyote, and they went quiet when they saw me.

"I—I'm..." I thought about running out the door again, but McMillan must've seen me looking because she sidled over to block the way out.

"Why are you here?" she asked. "You were in New Rutland, too, weren't you?"

The others were standing up now, peering out the dusty window or coming to stand in the doorway. I counted eight of them.

"What was that, McMillan?" said a deep voice from behind all the others. "Bring that girl in here. Bring her."

McMillan raised her eyebrows at me. "You heard him. Want me to come get you or you gonna come quiet?"

I didn't want to go into the glass room, but there was nothing else I could do. I stepped inside stiff and straight, trying not to look scared. The man who'd ordered me in was sitting behind a huge old desk from Before. He had a white mustache and a cowboy hat. I figured right away that he was the leader—the captain, I was pretty sure. The one the fiber committee had told me to go see.

All the other Greens watched me pass by and then sat themselves back down on stools or rickety plastic chairs. No one seemed particularly ill at ease except McMillan, who stood behind me like she thought I might bolt. Maybe she was right.

"Now who's this girl?" the captain asked in a booming voice. "McMillan, you say she was involved in the trouble in New Rutland?"

"No, sir," McMillan said. "But I can't think what she'd be doing here. She's from farther south. The Borough—that town that lost a constable and a deputy last week." She spoke as loudly as the captain, and I realized he must be hard of hearing. Some part of me realized it, at least. Most of my mind was twitching like a trapped rabbit, trying to think how to get free.

"So she was involved in that business? That what happened to her face?" the captain yelled.

"Well...I don't quite know, sir," McMillan said. And there was something in her voice that sounded uneasy now. Like she knew they'd done wrong when they brushed off the murders in the Borough, and she didn't want the captain to find out. I wondered if she knew what the circus had done, what Lee had done to cover for them.

The captain slapped the desk with the flat of his palm. I jumped. Everyone else just flinched, as if they'd seen him do this lots of times before and didn't like what it meant.

"I can't tolerate it!" he shouted, glaring around with his beady eyes. "Seven constables dead in the past season, and three mayors! Who knows why they all chose this season, of all the seasons, to croak? It's no coincidence, dammit. I want answers, and I'm tired of getting nothing but questions from you slags!"

The Greens all grumbled and took their time looking at their shoes and scratching their necks, but I was still thinking fast. The captain sounded upset, like he really was bothered by the deaths. And McMillan was unhappy too. So maybe they weren't all working with the circus. Maybe it really was just Lee.

"I have information—" I started, my voice croaky, but the captain said, "Huh?" and put a hand up to his ear. So I cleared my throat and yelled, "I have information!"

"McMillan, what's she talking about?" the captain barked.

"I don't know for certain," McMillan said. She poked me in the shoulder. "Information about what?"

"About the dying constables, and who's doing it."

"She says she knows who's killing the constables!" McMillan shouted at the captain. A few other Greens turned to look at me closely for the first time. The rest still looked bored, like they wanted to get to the party that crew seven was putting on.

The captain blinked, and I swear I could hear the noise of it—a sticky sound.

"Well, you got my attention," he said finally. "Out with it!"

They were all looking at me now, and I started getting nervous all over again. But I made myself look at the captain and nothing else, and I cleared my throat.

"I've been following a traveling circus for a week now, up Route 7," I said. "I've talked to them and everything. And wherever they go, people have been dying. It's them who've been doing it—killing everyone. They tried to kill me. And I know why. They're from America, and they're trying to make us weak so we won't be able to stop the Yorkers from taking over."

"Did she say circus? What circus?" the captain said, looking from me to everyone else, as if they'd know better than me.

"Anyone register a circus coming across the border?" a woman sitting closest to the captain asked. There was grumbling all around while everyone said no.

"We tracked the circus in our district, sir," said McMillan in a small voice. Then she had to say it again so the captain would hear her.

"American? Why'm I just hearing about this?" the captain barked.

"No, sir—domestic. Came from Bennington, or thereabouts. Came outa the hills."

McMillan wasn't looking at anyone now. She was staring at the ground.

"They were American," I said.

"Can you prove that?" the captain shouted.

"I talked to them—they said stuff about America, about killing people. I heard them."

"You said the circus had proper identification, McMillan?" the captain barked at the woman near the door. Everyone looked at her. She was blushing and blinking hard.

"Well—yes, they did," she said, but the words sounded like they'd been dragged out of her mouth with a hook.

"Why'd you have to say it like that? Did they or didn't they?" the woman beside the captain snapped.

McMillan paused again. "Well," she said again.

Then Lee walked into the room. I didn't have time to do anything but flinch before he met my eyes. He didn't look shocked to see me at all; he must've noticed me from the lobby and come running.

"'Pologies for the tardiness," he said to the captain, loud enough for him to hear. But he was still glaring at me, like he could trap me with just his eyes. "What'd I miss?"

"Sit down, Lee," the captain said. "This girl's just been giving us some troubling information about a rogue circus."

"Ah, hello, June," Lee said, his face twitching into a smile as he sat down in an empty seat near the captain.

"You know her?" the captain asked.

"Yes, she's from the Borough or thereabouts. In our district. She witnessed the, ah, event there last week."

"She's just telling us about an American spy circus, if you can call it that. Claims it's been marauding up the Route 7 corridor.

"Ah," Lee said again. He frowned down at his hands and then looked up again. "Cap'n, can I talk to you alone about this?" he said delicately, as if the matter were a private one—but of course he had to shout for the captain to hear him.

"Don't listen to him!" I yelled. "He's working with them! He's been helping them all along!"

Lee smiled at me again, but I could see in his eyes that he was angry. "Now, now," he said. "I've tried to help you, June, lots of times." He shrugged and looked around the room, shaking his head. "I'm sorry—I think I better explain here. She's a little out of her depth."

"I'm not—"

"Shhh, June, let me tell my side here," he said in a voice all soft and gentle. "Cap'n, I've run into June here a few times. She's had a rough go of it—lost her brother, kid ran away with the circus. But I can tell you for certain that the circus ain't done nothing wrong. Just folks trying to get by."

"They're not from America, then?" the captain asked.

"No, sir," Lee said, chuckling a little as if the thought was ridiculous. I opened my mouth, but I couldn't get a word in before Lee kept going. "She wants her brother back, Cap'n. Come up with some story 'bout that poor ol' circus to try and get us to bring him back to her."

"He's lying! He's working with them!" I shouted.

"Whoa, there, girl," the captain said. "We're looking at your word against his. This true about your brother going with the circus?"

"No! I mean, yes—they stole him! He didn't want to go with them, but they brainwashed him. They're planning something, and you gotta stop them!"

"Lee, you think there's any chance the circus might've had something to do with the terrorists you rounded up just now?" the captain shouted. Lee, who was right next to him, winced a little at the noise but shook his head.

"No chance, sir. The terrorist ringleader, Jacob, been on our list long before that circus ever came to town. Classic malcontent," Lee said, crisp as frost.

The captain sighed. He looked at me, looked back at Lee.

"What about all those mishaps in your district? Lots of dying for this time of year. Lots of killing, by the sound of it. You think that was all this Jacob fellow and his law enforcement defectors…?"

Lee nodded. "Sir, I investigated all them events myself. Jacob had a clear connection, and looks like he managed to get the New Rutland law enforcement in on it too. 'Nother reason why the Greens ought to have local power, sir—the locals are too easy to turn."

I hated him so much in that second that I could've scratched his stupid eyes out.

The captain nodded. "All right, that'll settle it. We've other matters to get to." He turned to me. "Kid, I'm sorry about your brother. But you best be heading home now."

"But, sir, please—" I said.

The captain stood up, shaking his head and smiling down at me. "I think you believe what you're saying, kid," he said. "And I thank you for trying your best. But we got this under control."

Lee stood up and walked over to me, putting his hand on my shoulder. I tried to shrug it off, but he held on tight. "Sir, I'm happy to find arrangements for her," he said. "She's from my district, after all."

The captain waved a hand. "I need you here, Lee. We've got to get this personnel distribution plan to the Town Meeting by tomorrow morning. She found her way here; she can make it back."

Lee opened his mouth to argue again, and his fingers dug into my shoulder. "It won't take long, sir," he growled.

But he'd said it too quiet for the captain to hear. The captain banged his hand on the table again. "Where were we? The Western Quarries? Stevens, you put in a request for five more Greens to patrol the area, right?"

I pulled myself free of Lee, hard enough that he would've had to make a scene to stop me. I backed out of the room, and he glared at me the whole time. But just before I turned away, I saw McMillan's face. She was looking at Lee like she'd just seen a ghost. Or like she'd just realized her boss was a monster.

23

I made myself stop beside the community college poster and look back. The Green Mountain Boys were all grouped around the captain again, listening to whatever he was shouting at them. But Lee was still watching me over the captain's shoulder.

With his eyes on me, there was nothing I could do but walk out the front door. But as soon as I was out of his sight I stopped and pressed myself against the wall by the entrance. The rain was coming down hard outside now, and no one was around.

My shoulder felt dirty where Lee had touched it. I was so mad I wanted to turn right around and go back and keep yelling at the captain until he listened to me, or until that coward McMillan said something to back me up. But I knew I couldn't. I was lucky I'd got out of there at all.

My breath was coming in big heaves, even though I hadn't been running. My throat ached like I'd been breathing smoke. Then my mom whispered in the back of my mind, the version of her that I'd held in my head for six years. And somehow, even though she didn't exist, the thought of her made me feel a little better. She wouldn't abandon me, and I couldn't abandon Jacob.

After I'd got my breathing under control, I peeked my head back around the door. Lee was leaning toward the captain, saying something loud in his ear. I didn't wait a second more—I rushed back in and down the dark hallway. I didn't stop until I found a gap in the metal lockers lining the wall, then I slid into the shadows there and waited.

No one burst out of the room, no one yelled that the backwoods girl had come in again. Glancing out, I saw that the captain's meeting was continuing as if nothing had happened.

Lee was still leaning over the captain's desk. McMillan hung back from the others, and I thought for a second that she was looking down the hallway at me. But then she turned away and stepped into the huddle around the desk.

I peered down the dark corridor, my heart pounding. It branched left a little ways farther down. I'd seen the prisoner guard go that way, so I did, too, slipping along as quietly as I could in the shadows. Water dripped somewhere nearby, but otherwise everything was quiet. The ground was slick with slime and the walls smelled rotten, like that leak had been here a long time.

I walked under a skylight and had to choose between two corridors. I picked the one that went further into the building, because that was the scarier of the two and I figured that was a good sign. Empty doorways lined the corridor, but someone had taken the doors away. The rooms on the right were lit by broken windows. The ones on the left were just black holes in the wall.

The hallway got darker as I went, and I had to feel my way forward. Maybe this wasn't the right way after all—it was so dark. Up ahead, two doors with glass windows let in some kind of dim filtered light. I decided to go that far and then turn around if I didn't find anything.

When I looked through the window on the double doors, I saw a horse. I hadn't been expecting to see anything, so the sight of it made me jump back and press myself against the wall. My heart beat like a trapped bird in my chest, but I tried to take even breaths so I wouldn't start to gasp again.

Gritting my teeth, I made myself look through the window again, and felt stupid for being so scared the first time. The Greens had to keep their horses somewhere dry, and I guess this was the stable they'd picked. The space on the other side of the doors was huge—the ceiling high in the gloom, benches rising up against both walls like wooden hillsides. I'd seen pictures and read about this—it was a gymnasium. People used to play sports here. Now one whole side had been scattered with hay, and horses were tied up to the wooden benches every six feet or so. The room was lit by high windows and a set of doors at the far end that opened onto the rain.

The horses' tails flicked and a few shifted their weight or shook their heads, but otherwise everything seemed still and quiet. I turned back, thinking I'd head for another corridor.

And then I heard the faint sound of someone humming.

I held my breath and pressed my cheek against the glass so I could see deep into the corners of the gymnasium. And there, tucked away beside the hill of benches, a Green was guarding another door.

I steadied my breathing again. The Green was sitting in a chair beside the door, leaning back with her arms crossed and humming some tune I didn't recognize. It was her—the one who'd gone to guard the prisoners, the one who wouldn't get to go to the party tonight.

So that meant that Jacob and Larry, if they were still alive, were on the other side of that door.

I backed up, stumbled down the hallway and into the nearest doorway. Then I stood there, hidden in a shadow, and tried to breathe. I was starting to feel my shoulders seizing up, and my fingers tingled. What could I do? I couldn't just charge in and try to fight her. She was bigger than me, and she was a trained Green Mountain Boy, and she might have a gun or a knife.

After a minute of silence, I made myself creep back out into the hallway. Back at the doorway, I peered in at the Green. She shifted her arms once and scratched her leg. But otherwise she didn't move.

I was here, I'd come this far, so I had to do something. I put my face in my hands and tried to think. She'd see me right away if I went inside. I snuck as quietly as I could down the hall a little ways, looking for another way to get into the room the woman was guarding. There wasn't one.

I had to get her away from the doorway long enough to get it open. Then, once I did, Jacob and the constable would know what to do.

But what if they were unconscious, or tied up, or not even there in the first place? What if she was guarding some other criminals, and when I opened up the door they attacked me?

I walked down the hallway again, shaking my hands at my sides. I came to a classroom with a window in it, and went in to try to get some fresh air. Desks lay piled up to the ceiling at one end, like someone had turned the room on its side and then stood it upright again. And there were books on a shelf. On any other day I would have wanted to look at them, but today I walked over to the broken window without stopping. Evening was coming on again, and the rain was still pouring down.

The window looked out on a field of junk from the nearby river: uprooted trees, mud, a gutted car, bits of buildings, and piles of trash. But the school itself was up on a rise, above the flood level. Sumac and puckerbush pressed against the building's brick walls, except where the Greens had hacked a path to the gymnasium for the horses. I could see the open double doors from here.

Maybe it was the fresh evening air or the sound of the rain, but my mind slowed down a bit, and I started thinking again. The rain reminded me of that first storm, back in the Borough when Jacob and I had looked for the dead girl in the woods. And that made me remember something else.

Jacob, with a ball of fire in his hands. The sudden warm light on his face, and then the darkness again as the flames choked out and the mess of wet rags and tinder started to smoke.

I took a deep, shuddering breath, then looked around the room again.

Right by the door, a wooden rod wrapped in cloth leaned against the wall. I unrolled it as quietly as I could, and saw that the cloth was an American flag. I almost laughed. That had to mean something, but I wasn't sure what. I used my knife to cut off a big chunk—the fabric was crumbly and stiff, so it wasn't hard—and then I tossed it out the window into the rain.

Now I needed tinder. I pulled a book off the shelf—it was a battered old copy of *Catch-22*, which I'd read and liked so much that I couldn't bear to ruin it. I put it back on the shelf and tried again. The next book was *The Adventures of Huckleberry Finn.* That one I wasn't feeling too fond of anymore. I ripped out a chunk of its pages and balled them up tight.

Then I pulled a chair over to the window and climbed onto the window, careful not to catch myself on the broken glass. My side ached as I pulled myself through, but then I was out in the rain. The world was bright and huge after the dark hallways of the school. I picked up the wet flag and wrapped it around the ball of paper.

No one was around, but I wasn't sure how long it'd be before someone needed a horse or the Green guarding the prisoners came to check that the coast was still clear. So I ran low and quickly to the big double doors that led into the gym. The gymnasium was dark and I had to let my eyes adjust.

Nothing moved but the horses.

I took a step inside, out of the rain. The closest horses looked up at me, and then all the others did too. I didn't move. A brown mare muttered, and a gray shifted hard enough that his rope made the wooden bench squeak. But that was the worst of it. The far horses got bored and looked away, and then the closer ones decided that their hay was more interesting than me and lowered their heads again.

I breathed out slowly, my chest burning from holding in spent air. My eyes had adjusted enough now that I could see the whole gymnasium, including the inner doors I'd looked through a few minutes before, and the slope of benches on the far side that just barely hid the Green and the room she was guarding.

I looked around. A pile of tack sat near the outer door—saddles and bridles and blankets. It stank of wet horse and wet people. It was as good a place as any for a smoke bomb.

I wedged the ball of wet flag and paper in between two saddles and then paused again to listen. Nothing. I reached back to get my matches, but of course I didn't have my pack anymore. I panicked for a second, but then an unlit lantern sitting on the end of the benches caught my eye. Sure enough, a box of matches sat next to it. The cistern was half full of oil, which I thought would probably make some good black smoke. I unscrewed the cistern and poured a bit of the oil into my smoke bomb, then pressed a lit match to it.

The thing went up just like Jacob's had, only bigger. I jumped back to stop it catching my hair on fire. The horses were looking over again, anxious and shifty, but I didn't wait to see what would happen. I ran back out into the rain.

At the classroom window I finally looked back. The gymnasium door looked just the same as it had a second ago—no smoke pouring out, no nothing. But I didn't have time to go back and check—either it was working or it wasn't.

It was harder getting back in the window than it'd been coming out. I should've put a chair outside too. Instead, I had to pull myself up and crawl over. My side ached and a shard of glass dug into my thigh, but I didn't have time to stop.

The hallway was dark after the outside, and I had to feel my way along the wall back to the double doors to get a look in the gymnasium.

The horses were all shifting and pulling on their ropes in the gloom, and the far end near the tack pile was building up with smoke. I pressed my cheek to the window to watch the Green. She was still just sitting there, digging at something under her fingernails.

I shifted my weight back and forth in the dark hallway. What if she didn't ever notice? What if the smoke bomb wasn't strong enough? Then all I'd gotten was a cut in my thigh and a lot of wasted time. I stared hard at the Green, trying to make her move just by wishing it.

Finally, after what felt like an hour, she looked up with a frown on her face. She sniffed the air. I wanted to scream at her. The whole end of the gymnasium was full of smoke by now, and the horses looked close to panicking.

Slowly, like she barely thought it was worth it, she stood up. She even sniffed the door she was guarding, as if the smoke was coming from there somehow. Then, finally, after so long that I almost burst in just to speed things up, she walked around the wall of benches to check the rest of the gymnasium.

She froze as soon as she saw the smoke, and then shouted, "Fire!" I hadn't expected that. Her voice echoed around the gymnasium, but no one came running. Everyone was on the other side of the school. The Green whirled around in a circle, looking for I don't know what. And then she ran across the gymnasium, toward the horses and the fire.

It took me less than a second to get through the door, and I was behind the benches in another second. I could hear the guard on the other side of the room, trying to calm the horses and coughing in the smoke.

The door she'd been guarding was locked, held shut by a padlock. I pulled on it, like that would accomplish anything. I could see it was new, made after the Fall, simpler than one from Before would've been. But I couldn't concentrate—half of my mind was focused on the Green at the other end of the gymnasium, trying to hear if she was coming back. I tugged on the padlock again. It must need a key, and she had the key, and so I couldn't open it, and so—

I didn't have time for this. I looked around, but the only thing nearby was the chair the Green had been sitting on. I picked it up—it was heavy. I aimed its leg at the padlock, and smashed at it as hard as I could. That was bound to have gotten her attention. But the padlock wasn't broken. I'd hit it wrong. I turned the chair over and hit the lock again, this time with the back of the chair. And finally the padlock broke.

I pulled the padlock free. The Green must've heard; surely she must be running over now.

But even so, I forgot everything when I fumbled the door open and saw Jacob and Larry sitting on the ground with their arms tied around a mess of metal pipes on the far wall. Up until that very second, I don't think I'd really believed I'd find them.

But I had found them. My arms ached from throwing the chair at the door, but my whole body felt like flying.

"June?" Jacob croaked, his voice ragged.

"It's me," I said, pulling my knife out of its sheath and taking a step forward—

And then something hard barreled into me from behind and next thing I knew I was on the ground, my nose smashed against the floor. The knife skittered out of my hand toward Jacob and Larry. Someone grabbed me by the shirt and jerked me around so hard my head knocked against the floor again.

"You rat, knew you'd come back here," snarled Lee. His face was lit up by the doorway behind, but I knew his voice and the feel of his hands on me.

He slammed the door shut behind him and then I screamed, but he had his hands on my face before I could take another breath. I heard Larry holler something and Jacob snarling at Lee to let me go—then I don't know what happened, but it hurt and it involved me and Lee wrestling in the dark. He was a lot bigger than me, but my blood was boiling so my arms and legs did things I didn't think they could do, kicking and scraping and punching.

The next thing I remember clearly was my face pressed against the cold concrete floor and something in my mouth bleeding onto the floor. Lee was on top of me, breathing heavy and swearing and holding my arms twisted around my back. Larry was shouting, "Release her, let her go!" but he and Jacob were tied up and couldn't reach us.

Where was the other Green? some part of me thought. She wouldn't let him hurt me like this. Or maybe she was right outside, waiting for him to finish up.

"Tried to shake you off nice," Lee spat, "but you couldn't let your shitty little brother go. This ain't my fault, what's happening to you. You stuck your nose in where it was bound to get cut off." He sounded strange. His voice was gravelly and tight.

I couldn't say anything except give a little moan. He was going to kill me.

"The Americans are doing what's best," he continued. "I don't want to break my back for this fucking Republic and get nothing in return. It's the end of the world—gotta side with the strongest. You'd damn us all, you bitch."

Then he flipped me over onto my twisted arms. I felt my left shoulder pop, and in that flash of pain his fingers wrapped around my neck. And then I stopped thinking, and the world shrank down to the size of my crushed throat, and my whole life was shaped like a breath. One breath. That was all I was.

I figured out later that I'd scratched his neck and face with my good arm, hard enough that he bled. I'm glad about that. But at the time I was far away from my body and whatever it was doing. Things went dark, and I felt like I was in a high field, looking down on a valley with a little town in its heart. The wind was blowing on my face, and the sun was shining, and all around me I smelled living things, and my heart was near bursting. Of course, it was near bursting because I was dying, but in that dream it felt good.

And then Lee's hands were gone, and the weight of his body was gone, and I was trying to breathe again but it was near impossible. I gasped and gasped, and that's all I wanted to do for a long time, until my head stopped spinning and my chest stopped burning. My arm was numb, so I tried to pull it out from under me but then it hurt so bad that I blacked out again.

When I came back Larry was beside me, saying my name.

"Jacob?" I croaked.

"Here," he said, swimming into view over my head. "I'm right here, June."

I sat up, my head spinning. Jacob was holding my knife. I'd dropped it when Lee grabbed me, and it must've fallen within reach of Jacob, close enough for him to pick it up and cut himself free. I could see the ropes on the ground where he'd been sitting.

I peered deeper into the room. It looked like the guts of the building—all pipes and hard angles. All hard angles except the heap in the corner that was Lee. His face had blood on it. He wasn't moving. Jacob and Larry must've gotten him off me.

"Sorry," I said, not sure why I was saying it.

"Junie girl, we owe you a debt of gratitude," the constable said. He hadn't gotten up yet. "However did you find us?"

"No time, we need to leave," Jacob said. He reached down and put his hands under my arms and lifted me up. "Can you walk?"

"Sure," I said, wincing from the new pain in my shoulder. I could move it, but it hurt bad. "Is Lee dead?"

"I don't know," Jacob said. He hoisted Larry to his feet. The constable's knees knocked together once, but then he steadied. Lee still wasn't moving.

The gymnasium was still smoky, but my bomb had petered out. We walked past the Green who'd been guarding the door. She was sitting in the chair again, clutching her head and moaning. I could see blood between her fingers. She didn't look at us or say anything, even when Larry stopped to ask her if she needed help. I guess Lee got to her too.

Jacob held on to my good arm as we walked, and I was glad for it. My throat was pounding and my head hurt where it'd cracked against the floor. But I was alive. And what's more, a minute later we were out in the floodplain, the three of us haring away as quick as our burned and battered and tired bodies would go. I looked back at the school, and the only sign we'd been there was a haze of smoke still hanging over the gymnasium.

24

"They arrested us the second we walked into that godforsaken town," Larry said. "Said there were active warrants out for our arrest. I told them, 'I'm the constable of New Rutland, and I haven't issued any warnings.' And they said that didn't matter on account of it being a *Green Mountain Boy* warrant, and the towns don't have overriding jurisdiction."

Larry rubbed at his wrists. I could see red marks on them from the ropes. We were huddled up in a copse of trees by the college, as far as we could get from the Green Mountain Boys camp before Larry needed to rest. His voice was sharp as ever, but his legs kept buckling out from under him. Jacob didn't look much better.

"So then I asked, 'What is the nature of the offense?'" Larry continued, "and the Greens who arrested us wouldn't say, they just threw us into that room and tied our hands. And Lee said, 'Jacob, I guess you'll finally buzz for this.' That charlatan accused us of conspiring to kill the mayor of New Rutland, and of attempting to replace her with *me*, of all people."

Larry shook his head. "Wherever did you come from? We thought the circus had you!"

I glanced at Jacob, who hadn't said anything since we'd stopped. He was watching me.

"I did go to the circus, with Thomas," I said. But I didn't want to talk about what had happened there. "I realized that Lee was working for them. He'd been working for Americans for years."

"The circus told you that? How'd you get away?" Larry asked, looking flabbergasted.

"I—I barely made it. There was this machine, full of electricity, and it killed the strongman, and I ran for it." That was hard enough to say, so I didn't even try to answer Larry's first question. I didn't want them to know about the LoTabs, about how I'd finally remembered why Lee scared me so much.

"Did they tell you what they were planning for Town Meeting?" Jacob asked.

"I don't..." I started, but then I stopped to think. Thomas had said they were trying to get rid of all the bad leaders. And when I'd seen Sebastian riding through Middlebury a few hours ago, he'd invited all the mayors and town officials to see the circus for free.

"I think it's happening now," I said. I made myself stand up, even though it hurt. "They're going to do something at the show—they've invited all the mayors."

"Damnation!" Larry said, struggling to his feet as well.

"What are they going to do, June?" Jacob asked. Somehow, his voice was still calm.

"I don't know, I—" My mind was spinning. How could I figure this out, when I couldn't even remember the color of my mother's hair? I didn't have all the pieces. I couldn't do this.

"Think back," Jacob said, interrupting my spinning thoughts. "What did they tell you? What did you see?"

All I could think of was the strongman, standing over me, not quite meeting my eyes because he figured I was as good as dead already. And the smell of his skin burning...

"They have that machine," I said. "Something that holds electricity, lots of it. They were collecting it from the solar panels."

"Is that what shorted our grid?" Larry asked. "Never seen anything that powerful."

"We'll have to find it, stop them from using it," Jacob said.

"We need reinforcements," Larry said, looking around at the empty woods and the pouring rain.

"The Greens won't help us, and there's no time," I said. It was already almost full dark, and back in the Borough the show had started right around this time.

Larry breathed out slowly through his nose. "Shit," he said. "This situation is looking more and more dire. We'd better get closer then. One way or another, we can't stop them from here." He took one more look around, straightened his soggy flannel, and started limping back toward Middlebury.

"June," Jacob said. I knew what he was going to say even before he said it. "Where's Thomas?"

I swallowed. "He's—" But I couldn't finish.

"He went back to them?"

I nodded.

"He's not with them against his will." It wasn't a question.

"I know," I said.

Jacob looked at me a moment longer, then nodded and turned to follow Larry. But as he passed me, he put his hand on my good shoulder and squeezed it.

Middlebury College was old, maybe older than anything else I'd seen in Vermont. Most of the buildings were made out of stone, and they probably looked just the same as they'd looked Before, and before that too. Even the windows still had glass in them, mostly. We came out of the woods and into the little forest of buildings, and for a second I thought about that girl in the poster again, the one who was going to college. Had it been this college? Even though I was scared and hurting and more tired than I'd ever been, some little part of me pictured it: the overgrown fields of grasses and parsnip drawn back into neat green lawns, and me with books in my pack, walking to class through sunlight.

But that didn't last, because I knew, deep down, that this might be the last day I ever saw. That I was already seeing more than I would have if Jacob and Larry hadn't stopped Lee from killing me.

The circus wasn't hard to find. We caught sight of the Big Apple between two buildings, set up in a cornfield right in the middle of the college. Dead cornstalks swayed and rattled, the little cobs shriveled, still attached. I guessed that the last drought had killed the crop, or maybe the double winter. Most of the stalks were freshly flattened, though, by the crowd of people flowing down from town and into the Big Apple.

The tent was lit up bright red from within. In the twilight it glowed brighter than any of the other lights in the town, and the last stragglers of the crowd were like moths to a flame. I could see the shadows of people floating along the walls of the tent. Music drifted through the air, mixing with the sounds of people laughing. The tent was almost full.

"It's starting already," Larry said. "You two've seen the show before? How will we know when they'll use the…the machine?"

"It won't be the same act I saw, probably," I said. "They said—oh!" I stopped, and Larry and Jacob turned to stare at me.

I did know what the circus had planned for tonight. I'd seen them practicing, way back in the Borough. Their world premiere, just for Town Meeting, Alexandra had said. I closed my eyes tight, trying to remember: the red light of the tent, the echoing of Alexandra's voice in the wide empty space…

"They're going to start a fire, just like in New Rutland, I think." I opened my eyes. "I saw them practicing the whole thing." I told them, quick as I could, what I could remember. Alexandra had said something about throwing a torch, and the tinker had stood at the door of the tent to keep it closed. Then Alexandra had told Thomas to flip a switch.

"Christ and Jeezum, we need to sound the alarm," Larry said. "There must be a hundred people in there."

"And they'll be trapped if it burns," Jacob said, pointing. "Look at the tent walls." They were staked down every three feet.

Then we saw something else. A clump of Green Mountain Boys was loitering outside the tent entrance, watching everyone go by.

"Damnation," Larry muttered again, turning away again so the Greens wouldn't see his face.

"They might not stop us," I said, even though I didn't really believe it.

"They must've found Lee by now. They'll be looking for the two of us," Jacob said, keeping his head low.

"But how will we get in?" I asked. Or at least I started to ask it. By the time I got halfway through the sentence, my voice had petered out because I knew Jacob and Larry weren't getting through the entrance. There wasn't time, with the circus starting any second.

Jacob looked down at me. He knew it too.

"I'll go," I said. "They won't recognize me." I pulled at my braids, and my tangle of hair fell down around my face. I'd be safe from the Greens, and maybe from any circus folks who might be hanging around. No one from the circus had ever seen me without my mom's coat on, after all.

"June, you can't go on your own," Jacob said. "We don't know what they're going to do, we don't—" He stopped, sucking his breath through tight lips. His eyes flicked to the tent, then back to me.

"I can do it. There's no one else," I said. I wasn't sure if I wanted him to stop me or not. But he didn't. He put a hand on my shoulder again.

"Be careful," he said, and he squeezed so hard it hurt.

"Try to warn them, then get out before the place goes up in flames," Larry said.

I nodded once, then turned and headed toward the tent. Almost everyone had gotten inside now, but the Greens were still there at the door.

"It's a dream to weave, I'm telling you! The plastic just flows right along," said one of the people coming down the path behind me.

"I don't care if it weaves itself—it's tacky."

I felt a tug in my gut— it was the fiber committee, on their way to see the circus. I wanted to turn to them in the dark and whisper that they should go home, get as far away from here as they could. But I couldn't make myself do it. We were almost to the tent entrance now.

I glanced through my tangle of hair and saw the Greens

looking past me, eyeing the fiber committee. I made myself walk by them slowly, keeping my head down. Then I took a last deep breath of cold evening air and pushed my way through the tent flap.

As soon as I stepped into the Big Apple, I had to clench my fists and grit my teeth to stop myself from turning right around and running out again. The space was hot and damp from the crush of people inside. Folks were milling about everywhere under the bright electric lights strung overhead. Most looked like delegates attending Town Meeting Day—mayors and treasurers and committee members, all dressed in their best clothes but looking a little worse for wear after the rain and mud of the day.

Already my chest felt tight and my head light from the lack of air. But I blinked hard, trying to remember what I'd seen at the rehearsal back in the Borough. A row of chairs. A torch. A network of wires.

I pushed through the crowd, trying to see what was happening at the end of the tent. Snatches of music floated over the chattering crowd, and I followed them toward the stage. A smell hung over the crowd, too—the same one I'd smelled in Alexandra's cart. Even with all the warm wool and wet leather in the room, the sweetness lingered.

I stopped when I caught sight of the stage. It was set up just the way I'd seen it before. The musicians were there, laughing as they played the same song from the Borough. My skin prickled. They didn't look like they were playing for an audience they meant to kill. They looked happy.

I heard a buzzing and glanced up—a big electric light was right over our heads, hooked up to a thick snake of wire that spun up to the top of the tent. I followed the wire back down the tent's sloping roof, along the wall, down to where it wound together with a dozen others and disappeared into the back room where the performers waited before the show. More wires came out of that room and snaked along the floor and out of sight under the crowd's feet.

A group of Abenakis were craning their necks at the stage right beside me, and beyond them the rest of the crowd was pushing forward like they all expected to get a front row seat. I felt a sudden stab of panic and all at once I wanted to shove and push and tear my way out until I was free in the night air again. I pushed that urge aside as best I could, and looked back at the wires under my feet. Then I saw the chairs.

They were positioned in front of the stage, the perfect place to watch the show—three neat rows of ten. In the electric light, they glinted. They were made of metal. These were the chairs from the rehearsal, the chairs the circus had said were for special guests.

Even as I watched, the chairs were filling with people: a man wearing a bulletproof vest over a striped suit, a woman with a constable's star on her chest, an Abenaki man wearing more beads than all the rest put together. They looked like all the most powerful folks in the tent—mayors, constables, and delegates. None of them seemed to have noticed that their chairs were standing in a nest of electricity. None of them, apparently, had thought to look.

I pushed people aside, almost knocking a woman over and not even stopping to apologize. I had to warn the special guests, to get them out of the chairs before the show started.

I tried to shoulder past the last row of people between me and the chairs, but this time the crowd didn't budge. I pushed harder and felt an arm push back on me.

"Watch it," the person said. I looked up through my hair and came face-to-face with the jacket of a Green Mountain Boy. There was a row of them standing between the special guests and the rest of the crowd.

"I need to get through," I said, trying to keep my face covered by my snarled hair.

"Back up. This is the Town Meeting council, and you don't have access."

"I need—" I pushed forward again, but the Green grabbed me by the shoulders and pushed me back. I stumbled, hissing in pain, and then out of the corner of my eye I saw Sebastian. He had changed into his striped and starred suit and a wore a shining new top hat. He hadn't seen me, but he had seen the struggle and he was making his way over, smiling at everyone but keeping his eyes fixed on the Greens who'd bunched up in front of me.

I turned and ducked into the crowd again, barely seeing where I was going. And just then all the lights turned off with an electric pop. I had that panicked sense again, of too many bodies standing too close together. I couldn't breathe. Then a spotlight tore through the darkness, lighting the stage. Sebastian leapt into the light.

"Welcome!" he cried. "In this tent, the end of the world ain't so close anymore. We've got the start of something here. But before we titillate you with our tales of triumph, we must have a toast to our beautiful guests of honor—the mayors and lawmen of this great Republic! Give these honorable men and women a round of applause! To the continued prosperity of your great land!"

The crowd cheered and whooped while the folks sitting in the metal chairs stood and waved. I put my head down and struggled toward the tent wall.

"And to the Green Mountain Boys, our brave protectors!" Sebastian shouted. I glanced up in time to see Sebastian reaching his hand down to shake the hand of the Greens' captain—the same one I'd just tried to warn. His face was lit up by the stage light and he was beaming.

I reached the tent wall and sagged against it, feeling the cool of the night air on the other side of the canvas. I was panicking now. The show had started, and the metal chairs were full of mayors and constables. They were all going to buzz. That was what the circus had rehearsed. And then the tent was going to burn, and I was going to burn too. I couldn't get air. I felt my head spin, my face prickle with fear. I had to get out.

"And now, from the exotic beyond, put your hands together for Alexandra, Queen of the Hudson!" Sebastian crowed. The crowd went wild. The cheers smashed into my aching head, drowning out any thoughts or plans I might've had. I couldn't do this.

Up at the front of the tent, Alexandra was floating down from the shadowy heights of the tent, holding a flame up over her head. Sebastian was at the edge of the stage. The musicians were behind it, strumming dramatically on their guitars. And finally something made it through the panic blinding me. It was a scrap of a memory: Thomas, standing at the back of the Big Apple alone, watching the circus rehearse. His back to me, his corncob pipe in his hand.

Where was he?

My breath came in ragged gasps. I blinked and looked around, trying to get my bearings. Beside me on the tent wall, a cord snaked up to the electric light way above me. My eyes followed it down, along the bottom of the tent wall, and off behind the stage. The electricity machine had to be back there, in the small room behind the stage. Filled with enough electricity to kill everyone in the metal chairs and light the whole tent on fire.

I tried to breathe deeply, but it was impossible in the close darkness of the crowd. So instead I made myself move. I slid along the tent wall, keeping myself pressed against it to avoid the crowd. Up on stage, Alexandra shone in a spotlight. I slipped behind the stage, just another piece of the dark canvas, and through the flap into the back room.

The chamber was dim, lit by a few flickering oil lamps, and the air felt cold and fresh after the crush of the main tent. But that was about the only comforting thing about it. Wires ran under my feet and back to the huge electricity box, which stood like a warning in the middle of the empty space. The wires were latched onto the machine with metal teeth and wire jaws.

Thomas was there. He crouched beside the machine, clamping wires onto it like he'd been using electricity his whole life.

I stood still for a long second, but Thomas was so engrossed in whatever he was doing that he didn't see me. Half the wires were plugged into the machine, and he looked like he was trying to get the rest connected too. Sweat ran down my face, and I felt my legs quivering under me.

"Thomas," I said finally, and he jumped about a mile and looked around at me.

"June," he said. He let go of the wires, but he didn't stand up or move away from the machine. "What're you doing here?"

"Get away from that thing," I said. "It's dangerous."

Thomas looked at the machine. "I know," he said. "That's the whole point."

I was scared to move, scared of what he'd do if I took a step toward him. "Come away, Thomas," I said again.

"You need to leave," Thomas said, his words sudden and sharp. "You aren't supposed to be here."

"You don't have to do this," I said, and I took a step forward. Thomas held out a hand and stood up, putting himself between me and the machine.

"No," he said. "You don't know what this is. You don't get it. It's my job."

"Thomas, you don't want to hurt people," I said, but it came out as a question. "The circus is evil—they're—"

"They're not evil!" Thomas shouted. "They're my family."

"I'm your family," I said, but right when I said it a huge, excited shout came from the crowd in the main tent, and my words got swallowed.

"Will the flame survive?" Alexandra's thin, high voice split the applause.

"They're killing people," I said when the applause had faded. "They want the Republic to fall."

"They're right," Thomas said, and he took a step toward me. "We're being oppressed—and we don't even know it." He said the word *oppressed* carefully, and I knew it was a word he'd just learned.

"But this is your home," I said, not knowing what else to

say. I didn't understand how Thomas could say what he was saying. He had to know by now that this wasn't a story or a game anymore.

"What home? Slaving for Bob and Denise? Not being able to do what I want?" He sounded earnest now, like I was stupid and he was explaining something obvious. It made me mad.

"Would you kill Bob and Denise if they were in this tent?" I asked. "That what you want?"

Thomas blinked. "Sure," he said. "For the good of the people. But they're not here, and when we destroy the corruption they'll be free too. That's what America is."

"No, it's not, Thomas," I said sharply. "Whatever these people are, they're not trying to set us free. They're killing us."

Thomas's face twitched when I said that, and for a second he opened his mouth and looked like he used to do, like he was about to ask me to read to him. But then he closed his mouth again and turned back to the machine.

"Get out of here, June," he said over his shoulder. "Or you'll be sorry."

He picked up the last of the wires and attached them to the machine.

"Stop!" I yelled. I grabbed his arm and pulled it, but he shook out of my grip. So I wrapped my good arm around his shoulders and pulled.

"The light will never go out!" Alexandra shouted from the stage. "The flame only grows!"

"Let me go!" Thomas snarled, and then we were on the ground, tangled up and furious. Thomas was stronger than me, I realized right away, and my whole body was hurting already. I couldn't hold him. He pushed me off every time I grabbed him, and each time he pushed me harder. He threw me on the ground and turned back to the machine, reaching for a lever on its side.

"Stop!" I said, trying to stand again. I took his arm and held it as hard as I could.

"You're ruining it!" he snarled at me, and there was more

than anger in his voice—there was desperation, I realized; the sound of someone whose whole life was slipping through their fingers.

"Thomas, I—" I started, but then the flap from the main tent whipped open.

Lee was there, filling up the doorway. One of his eyes was red and puffy and he had blood caked under his nose. So he wasn't dead after all. "What's going on, that was your cue—" he started, and then he saw me holding on to Thomas.

"Bitch," he said, and let the tent flap fall shut behind him. I backed up, dropping Thomas's arm and stumbling over another bundle of cable. Lee was going to kill me for sure this time. He took a step toward me, making a wide arc around the machine as if he didn't want to get too close.

I felt something hard under my foot and looked down to see one of the clawed ends of the wire. The wire was coiled up, one end bare, with metal wires sticking out past the rubber coating. I looked back up. Lee was coming for me, and Thomas stood silently beside the machine, watching.

I did the only thing I could think to do. I grabbed the two ends of the cable and reached past Thomas, clamping one end onto the machine before he could do anything. Then I held the bare end out like a gun.

"Stop, or I'll buzz you," I said.

In the main tent, the crowd gasped. "The flame only grows!" Alexandra shouted again.

Lee stopped dead. I took a step, putting myself between Thomas and the machine.

"It's not on," Lee said. His swollen eye was bloodshot, flicking between my face and the bare wires at the end of the cable. I felt sweat in my palm, and had to force myself not to drop the cable. It felt evil.

"It is on. The current is just waiting to touch something." I didn't know if it was true or not. Jacob had explained electricity to me back in the cave, but it felt so long ago and I didn't have time to think properly.

Lee glanced over his shoulder into the Big Apple. When he turned back to me, his teeth were gritted in a snarl under his black mustache. I knew he was about to jump at me. Thomas had backed up beside Lee, and still hadn't said anything, but I met his eyes for one tiny instant.

And then the crowd started screaming. Lee turned again, and we all saw smoke billowing under the flap into the Big Apple. In the second we watched, the wall of the tent burst into flame.

Alexandra and the others had lit the Big Apple on fire, even though the electricity hadn't buzzed the special guests yet.

"Don't—" I shouted, brandishing the cable at Lee. But it was too late. He grabbed Thomas by the front of his shirt and dodged around me, out the back flap and into the night.

"Thomas!" I cried, dropping the cable and staggering after them.

The field and the stone buildings of the college were already lit up like daylight by the flaming tent. I ran a few steps and looked back. The Big Apple was burning hotter and brighter than should have been possible in the rain. But people were pouring out the exit, and more were crawling out from under the tent sides, which had somehow come unpinned. I caught a glimpse of the Green Mountain Boys' captain, pushing people ahead of him and roaring at them to hurry. I didn't see Alexandra or Sebastian or any of the others.

Thomas and Lee, though, were running away between two buildings, disappearing into the dark. Lee dragged Thomas by the arm.

I sprinted after them, as fast as my legs would take me. My breath tore in my throat but I didn't slow down.

I caught sight of them again on the road beyond the college. They were headed for a bridge that led out of town—they were headed west. Thomas was struggling against Lee, so I knew I could catch up to them. But then what?

I didn't have time to think. I ran and caught up to them just as they reached the bridge. I pushed Lee from behind. He stumbled but didn't let go of Thomas's arm. I pulled my knife out and darted past them onto the bridge, between Lee and the York border I knew he was shooting for.

"Let Thomas go," I said. "I'm arresting you." My voice came out a rasp. I wanted to bend over and gasp, but I knew I had to keep my eyes on them.

"Hell no," Lee said. "You're going to let us go, or you'll be sorry." He'd lost his flat-brimmed hat, but his Green Mountain Boys uniform still glistened in the rain.

"I won't," I said. A trickle of rain slid down my neck and into my shirt. I held the knife as steady as I could. I didn't know if Lee had a knife too.

"You wouldn't hurt your little boyfriend," Lee said. Thomas was silent, tears streaming down his wet face.

"He's my brother," I said, and anger flared up in me, made me braver. "Thomas, it'll be okay."

"This Republic will fall," Lee said. "Just a matter of which way. World's a new place. You'll have to join us soon enough."

"Let go of him. You're under arrest," I said again. I knew the moment was slipping through my fingers, that there wasn't anything else I could do. Then I heard hooves pounding on the road from the direction of the college. Lee laughed, and I looked behind him as Alexandra's cart came careening down the road, the contortionist, in the driver's seat, squinting through the rain. No one else followed.

The horses struggled to a stop behind Lee, and the door flew open.

"Get in," Alexandra gasped. Her hair was coming down from its crown on her head, and her green dress was torn.

Lee started backward, pulling Thomas.

"No!" I yelled. "Leave Thomas. I'll let you go, just leave him!"

Thomas stared back and forth between me and Alexandra. I'd never seen him look so young, not even when he first crawled out from under the porch back at Bob and Denise's so long ago.

"Don't be an idiot," Alexandra snapped. "He's ours, and you should be thankful."

"He's staying with me—" I said.

"You want him?" Alexandra interrupted. "You can have him for the week between now and when he buzzes. That's what happens to little boys who murder mayors."

"He didn't," I said, although I was suddenly doubtful. Thomas had gone with the circus of his own free will. And he'd been in the Big Apple, about to activate the machine. If he stayed, he'd be arrested, and people buzzed for less than attempted mass murder.

"He was kidnapped," I said. "He didn't do anything wrong." I looked at Thomas, and he looked back at me, still not saying anything. I wished he'd say something.

"Do you want to test that belief?" Alexandra asked impatiently.

I didn't know what would happen if I brought Thomas back to Middlebury, back to the Greens and the local law and however many town leaders were still alive. I didn't want to find out.

"Thomas, I—" I said, and I felt my knife lower to my side. He couldn't stay with me. It was too dangerous. My vision blurred, and before I could stop myself I thought of my mom. She hadn't looked for me, and I'd thought that was a betrayal. But what if it wasn't? What if she'd gone through this same moment, had this same choice? What if she'd known I'd be safer without her?

Alexandra reached for Thomas's arm and pulled him into the cart, Lee right behind him, and I heard a terrible noise escape from my throat.

"June," Thomas said as he stood in the doorway of Alexandra's cart. That was all. Then Lee pulled the door shut and the contortionist whipped the horses and they rushed past me across the bridge.

"Stop!" I yelled, even though I knew they wouldn't, couldn't. I felt the knife in my hands, trembling, as the cart disappeared into the night.

I don't know how long I stood there.

I don't know how many times I yelled into the darkness for the cart to stop, for someone to come and help me. But eventually, I must've turned and walked back up the road to where the Big Apple was smoking in the rain.

Jacob found me wandering through the crowds of people who had come to watch the Big Apple burn.

"June!" he shouted, his voice choked.

I turned as he came running up. His face was twisted and pale, and his hands shook as he reached for me.

"You're all right," he said. "We didn't know—we didn't see you come out."

He'd thought I was dead, I realized. He'd thought that the fire had finally got me after all.

"Did everyone…did anyone…?" I wasn't sure what to even ask.

"Come over here, get out of the rain," Jacob said, and he led me over to an awning along one of the brick buildings.

"We won't know for certain till the fire stops, but most everyone got out. Larry got the tent doors open, and when the fire started I cut through the ropes holding the walls down. As soon as he saw the fire, the Green captain figured he'd rather deputize us than arrest us."

I nodded.

"Something went wrong with their plan. You slowed them down, didn't you?" Jacob asked.

"It was Thomas," I said.

Jacob looked out into the rain, as if he expected to see Thomas standing there. "Is he—?"

"He's gone," I said.

Out in the rain, someone was struggling against a group of Greens. I watched, though I didn't really care much who it was. The Greens wrestled the man down into the mud and tied his hands before they let him up again. He looked my way and I saw that it was Sebastian. He spat on one of the Greens, who smacked him across the face. I recognized McMillan. They dragged him away across the cornfield, back toward the school.

"I'm sorry," Jacob said. He put his arm around me, wincing, and I winced from the weight of it. But I didn't pull away. We stayed like that a long while, until the rain had put the Big Apple fire out and the only thing left was the wreckage.

Epilogue

The sun felt good on the back of my neck as we walked up the rocky path in the afternoon light. The rains hadn't come for the past week, and things were finally drying out. Benny was already talking drought, but I was happy enough calling it sunny without getting apocalyptic about it. Benny loved everything to be dramatic, and I'd grown to love making fun of him for it.

Beside me, Jacob was quiet. Quieter than usual. Somehow, he'd been more worried about this day than I was. I'd been getting used to seeing him smile, to hearing him laugh in the three months we'd been working together, but since Benny came by with the tip Jacob had been sad and drawn again. I didn't need him making me more anxious than I already was, and I was grateful to have the library to go home to at the end of each day.

Jacob had offered me a place to stay with him once we got back to the Borough, but I'd said no. He'd moved into the constable's rooms over the jail, where Sarah had lived, and I'd found myself a place nearby instead. It turned out the Borough had had a library once upon a time, and the building was still full of dusty books, dumped on the floor when folks had looted the shelves for fuel. Once we'd cleaned out some of the rooms to make a living space, it suited me fine.

The jail itself suited me fine, too, since the first thing Jacob and I had done when we got back was gut the electricity from the building. We'd sawed a few more windows out of the walls to let in more light, and the place felt bright and comfortable now, except in the last few days. We'd known this day was coming, but it didn't make it easier.

We reached the top of the rocky path and started through a

meadow overgrown with sumac. The place we were headed was far off the beaten path, just a few miles north of the Borough. We were high enough in the hills that when I looked back I could see the Hollow on the far side of the valley.

"Look," I said to Jacob. "They're haying." Even from here I could tell that the Hastings' field was half shorn. Jacob squinted back and nodded, but still didn't say anything.

I looked a little longer, trying to make out people. I'd been back to see Bob and Denise a few times. Bob hadn't been able to find his voice for the first five minutes after he saw the silver deputy badge on my chest. He'd always wanted Thomas to be a Green Mountain Boy, but apparently hadn't imagined I'd be anything but Cyrus's wife. Denise, though, hadn't been able to stop talking. Said they'd waited a few weeks for Thomas and me to come back before Bob walked over the mountain trail to Dorset and picked up a new orphan from the home over there. Said I could come back whenever I wanted. She cried when she first saw me, and then cried some more when I told her Thomas was gone. Finally Bob found his voice and said they'd had some tools stolen since I left, and would I look into it for them. I said I would.

I'd seen Gemma too. She must've heard I was back, 'cause she was waiting for me at our spot when I went out there. She said she'd missed me, and she was angry at me for leaving and not telling her. For a minute it was like I'd never left, like we were still stealing moments in between chores and storms and nothing had changed. But then I told her I was moving into the library, and she looked at me like I was a stranger. I told her to come visit me, and she said she might. We spent some more time together after that, but it felt like goodbye. And when I walked down from the Hollow that last time, I found I was light as air.

Jacob and I reached the top of the meadow and paused. Jacob frowned down at the map Sebastian had finally agreed to draw for us. Most everyone who'd helped the circus had been rounded up by now—most of the Greens on Lee's crew, a few Yorker sympathizers on the border, the shepherd from the Borough who'd planted the cowbane and killed his own sheep as a cover—but Sebastian had held out. He hadn't said where Alexandra, Lee, and Thomas might have gone. They had to be across the border by now anyway, where none of us could reach them. Didn't stop me glancing out at the road a few times a day, looking for a boy with a corncob pipe.

In the end it was the Alt-Zs who gave Benny the tip about where she was, not Sebastian. Then Benny came to tell us as quickly as he could.

Jacob cleared his throat. "Almost there," he said. "Just through these trees."

He paused, still not moving.

"It's all right," I said, and I meant it. I was glad, now that we were here. Once it was over, I'd feel better. I stepped forward, and Jacob followed behind me.

The settlement was small, just five or ten shelters made of logs, tarps, and piled spruce boughs. Smoke hung in the trees around the shelters, but no one was outside. The ground was hard-packed from years of footfalls, the trees around the settlement dead or dying, stripped of low-hanging branches. But the whole place looked halfhearted, temporary. A wooden cross stood crooked in the center of the clearing. An orange pill bottle lay on a pile of trash outside one of the shelters.

We went straight to the furthest shelter, the one that looked the oldest. Its log walls were weathered and cracked, but neatly caulked with clay. A blue feather on a string hung from the edge of the roof, and the word *Welcome* was written in charcoal over the doorway. I'd been calm up until then, but the shape of the letters made my breath shudder and my chest tighten. I hadn't thought that I'd recognize her handwriting. I looked back at Jacob. His face was stiff, but when he saw me hesitate he came up beside me. I took one more breath, then nodded.

"This is the constable and deputy of the Borough," he said,

knocking on the door. "We've got some questions about the American circus. We can help you. Please come out."

We stood there in silence, and above me I heard the breeze whistling through the trees. The sun dappled through the leaves and branches, sending light and shadow over everything.

Then the door swung open, and she was standing before us. Her eyes, LoTab soft, sharpened as she saw Jacob, then widened as they moved to me. Her hair, like I should've always known, was exactly the same shade of brown as mine.

ACKNOWLEDGMENTS

The writing of this book has been so much a part of my life that I wonder where to start this task of thanking those who've helped me. Either directly or indirectly, everyone who supported me in the years I was writing *After the Fall* supported this book. If you're one of those people, thank you. Specifically, I'd like to thank Jaynie and the team at Regal House for believing in my story and turning it into the book it is today. Thanks also to all those who added their own elbow grease to the effort—I'll try to name most of you here: Thanks to my mentors and friends at the Solstice MFA Program, including Laura Williams McCaffrey, Steve Huff, David Yoo, Laure-Anne Boselaar, and Meg Kearney. Thank you to Tom Slayton, who allowed me to use some of his wonderful writing from *Vermont Life* in these pages. Thanks to Kate and Noah, the intrepid members of HENK who gave me feedback on many iterations of *After the Fall.* To the Equinox Writing Group—Cindy, Megan, Charlotte, Rhonda, Jim, and Dean—thank you for your invaluable advice, encouragement, and friendship. Thanks to my mom for being a constant cheerleader and to my dad for talking me through the intricacies of crayfish and poison parsnip, and to both of you for your unwavering support, always. Thanks to Molly, specifically for giving me feedback on *After the Fall,* and generally for everything else, too; and thank you to Erich for being my favorite brother. Thank you to Autumn, whose increasingly rowdy presence in my uterus inspired me to get a move on with this whole thing. And, most of all, thank you, Hunter, for always encouraging and believing in me, for reading this story over and over again to help me make it better, and for being my partner in writing and in life.

Book Club Questions

1. How is June's perception of her relationship with Thomas different from reality? How does this difference affect the story?
2. Why is Jacob so drawn to June in the first act of the book? How does his past relationship with her affect his actions in the story?
3. How do the various settings in the novel affect the story's mood?
4. Consider the role of electricity in the novel. When is it a positive force? When is it a negative force? How might the role of electricity illuminate the themes of the book?
5. Does *After the Fall* take a hopeful or pessimistic view of humanity? How?